Malice

A Southern Comfort Prequel

Book One

Lisa Clark O'Neill

Copyright 2015

With special thanks to Brian Koch for his incredible graphic design work and for being a rock; to David Rusev for his photography skills and for his patience with answering my questions about all things Russian; to Sandra Clark for her eagle eye and too many other things to enumerate; and finally to Kristina Costello and Catherine Hudson for their very helpful feedback.

This book is a work of fiction. Names, places and incidents are the product of the author's imagination or are used fictitiously.

Other Novels by Lisa Clark O'Neill

The Sweetwater Trilogy:
Mr. Write
Admit One
Circumstantial Evidence

The Southern Comfort Series:
Serendipity
Forbidden
Deception
Nemesis
Obsession

CHAPTER ONE

IF there were any benefit to living as a homeless man, it was the ability to scratch your ass on a public street without having people look at you as if you were crude. Mostly because people looked past, around and through the homeless.

An unfortunate fact, but one that currently worked to the benefit of FBI agent Jesse Wellington.

Cursing the cold December rain which had started sometime around two a.m. and hadn't let up since, Jesse proceeded to scratch his left cheek. Sitting in a wet cardboard box in the alley half the night had given him a rash.

Muttering to himself, Jesse pushed his shopping cart to the mouth of the alley, hunching his six-three frame to better project the image of a harmless old man. Not that anyone was paying any attention. Aside from people's tendency to avoid looking at the homeless, they also – mostly – had the sense to stay out of the rain. The street was basically deserted. This part of Savannah wasn't exactly bustling with activity at this time of the morning under normal circumstances, given as it was toward activities that were better conducted under the cover of darkness. The weather kept all but the most intrepid locals tucked away inside.

The repeated thump of ball hitting pavement drew Jesse's attention to the bulldozer-sized man shooting hoops on the corner. Rain slid off his bald head, water splashing from the cracked court every time he dribbled. Seemingly heedless of the uncomfortable damp, the man tried for a three pointer. The ball hit the rim, bouncing off and rolling toward Jesse.

He bent sideways and scooped it up.

"Hey, old timer," the bald man called. "That's my ball."

"And I wouldn't have it if you could hit the broad side of a barn."

Eyes narrowing, the man sauntered across the court, mile-wide shoulders back, ham-sized hands spread in a contentious gesture. He was a walking, talking poster boy for Badasses of America.

But he pressed his wet black T-shirt against his wrinkled nose as he drew closer.

"Shit, Wellington," he said in an undertone. "Did you sleep in the dumpster?"

Jesse indicated his old, wet Army jacket, a tattered relic that he'd picked up at a thrift store and which probably hadn't been laundered since the Nixon administration. "You try wearing this and see if you don't smell like ass. Some of us weren't tucked up inside a cozy apartment all night, watching the goings-on through binoculars."

"I'd hardly call that place above the tattoo parlor *cozy*. And might I remind you that you volunteered for this."

"Yeah, yeah." Mostly because Jesse hated surveillance, the unutterable tedium of it, and the opportunity to disguise himself as a bum and keep an eye on the back door to the building seemed more proactive.

Not that he'd accomplished much of anything other than freezing his ass off and giving himself a rash. The subject of their interest hadn't shown hide or hair since he'd disappeared into his apartment above the Fluff & Fold laundromat yesterday afternoon. It reminded him of another case he'd been involved with recently, in which he'd taken down a killer who was holding a woman hostage behind a row of washing machines.

"I need to stay away from laundromats," Jesse muttered.

"What?"

Jesse waved a hand to indicate that it wasn't important. The laundry machines running at all hours of the day and night generated too much white noise for their audio equipment to be effective, so at this point they were stuck doing surveillance the old fashioned way – they watched and they waited. "Losevsky has to show his face sooner or later."

Miron Losevsky was the little toad who lived above the laundromat. The management company he worked for maintained the Fluff & Fold and a string of others like it, as well as some self-serve car washes. All cash-rich operations.

They suspected, quite strongly, that the businesses served to launder more than dirty clothes and cars. They were part of the legitimate business front for one particularly nasty Russian import, whose real business was anything but. Massage parlors that functioned as prostitution rings, drugs – the man had his fingers in any number of criminal pies. They knew that much, but they didn't know *him.*

The Ghost, as some members of the task force had taken to calling him, because the bastard seemed to be able to disappear at will. His identity was hidden behind dummy corporations and grunts like Miron who did his dirty work.

They wouldn't even know that much if one of the girls who worked – involuntarily – at one of the massage parlors hadn't escaped and subsequently been picked up by local law enforcement. Her name was Irena, and though she'd been terrified of the cops, she was more terrified of being returned to her former "employer." With the help of a translator they'd learned that like many of the victims of human trafficking, she'd been promised a better life in the U.S. When that better life turned out to be sexual slavery, her life and – more effectively – the lives of her family back in Russia had been threatened in order to keep her in line.

They'd gotten Losevsky's name from her, as he was one of her regulars. She didn't know who Losevsky's boss was, though she said one of the other girls had spoken of servicing him.

That girl hadn't lived long afterward, but Irena refused to say more on the subject, and no amount of cajoling or legal threats could persuade her. Whatever she'd seen had been sufficiently horrifying to ensure her silence.

Unfortunately, by the time they had enough information to raid the parlor, a convenient fire took the building and any evidence it might have contained to the ground.

And Irena – who was supposedly safe in police custody – had been shanked by another inmate at the jail.

Realizing they had a bit of a problem, the locals gave the FBI a call.

Because they didn't want a repeat of the fiasco with the massage parlor, they were taking a more covert approach to surveilling Losevsky. Without their witness's testimony, they had a lot of suspicions but no actual grounds for bringing him in.

Jesse scratched at the straggly gray wig covering his dark hair, and Brian took the ball back. "Why don't you head out, grab some coffee, something to eat? I can call Bristol in, have him back me up for a while."

Because the thought of coffee – and possibly even a shower – sounded like nirvana, Jesse opened his mouth to agree. But then the glass door to the Fluff and Fold banged open, discharging a woman who yanked at her long dark hair, shouting her head off in hysterical Spanish.

"La sangre! La sangre!" She ran into the street, looking wildly over her shoulder.

"That means blood," Brian contributed uneasily, and the hair on Jesse's neck stood up. "She just walked in a few minutes ago."

"Let's go. Now." Jesse unholstered his weapon from beneath the grungy jacket that he wore, holding it against his leg as he ran toward the open laundromat door. After a nod from Brian he went in high, Brian going low. A tinny version of *Deck the Halls* piped from the speakers, but the room appeared empty aside from the basket of clothes turned over on the floor, presumably dropped by the woman.

"There," Brian said, gesturing with his chin.

A choir sang *follow me in merry measure* as they approached the artificial Christmas tree covered in shiny tinsel. The angel topper held an unfurled scroll that declared *Peace on Earth*.

Blood dripped from the ceiling, staining her white dress.

Jesse grimaced, then examined the ceiling. The blood was obviously leaking through from the floor above. "Stairs are in the back, through that door."

In this type of situation stairwells were like a barrel, whoever entered them the fish, but they had little choice. With a hand signal, Jesse indicated he'd take the lead, Brian bringing up the rear. In contrast to the bright overhead light and artificial cheer of the laundromat, a bare light bulb shone, casting grim-looking shadows. Jesse spotted Miron's front door, a crack of weak, watery light indicating it was open.

"*FBI*," Jesse announced as they gained the landing. Though from the smell creeping out the door like a malodorous fog, he was pretty sure whoever's blood that was couldn't hear him. *"We're coming in."*

Jesse shouldered the door aside, crouched low and Brian went past him. The room was a living/dining combo, an absolute pigsty, and visibly empty. Brian moved to the adjoining galley kitchen, examined it and then shook his head at Jesse. Steeling himself, Jesse eased toward the bedroom. The door was closed, but the room wasn't quiet. After a couple moments listening at the door, Jesse determined the sound came from a TV.

But he wasn't about to take chances. He waited for Brian, then kicked open the door.

The smell nearly knocked him over. Excrement. Blood. Death.

"*Shit,*" Brian swore, the color draining from his face. "Oh, hell."

Jesse, whose stomach was much stronger than Brian's, felt a little sick himself.

"Clear the bathroom," he said, because it needed to be done and because Brian looked like he needed a moment to get his gorge under control.

When the other man moved away, Jesse forced himself to look at the bed.

Miron Losevsky had been tied to the frame, spread-eagle, and then filleted like a fish. Blood soaked through the mattress, pooling on the floor and dripping through the laundromat ceiling beneath. Duct tape covered his mouth, and a few intrepid flies crawled and buzzed around what was left of his body.

Jesse studied the wall behind the bed, the ceiling. No arterial spray. So the perp hadn't cut Losevsky's throat and then carved on him. He'd carved him first, let him bleed for a while, and then severed the carotid artery just to make sure the poor bastard was really dead.

"How'd this happen?" Brian said from behind him. "We've had this place under twenty-four hour surveillance."

"Hell if I know." But the thought of it pissed him off. Someone had snuck in here – and they *would* discover how –

murdered Miron Losevsky in the vilest possible way, all while he'd been right outside, scratching his ass.

Literally.

Jesse spotted some square, brightly colored sheets of blotter paper on the nightstand and stepped as carefully as possible around the bed. The paper, perforated into individual tabs measuring about a quarter of an inch square, bore a smiling brown bear.

"Drugs?"

Jesse nodded in response to Brian's question. Hallucinogens – usually LSD or a chemical relative – seemed to be the Ghost's particular niche. Given the drug's popularity with the artsy crowd – a significant part of Savannah, which boasted one of the most successful art and design schools in the country – it was a profitable niche, indeed.

"Looks like the same design the Counter Narcotics Team has been tracking." The brown bear, of course being a well-known symbol for Russia, dating back to the age of the tsars.

"Maybe Losevsky was sampling the merchandise a little too freely," Brian suggested.

Jesse glanced at the remains of the man on the bed. "Maybe. Maybe this is his boss's way of sending a message."

"I'd say it's a pretty effective one. Messy, but effective."

"Not that messy," Jesse said as he studied the carpet. "This much blood, you'd think he would have tracked it." A blade was an intimate weapon, one frequently used in anger, in passion. But even if there was anger here, it was icy. Controlled. Forensics would come in, vacuum, find any stray hairs or fingerprints – maybe the duct tape would be good for that, unless he'd worn gloves – but the scene, for all its brutality – did not look like the evidence bonanza typical of most fatal stabbings.

"*Shit,*" Brian muttered.

Jesse heard the siren, too. Evidently the woman who'd run out of here earlier had found a squad car and alerted them.

"We better go down and meet them," Jesse said. "Let them know who we are. I don't feel like getting shot today." They didn't exactly look like officers of the law at the moment, and the last thing they needed was a run-in with a trigger happy beat cop who wasn't aware of the situation.

He turned, but the TV on the dresser caught his eye.

It took him a moment, but then his fist clenched of its own volition as what he was seeing registered. "Son of a bitch. Son of a *freaking* bitch."

"What?" Brian's bulk eased up behind him. "What's wrong?"

Jesse jerked his chin toward the screen.

From between two buildings, a giant Stay Puft Marshmallow Man emerged, terrorizing a busy city.

"You have to be kidding me." Brian's tone echoed Jesse's.

Jesse wished it was a joke, he really did. But it wasn't the least bit funny. Because it meant that they had a real problem.

As *Ghostbusters* continued to play, Jesse seethed. Not only was this evidence that the task force had a leak, but the bastard was cocky enough to let them know it. "He's thumbing his nose at us," Jesse said. "He thinks this is some kind of game."

CHAPTER TWO

JILLIAN Montgomery had always heard that when life gave you lemons, you were supposed to make lemonade.

She wondered what you were supposed to do with acorns.

She straightened from her post-run stretch, rubbing the spot on her scalp where the missile had landed. Looking up, she spotted a familiar gray form lurking behind a curtain of Spanish moss.

He shook his bushy tail at her.

"Is that any way to greet me?" She'd run out of trail mix a few days ago, and the squirrel she'd nicknamed Killer due to his aggressive personality clearly wasn't happy. "I'll go to the store this afternoon, you demanding little rodent."

"You really shouldn't encourage him, dear."

That admonition indicated that her neighbor, Mrs. Franklin, had been watching from her window. Jillian turned to see the elderly woman hobble onto her front porch, holding Ruffles the dog in her arms. Although really, *dog* was something of a misnomer. The little animal looked more like a rodent than the squirrel.

Mrs. Franklin's floral housecoat flapped in the brisk November breeze. The riot of gray curls around her head gave her the look of an aging medusa. "Mr. Pratt said that your little friend is becoming a nuisance."

It was Mr. Pratt, her neighbor on the other side, who was the nuisance.

"If Mr. Pratt is worried about the squirrels getting into his birdseed, he should use the new feeder I got him last month. It's guaranteed to keep them out. I made sure before I bought it."

"I know that, dear. But you know how some old people can be. Set in their ways."

She could probably write a book on the subject, after living between those two. At least Mrs. Franklin was sweet. Mr. Pratt was the type who needed a lawn so that he could yell at kids to get off of it.

"If I stop feeding the squirrel," Jillian pointed out "it seems to me that he would be *more* likely to get into the bird feeders."

Mrs. Franklin gave a little shrug. Jillian didn't think she actually cared about the squirrel or Mr. Pratt's feeders. She just liked to have something to gossip about.

"Are you sure it's safe for you to be out running around the neighborhood by yourself, what with all the crime lately? It's terrible, I tell you. Decent people having to be afraid to go out their own front door. Pretty girl like you, I just hate to think what could happen."

The crimes were mostly vandalism, nothing overtly violent, but she was touched by the older woman's concern. "I always carry pepper spray with me." She held up her wrist to show the bracelet she wore, which contained a concealed canister. Jillian had learned, the hard way, not to take her personal safety for granted.

Unconvinced, Mrs. Franklin sniffed. "I'd feel better if you had a man with you. Or at least a dog. You could take Ruffles with you any time you want."

Jillian eyed Ruffles, who shivered despite his little sweater. She wasn't sure how exactly he would defer an attack, unless the assailant tripped over him.

"I appreciate it," she told her neighbor, reminding herself that the woman really did mean well. "And I'll keep that in mind. Have a nice day, Mrs. Franklin."

Jillian gathered the neglected mail from the box and started up the steps. The curtains twitched in the front window next door, and Jillian barely restrained herself from rolling her eyes. Rather than pretending like she hadn't seen Mr. Pratt spying on her, she stopped and gave a little wave.

The curtains twitched closed.

She lamented, for possibly the hundredth time, that Mr. Pratt's brother – the elder Mr. Pratt, Robert – had suffered a stroke six months ago, precipitating this extended visit from his younger sibling, Adam. The older brother was a sweetheart. The younger, not so much.

Dropping the mail on the entry table beside the *matryoshka* – the wooden nesting dolls she'd inherited from her mother – Jillian looked up at the sound of a squeaking stair tread. She frowned as her housemate staggered toward her. With her freckled face and ruffled pajama pants, Katie resembled Little Bo Peep with a hangover.

"I thought I fixed all of the squeaky treads."

Katie grunted. "I guess you missed one. I'll dock your pay." With that she headed toward the kitchen and the life-saving caffeine it promised. Knowing Katie as she did, Jillian had set the coffee pot on a timer before she'd left for her run.

Then she winced, hearing Katie sigh when she opened the fridge.

"I'm going to the store as soon as I shower," Jillian called out, recalling that she'd used the last of the cream.

Katie reappeared momentarily, a mug clutched between her hands.

"Sorry about that."

"It's probably better that I drink it black," Katie said. "Less caffeine dilution."

"Maybe you should just start running it through an IV."

"Don't think I haven't considered it." She sat down on the bottom step. "The next time I get a bright idea like opening my own restaurant," Katie said "just shoot me, okay?"

"Since you've already opened the restaurant, I think it might be a little late."

"You know better than to use logic before I'm adequately caffeinated."

Jillian only smiled. Katie had indeed been working her butt off, but Jillian knew that she loved every minute. After cooking professionally for other people for years she was finally realizing her dream. Parker's on the Park was little more than a hole in the wall, but it was also a wildly successful hole in the wall. Less than a year after opening, Katie was already looking at expanding into the second floor space above the restaurant.

"I put the mail on the hall table," Jillian said. "Looked like Christmas cards, mostly."

Katie dropped her head onto her lap. "It can't be time to do that yet."

"Tis the season." Taking pity on her friend, Jillian patted her on the head. "I'll be happy to do a photo card – maybe you and the staff in front of Parker's – for you to send out. That would work for both personal and business purposes."

Katie's tired eyes lit up like holiday candles. "Would you?"

"No problem. Just tell me when you want to do the shoot. I'm going to run up and hit the shower and then I'll go to the store. I started a list and pinned it to the fridge if you want to add anything."

She started to move past, but Katie stuck out her mug, blocking her path. "Before I forget, Brian stopped by the restaurant last night."

"Oh?" Brian was Katie's older brother.

"He's having a little get-together later today on Tybee. Kind of an early Christmas thing before everyone's schedules get totally crazy. He told me to invite you."

Jillian frowned. Huge, bald and tattooed, Brian Parker was Jesse James to Katie's Bo Peep. And while underneath all the testosterone Brian was actually a total sweetheart, he was also a cop. FBI, technically. But still a cop. And likely to invite other cops.

Quite frankly, Jillian had had enough dealings with law enforcement to last her a lifetime.

"That's sweet," Jillian said, as casually as possible. Not that she had a single thing against Brian – she thought of him as an honorary brother – but she didn't particularly want to socialize with his friends. "I think I'm going to stay in tonight, though. I still have to edit the photos from that engagement shoot I did last week."

Katie shook her curl-covered head. "Brian said that you're not allowed to bow out, and to remind you that you owe him."

"Can't he ask for something easier, like one of my kidneys?"

Katie gave her a retiring look.

"Fine." Jillian capitulated with a sigh. She'd stay for an hour. Two, tops.

But when Katie looked smug, Jillian narrowed her eyes. "This wouldn't have anything to do with any single, available friends of his, would it?"

"No." Katie squirmed under Jillian's stare. "But there's nothing wrong with putting yourself out there. I think it's time for you to start seeing people again."

"I see people."

"Through the lens of your camera, which doesn't count. Nor does the resident geriatric set." She indicated their neighbors. "The goal is to get you socializing with people who aren't marrying other people and who still have a full set of teeth. And don't look at me like that," Katie complained. "It's been almost two years since Cooper."

"I know how long it's been," Jillian said dryly. "I was there when the divorce papers were signed. And besides, it's not like I haven't dated. I even let you set me up."

Katie winced. The last man whom she'd convinced Jillian to meet for dinner was currently sleeping in Katie's bed. And had been more often than not for the past six months.

"You're never going to let me live that down, are you?"

"It's the gift that keeps on giving." But because Katie and Davis were smitten with each other and Jillian bore no ill will over that fact, she smiled at her friend. "I'll go for a little while, okay? That way Brian can't accuse me of welshing and you can assuage your misplaced guilt."

"If it's any consolation, I'm pretty sure none of Brian's friends wear dentures."

Jillian shook her head. "If that's the standard we're using now, maybe you should be the one to shoot me."

She continued up the stairs – and damn it, one of the treads *was* squeaking. She bent down and examined it. Somehow, the new screws she'd put in had worked their way loose.

"That makes no sense," she muttered. She'd just replaced them last week. Maybe the wood was too worn? The house was pretty old. Sighing, she made a mental note to get some wood glue to drop into the holes before she tightened the screw again. Hopefully that would do the trick.

Jillian rounded the corner toward the hall bathroom just as the door to the master bedroom opened.

"Unh," Davis said by way of acknowledging her presence, scrubbing a hand through his dark blond hair, currently standing in spikes. A creative manager with one of the local theaters, his schedule involved a lot of late nights. He wasn't one to greet the day before he absolutely had to.

"You're up early," she told him.

"Dress rehearsal tonight. Do I smell coffee?"

"As long as Katie didn't get the last cup."

"Unh," he repeated, staggering toward the stairs.

Jillian watched him go, a little smile on her face. Katie had met him when he'd hired her to cater a cast party he was hosting, and Katie had been sure that he and Jillian would click. And they did click – when the possibility of any sort of romance was taken off the table. Jillian suspected it was a case of them being *too* much alike for any sort of spark to ignite. Davis seemed more like her brother.

A little wave of sadness passed over her at the thought, but Jillian shook it off. She needed to shower and run her errands if she was going to have time to get some work finished before Brian's party this afternoon.

Locking herself in the bathroom, she turned on the shower, removed her pepper spray bracelet and stripped out of her sweaty clothes. Her thighs burned, reminding her that she'd been less than faithful about her exercise routine lately, a consequence of too much work. Not that she was complaining about the work – she'd put in a hell of a lot of effort to build her photography business.

But she knew better than to let her physical fitness, speed and agility slide. Those things were every bit as important to her ability to defend herself as the can of pepper spray. In fact, maybe she should consider taking a self-defense refresher course.

Reaching back to pull free the ponytail holder which held her mass of hair, Jillian glanced out the bathroom window.

And froze.

Changing the angle on the plantation shutters so that she could get a better look, she blinked to make sure that her eyes weren't deceiving her.

"You have to be kidding."

Yanking her robe off the hook on the back of the door, she wrapped it around herself and then reached into the shower to shut off the water.

Flying down the stairs, she strode into the kitchen where Katie and Davis were canoodling against the counter.

"Hey," Katie said, peeking around Davis's bare shoulder. "What's wrong?"

Jillian yanked open the back door, too angry to adequately respond. Crossing the little courtyard, she winced as stray pebbles bit into her sole, but didn't let it deter her from her march toward the back gate.

She unlatched it, glaring at the sight that greeted her, a sight confirming what she thought she'd seen from the bathroom window.

Some... *asshole* had shattered the back window of her car.

More cautious now, seeing as there was broken glass scattered over the parking pad, Jillian picked her way around to the back.

Her back window *and* her rear taillights, she amended. Just freaking great.

"Ouch," came Davis's deep voice from behind her. "That sucks."

"Oh no," Katie added. "I guess they got you, too."

They were the perpetrators behind the recent spate of vandalism – soaped windows here, a spray-painted mailbox there. It appeared they were upping their game.

Jillian sighed. She could file an insurance claim, but figured that by the time she met her deductible she'd be better off just paying it out of pocket so that her rate didn't go up.

"Do you want me to call the police?" Davis said and then added "I guess not" when Jillian glared at him over her shoulder.

"At least they didn't get anything," she said, considering she never left valuables in her car. That was another thing she'd learned, having been targeted before.

A chill ran over her as memory wanted to intrude. She pushed it back. This was nothing like that. It was random. An unfortunate byproduct of her car being parked outside when some hooligans were looking for somebody to mess with, something to destroy.

There was nothing left to be done except place a call to her garage and see about getting the glass replaced.

She turned toward Katie with resignation. "I'll get your cream," she told her. "But it looks like I'll have to borrow your car."

JILLIAN also had to bum a ride to Brian's party, which put her at the mercy of Katie's schedule far more than she liked. At least Brian's friends did have all of their teeth, she acknowledged. And most of them were single. With the exception of one engaged couple and two marrieds, they met Katie's criteria for Jillian's target demographic.

So Jillian mingled, appreciating the festive atmosphere of the funky little beach bungalow that had originally belonged to Katie and Brian's grandparents. She was also relieved to find an eclectic mix of people – none of whom appeared to work with Brian – rather than the sausage fest she'd feared. A sausage fest in which she'd expected to play the role of sacrificial virgin.

Maybe she'd grown cynical, she mused as she carried her glass of red wine through the crowded kitchen, toward the doors leading onto the screened porch. She'd become accustomed to being alone, or to being Davis and Katie's third wheel.

It was… easy, she guessed, to keep to her safe little routine.

Rut, she admitted. She was in a rut. Because even as her professional life continued to grow and expand, her personal life became progressively narrower. Maybe Katie was right – not that Jillian was going to come right out and admit it. Regardless, she couldn't feel sorry that Katie and Brian coerced her into coming tonight.

She stepped through the French doors, which had been left open to catch the salty breeze off the beach and to allow guests ease of movement between inside and out. The weather gods had cooperated, bringing sunshine and milder temperatures. Tiny lights glowed like lines of fireflies around the ceiling, and Jillian couldn't help but smile at the image of big, bad Brian Parker stringing them up before his party.

Speaking of Brian, Jillian looked over to see him speaking with someone in the corner. Brian's back was to her, but both his size and his Santa hat were unmistakable. She couldn't make out the identity of the other person, but it was clear by the well-muscled arm that reached out to sit an empty beer bottle on the porch ledge that it was a man with whom he was engaged in conversation.

Jillian hesitated. She hadn't had a chance to talk to Brian beyond thanking him when he'd handed her a glass of wine, but she didn't want to interrupt. She'd wait a minute, see if the other man left. Right as she had the thought he stepped around Brian, making a gesture she took to mean that he was getting another beer.

He saw her standing there and stopped.

Jillian thought that her heart may have stopped as well.

It started again with a great thump against her ribcage, a thump that picked up in pace when his gaze locked onto hers and stayed there. He wore glasses over eyes that she couldn't quite discern the color of from this distance, under a mane of dark, unruly brown hair. Tall. He was almost as tall as Brian, though built along leaner lines.

Sensing his friend's arrested motion, Brian turned, saw Jillian standing there, equally frozen. He shot a quick glance at the other man and then turned a smile on Jillian.

"Jillian! There's my best girl."

His words knocked Jillian out of her reverie. She gave him a wry look. "I've heard you say that to at least three other women tonight."

"A man can't have more than one best girl?"

"Not according to the definition of that particular superlative."

"In that case, I was lying those other times." He extended an arm in invitation. "You're clearly the best girl here."

"On the porch, maybe." But she moved forward, snuggled against his familiar and comforting bulk.

Brian bent down to plant a smacking kiss on top of her head and then cleared his throat. "Hey. Let me introduce you to my friend, Jesse."

Jillian let go of Brian, looked at the other man. Blue. His eyes were blue – a really unique shade which eased toward something floral. Violet, or maybe chicory.

Jillian shifted her glass to her other hand to shake the hand he offered. "It's a pleasure to meet you."

"I'm pretty sure the pleasure is mine."

His palm was callused, suggesting he worked with his hands, and it scraped against hers as he slowly released it. Jillian swallowed. She thought she might be blushing, which was mortifying. It hadn't been *that* long since she'd talked to a good looking man.

Okay. A *really* good looking man.

But that was beside the point.

"I, uh, can go get you that beer," Brian said to Jesse. "If you want."

"That'd be great."

"Jillian?" Brian said, a bright, bright smile on his face. "More wine?"

Regaining her mental balance, Jillian narrowed her eyes. Brian was about as subtle as a buffalo stomping through a field of daisies. "I'm fine. Thanks."

"Okay, then. I'll be right back. With that beer."

He scampered off as quickly as a man his size could scamper, and Jillian was left standing in the shadowy corner with a man whom she'd just met. She hadn't had nearly enough wine to become chatty, and realized, to her returning mortification, that she had no idea what to say. The sound of breaking waves filled the ensuing silence, the equivalent of crickets chirping.

"I would make a comment about the lovely weather we're having this evening, but as far as conversational gambits go, that's about as lame as it gets."

Jillian found herself smiling. "It's better than what was running through my mind, which I'm ashamed to admit was somewhere along the lines of *do you come here often?*"

"That is bad." He shook his head in disapproval, though a smile lurked in his eyes. "At least neither of us asked for the other's sign."

"Stop," she said. "If someone used that line on me, I think I would have to say that my sign is *Stop.*"

He grinned. "Well then I'm doubly glad I didn't say it."

Jillian rocked back on her heels. Cleared her throat. "I'm sorry. I guess I'm out of practice talking to people."

"Recently released from a vow of silence?"

"What?" But she laughed. "No. I don't think I'd make a very good monk. I've just been…" in a rut "focusing on my career, I guess. Which involves talking to people, of course, but that's professional. If you'd like to discuss the golden hour and why it's the best time of day to do an outdoor shoot, I'm your girl."

"Since I don't think you're talking about gun ranges, I'm guessing you're a photographer." He had a way of zeroing in, she noticed, as if you were the only other person in the room.

Which, she considered with chagrin, she actually was. They were currently the only two people on the porch.

"Guilty. Mostly portrait photography – weddings, engagements, babies. Senior photos. That sort of thing." She took a sip of her wine. "How about you?"

"I'm a crappy photographer," he told her. "I always cut off the tops of everyone's heads."

She looked at him over the rim of her glass. "That wasn't quite what I meant."

He grinned again, quick and easy. "Sorry." He had a fabulous smile. "Smartass is sort of my default setting."

Jillian leaned that direction as well, when she wasn't tongue tied because she'd spent the past two years avoiding small talk in the way some people avoided contagious diseases.

"Your hair is… striking," Jesse said, catching her off guard with the unexpected compliment. He reached out, lifted a loose strand from her shoulder. "The setting sun was hitting it when you were standing over by the door. It looked like flame."

He smiled, a little rueful, noticing that he'd flustered her. He dropped the hair, stuck his hands in the pockets of his jeans. "I guess that makes me the moth."

"Ah. That's…" God, why was she having so much trouble forming complete sentences? "Thank you. I hated it, growing up. Not quite red, not entirely blonde. And so much of it. I…" Honestly, his smile was making her stupid. "I swear I'm not normally this incoherent." She peered into her glass. "Must be something in the wine."

He tilted his head. "And here I was hoping it was me."

He said it with just the right amount of self-deprecation to keep from coming off as a line. It would be easier if he'd intended it as one, because she had plenty of experience fending off creeps.

But he didn't appear to be a creep, she thought as he continued to hold her gaze. In fact, he seemed very un… creep-like.

"Here we are," said a voice from behind her, and Jillian whirled, bumping into Brian.

"Ah, shit," he said, wincing as red wine soaked into the pale gray fabric of Jillian's dress. "I'm sorry, Jillian. I didn't mean to startle you."

"It's as much my fault as yours," she said, suffering a brief but intense period of mourning for one of her favorite dresses. "I don't guess you have any vinegar on hand, do you?"

When Brian looked blank, Jillian just shook her head. "Never mind."

"Let me go find a towel or something," Brian said, handing the beer to Jesse. "Be right back."

When a wad of white cloth appeared in her field of vision, Jillian looked up. She blinked, trying to process the fact that Jesse was now shirtless.

"Take this," he said, when she didn't make an immediate move to accept it. "You need to blot it or whatever right away, right?"

"What?" She shook her head again to clear it. "Yes, but… really, you should keep your shirt." Please, so she could keep some brain cells.

"I have this one," he told her, lifting a long sleeved plaid from the back of a chair. "I took it off because I got too warm inside. And I have probably a hundred T-shirts. So really. Take it."

Frowning a little, Jillian accepted the shirt and set her empty wine glass on the table next to his full beer. "Thank you."

"No problem. I, uh, have four brothers, so somebody was always spilling something growing up. My mom was real big on blotting."

She smiled. "I'll bet." Jillian did her best to absorb the wine, but realized there was no way she was going to be able to salvage the dress enough to last the rest of the evening. Her entire front was soaked.

"Um, I appreciate you sacrificing your shirt, and it was really nice to meet you, but I think I'd better... shoot."

"And now I'm guessing that you're not talking about the golden hour," he said and she sighed.

"I just remembered that I don't have my car." The reason behind which still pissed her off. "I rode over with a friend. And I hate to ask her to leave, seeing as how she's the host's sister."

"I can give you a ride. Where do you live?"

"Oh, I wasn't angling for... That's very nice of you to offer, but you should enjoy your drink."

"I'll survive without it."

"No, really. I'll work it out."

He considered that a moment. "Are you worried about getting in a car with a stranger? Because I can have Brian vouch for me."

She just bet. "I can't ask you to leave the party so early."

He shrugged. "I'm not worried about it. Crowds and I don't really get along that well, anyway. And that was going to be my second beer, so I'm fine to drive."

Jillian hesitated. His eyes were indeed clear. He appeared sober, and unlikely to be the type to keep shrunken human heads in a display case in his basement.

Brian rushed back out, an old beach towel clutched in his big hands. "Sorry it took me so long. Oh." He looked at the shirt Jillian pressed to her chest. "Good idea," he said to Jesse.

"Can you tell Jillian here that I'm not a serial killer? She needs a ride home, and doesn't want to bother your sister."

"He's not a serial killer," Brian dutifully repeated, flashing a quick glance at Jesse that Jillian couldn't quite interpret. "But I hate to see you leave. Especially because I'm such a clumsy oaf."

"I have some editing to catch up on this evening, anyway. If the vandals hadn't gotten my car, I probably would have only stayed for an hour or so."

"Vandals?" Jesse said.

"Some asshole smashed her rear window and her brake lights," Brian explained.

"At least they didn't steal anything this time. And the glass is replaceable."

"See, this is why you're my best girl," Brian said with approval. "Always looking on the bright side." He shuffled his big feet and glanced down at the beach towel with uncertainty. "I guess you don't need this. I'll tell Katie that you're taking off." He leaned down and kissed her cheek. "Thanks for coming. Catch you later, man," Brian said to Jesse, and then headed back inside.

Jillian blinked. And then slid her gaze toward Jesse.

His dark brows arched over his glasses. "Ready?"

She played the whole thing back in her head, trying to remember when she'd actually agreed to accepting a ride from him. She was pretty sure she hadn't. But somehow, here she was with his hand on her elbow, steering her out the screened door.

She felt… maneuvered.

Jillian halted on the top step. "That wasn't" she gestured back toward the porch "some kind of… set up, was it?"

His eyebrows arched again. "Set up?"

She shook her head. She probably sounded like an idiot. A paranoid idiot. After all, she was the one who'd bumped into Brian and spilled her wine. "Never mind."

"My car's right over here," he said, angling toward a black four-door Jeep with fat tires and a trailer hitch on the back. He opened the passenger door for her, but then cursed under his breath. "Hang on. Sorry." He removed what looked to be a fishing tackle box from the seat, slid it onto the floorboard in the back. He smiled as he stepped back. "Wasn't expecting company."

Jillian shot him a look.

"What?"

"Nothing," she said after a moment. Her imagination was working overtime if she thought that he and Brian had somehow planned this whole thing out. And what a ridiculous notion, anyway. Unlike Katie, Brian wasn't overly concerned with Jillian's social life – or lack thereof. And men who looked like Jesse… she never had learned his last name, had she? Anyway, men who looked like him didn't need help from their friends to get dates.

Not that this was a date. It was simply a nice gesture from a man she'd met all of thirty minutes ago. And in whose vehicle she was now sitting.

The knock on the window beside her caused her to jump.

"Sorry," Brian said when Jesse rolled down the window. "You forgot your purse."

"Oh," Jillian said as he passed it through. "Thanks, Brian."

"No problem." He pointed a finger at Jesse. "You take care of my girl."

Jesse's tone was droll when he answered. "I'll do my best." He pulled away from the curb, and then glanced at Jillian. "So where to?"

"What would you do if I told you I lived in Charleston? Or... Kansas?"

"I'd fuel up, because it sounds like we're going on a road trip. But you don't live in Kansas."

"No, I don't. But I *could.* You know nothing about me, aside from my name, and that we have a mutual friend. But you didn't hesitate to leave the party to offer me a ride."

His lips twitched as he glanced over. "Are you always this suspicious?"

"No." Probably. "I just... like to understand people's motives." Because she'd been at the mercy of the incomprehensible actions of others too many times before. "Especially when I'm trapped with them inside a moving vehicle and I met them less than an hour ago."

He nodded. "Fair enough. What I said about me and crowds, that was no lie. I'm not the most social of animals and after prolonged exposure to a bunch of loud, giggling drunks, I start to break out in hives. Not that many of Brian's guests were intoxicated, but they were headed that way. And there were definitely some gigglers. Better to get out before I was tempted to run screaming down the beach."

She smiled. "You're an introvert."

He looked appalled. "I just don't like to be around a bunch of random people for too long if I can avoid it."

"Same thing. And I can say that because I'm the same way. It has to do with energy. Introverts gain energy from being alone. Interacting with groups drains us."

He stared at the road, brows drawn low in an expression that radiated skepticism. "If you say so."

"I do." Jillian wasn't entirely sure why the revelation made her feel more comfortable with him, but it did. Her shoulders relaxed a little. "I live on East Henry, by the way. Katie and I are housemates."

"That's right. Katie got the townhouse and Brian the beach place when their grandparents died."

"They were such kind people." They'd been killed in a car accident. Katie's grandfather suffered a fatal heart attack at the wheel, driving off the road and into a tree, also killing her grandmother instantly. "Did you know them?"

Jesse shook his head as he drove down the long, low road – surrounded by miles of winter brown-marsh grasses – that connected Tybee to the mainland. The sun hung like a fat ball just above the horizon, painting the sky with pink and orange as it made its final descent. "I didn't meet Brian until a few years back," he explained "so that was before my time. You've known Katie a long while then?"

"Since college."

"I thought Brian said that she went to one of those cooking schools."

"She did," Jillian agreed. "And I went to SCAD." The Savannah College of Art and Design was what had brought her to the city. "I had an assignment in one of my classes to photograph prepared food, like for restaurant advertisements and menus, and that's how I met Katie. We clicked. Been best friends ever since."

Jillian glanced down. She'd tucked his T-shirt between her dress and her skin to try to keep the wine from saturating her bra as well, but she didn't think she'd been successful. Her breasts felt damp and sticky. She pulled the shirt back out and then glanced up to find Jesse looking her direction.

"Sorry," he said. "I'm trying to pretend you're not wearing the equivalent of a wet T-shirt."

Her cheeks heated a little. "How's that going for you?"

"Not all that well."

"At least you're honest."

He returned his attention to the road.

Resisting the urge to clear her throat, Jillian sat the ruined T-shirt on her lap and tried not to notice that he smelled really good. Aside from the wine permeating the air inside the Jeep, she detected the clean, warm scent that struck her as uniquely male. What was it about a recently showered but slightly sweaty man? Something to do with pheromones, she was sure. He seemed to produce an abundance of them.

"So how do you know Brian?"

He glanced her way as they entered the city limits. "I own a fishing boat, and he was my partner in a charity tournament a few years back."

"Oh? I guess I didn't realize that Brian was that into fishing."

"He's not. Well, he is, but let's just say that fishing isn't that into him."

"I take it you didn't win the tournament?"

"Sadly, no. Brian got sick as soon as we hit some rough seas about three miles out. He failed to mention that he has the constitution of a Chihuahua inside the body of a Great Dane."

Jillian smiled at the description. "Do you operate out of one of the local marinas?"

He waited a beat before answering. "I'm docked on Tybee."

"Oh. Do you live on the island?"

"For the moment. I've been getting the home ownership itch recently, so I gave up the lease on the place I was renting and have been staying on my boat until I figure out where I want to buy."

"Now I feel even worse about you driving me home. You'll just have to turn right around and head back out there."

He glanced her direction. "I wouldn't have volunteered if I minded the drive. Especially when I have a captive audience to regale with my fishing stories."

"The only story I heard didn't involve much fishing."

"I'd be happy to take a detour and correct that oversight."

"Too late," she said, realizing that they'd already turned onto East Henry. Then she frowned when she saw the two men dressed in shirts and ties standing on the porch in front of her townhouse, talking to Mrs. Franklin across the adjoining rail.

"Problem?"

She glanced over at Jesse. "I don't know. Those look like cops."

"Judging from your tone, I take it that you're not a fan."

"Of cops?" She shook her head. "Let's just say that I prefer to avoid them whenever possible. And not because I'm a criminal," she added.

"I didn't think you were."

"I had an... unpleasant experience," she felt the need to clarify.

"I'm sorry to hear that."

So was she. And despite the fact that it had been years since that experience and she knew, theoretically, that not all cops were bad, her palms began to sweat. She hated the automatic nervous reaction, but had come to accept it. Surreptitiously, she rubbed her hands on her thighs, remembering too late that she'd laid Jesse's wine-soaked T-shirt there. It fell onto the floorboard and when she bent to retrieve it, she hit her head on the dash.

"Are you okay?"

"Fine." She rubbed her scalp and then offered him a quick smile that she hoped didn't betray her embarrassment. Leave it to her luck to have a mini-meltdown in the presence of the first guy she'd been attracted to in...

Well, in a really long time.

"You can just drop me off here."

He pulled to the curb and the two cops turned around, stared at them through the windshield. Jillian tried to swallow, but her throat felt thick. *Stupid, stupid* she told herself, pushing back against the memory of rough hands, hard fists. The sound of tearing fabric. Blood and water clogging her nose.

Judging by their street clothes they were probably detectives, not beat cops. Maybe they were talking to people in the neighborhood about the vandalism, and someone had mentioned her car. Maybe they had the wrong address.

Both perfectly plausible scenarios. There was no reason to be afraid.

"Jillian?"

Despite the soft tone, Jillian jumped. She'd been so lost in her thoughts – in her paranoia, she admitted – that she'd all but forgotten he was there.

He must think she was crazy.

"Um, thank you for the ride. And the… T-shirt."

When she turned to reach for the door handle, he laid a forestalling hand on her arm. "Let me come with you."

"Oh, no. That's not necessary." She glanced at the cops, who'd started moving down the steps, heading in their direction. Did that mean they recognized her? How? Why?

"If your face gets any whiter you'll be able to audition for the role of the Ghost of Christmas Past." He turned off the ignition. "I'm going to come around, open your door, and stay with you until we find out what they want." He looked grim. "And sometime I'd like you to tell me just exactly what happened to put that look on your face."

Muttering something that sounded like *unpleasant experience, my ass,* he climbed from the Jeep. Jillian wanted to protest, wanted to laugh it off, wanted to get out of the vehicle and talk to the police like any normal person. She hated this fear, and usually managed to control it.

When the door opened she glanced up at Jesse, tried to smile. His eyebrows slammed together, and then he leaned in to grasp her by the elbow again and help her from her seat.

Even though it was humiliating to be treated like an invalid by this man she barely knew, she had to admit that she was grateful. Her legs seemed to have turned to rubber, and she wasn't sure she could stand on her own.

"Breathe," he said and she did.

She flicked a glance his direction, woefully embarrassed. "Thank you."

"We've got company." He nodded in the direction of the approaching cops. "Remember that you don't have to answer anything you don't want to. You have that right."

Blinking in surprise at the murmured advice, Jillian found herself somewhat steadied as the two men stopped a few feet away from them. "Jillian Montgomery?" the older one said.

"Yes." She cleared her throat. "I'm Jillian Montgomery."

"Detectives Axelrod and Gannon, SCMPD. We'd like to ask you a few questions."

CHAPTER THREE

JESSE settled onto the sofa next to Jillian after she'd directed the two detectives into the arm chairs on either side of the fireplace. The chairs looked to be holdovers from the days in which Brian's grandparents had inhabited the townhouse, and he knew, from experience at his own grandparents' house, that that particular style of chair was about as comfortable as a pile of bricks. Given her obvious aversion to law enforcement personnel, he wondered if Jillian had suggested the formal parlor for that specific reason.

He'd expected her to object to his presence, to tell him that his assistance was no longer required, but she hadn't. Probably an oversight on her part, as she looked a little surprised when he joined her on the sofa, but he offered a reassuring smile. She blinked, her pale cheeks coloring a little, and then turned her attention back to the detectives.

"Accident?" the detective named Axelrod said, nodding at Jillian's stained dress.

She glanced down, seemed surprised to realize that she was still holding Jesse's shirt on her lap. "Yes. I spilled a glass of wine."

The detective waited for her to elaborate and when she didn't, said: "Would you like to change? We can wait for you."

"No, thank you. I prefer to answer your questions first."

And get this over with, was the unspoken subtext. The trembling fear she'd exhibited earlier had been tucked away behind a polite mask. She was composed, direct and thus far not offering one shred of information aside from what was specifically asked. Obviously this wasn't her first time at the interview rodeo, and the two detectives realized this as well.

Axelrod's gaze shifted Jesse's direction. "And you are?"

"A friend of Jillian's."

The dark eyes narrowed, displeased with that response, but he didn't make an issue of it. Jillian had invited them in and was prepared to answer their questions voluntarily, without the presence of a lawyer. Any cop worth his salt knew to take advantage of that kind of situation as quickly and thoroughly as they could.

The detective named Gannon leaned forward, the lamp beside his chair reflecting off the balding crown of his head. He frowned at Jesse. "Do I know you?"

"I don't believe so."

Gannon's brow furrowed. "You seem familiar. I could swear I've seen you somewhere before."

"Maybe I just have that kind of face."

The man studied him for several more moments, visibly trying to place him, before eventually sitting back. Then he glanced at his partner, passing the invisible baton.

"Are you familiar with a man named Myles Lewis, Ms. Montgomery?"

Jillian considered, and then shook her head in response to Axelrod's question. "The name doesn't ring any bells."

Gannon pulled a photo from a folder he carried, slid it across the ornate mahogany coffee table. "Well, Lewis is an alias. Maybe you know him by the name Miron Losevsky."

She glanced up sharply and then leaned over, studied the photo which had been pulled from the man's driver's license.

"No." She shook her head again, lifted her shoulders in a slight shrug. "I'm sorry, but to my knowledge I've never seen him before."

"Have you ever used the Fluff and Fold laundromat on Martin Luther King?"

"I don't believe so."

"Never?"

"I haven't used a laundromat since college, Detective. To the best of my recollection, I never patronized that one."

"You went to college locally?"

"Yes. SCAD."

"That's right, that's right." Gannon snapped his fingers, acting as if he'd just remembered a detail which Jesse knew he'd never forgotten. "You're a photographer."

Jillian stared at him a moment, clearly trying to figure out where this was heading but loathe to come right out and ask. "Yes."

"What sort of things do you photograph?"

"Weddings. Babies and children. Graduation photos. The occasional magazine spread for a lifestyle section or personal spotlight. Portraits, essentially. You can find all of that information on my website."

"Ever do any work for Thrifty Car Wash? An… advertisement maybe?"

"No."

"How about the All American Spa?"

"No."

"You're sure?"

Annoyance briefly flickered across her face. "Yes, I'm sure."

"The spa.... they had these photos in the windows, of some of the... ladies who worked there? Before it burned, that is. You didn't maybe take their pictures? Or portraits, to use your word. They were real professional looking."

Annoyance returned and set up camp in the form of a line on her forehead. "Perhaps one of the other of the hundreds of professional photographers in the area took them."

"Could be, could be." Gannon met her gaze, and then slid a bag from his pocket. "I'm just trying to figure out why Lewis – Losevsky – had this in his wallet."

Jillian picked up the bag. Inside was one of her business cards.

She stared at it a moment, and then carefully set the bag back down. "I've distributed boxes of these cards all over the city. I hand them out to clients, who pass them along to friends. I post them on coffee shop memo boards. Pass them out at bridal expos. There are almost limitless ways someone could come by one."

The detective picked the bag back up. Turned it over. And passed it to Jillian again.

Jesse leaned close enough to read over her shoulder. The name of a local dive was written in a sloppy hand along with last Thursday's date and a time. "I'm sorry." She returned Gannon's steady gaze, though Jesse detected a fine tremor in the hand that held the bag. "Is this supposed to mean something?"

"I was hoping you could tell me. When people write down a time and a place for a meeting on the back of a business card, the person whose name is on the card is usually the one that they're planning to see."

"But as I've already told you, I don't recognize this man. And the Shady Lady is hardly the sort of venue in which I would choose to meet with clients."

"So you're familiar with it?"

She gave him a cold look. "I'm familiar with many businesses in the area, even the ones I don't patronize."

"Huh. Most people, unless it's their dry cleaner or their coffee shop or a restaurant they keep meaning to try but haven't gotten around to it, seems they just drive by places without paying much attention. Especially little hole in the wall places like that. No neon, nothing much to look at. I guess photographers are unusually observant."

Rather than responding to that, she returned the bag to the table, and then clasped her hands in her lap. Tightly enough that her knuckles turned white. "What division do you work with, Detectives?"

"Criminal Investigations," Axelrod said.

"And specifically, in this case?"

"Homicide."

"The Fluff and Fold. I remember now. I caught the tail end of the news the other night. A man was murdered." She divided a look between the two men. "Was it the man who had my card?"

"What makes you think that?"

She opened her mouth as if to answer Axelrod's question, but then blew out an audible breath. "I believe I'm all finished answering questions. I'd like you to leave."

Axelrod slowly reached over to pick up the bag as Gannon stared Jillian down. "It would look better for you if you cooperated."

"I have cooperated, Detective, to the extent which I am able. I do not know Myles Lewis or Miron…"

"Losevsky," Gannon offered with a little smile, as if amused by the fact that Jillian had conveniently forgotten his name.

"Losevsky," she repeated coolly. "I also do not know how he came to be in possession of my card or why he used it to write down an appointment, or whatever it was.

51

However, given the nature of your investigation and the... tone of your questions, I believe it would be wise for me to have an attorney present should any additional questions be necessary." She stood, and Jesse followed suit. He almost grabbed her elbow again, but the rigidity with which she held herself suggested that his touch wouldn't be welcome this time.

"I'll show you to the door," she informed the cops.

The two men went, though not happily. Jillian opened the door and stood beside it, her expression stony. Axelrod murmured his thanks as he left, but Gannon paused, his attention caught by the grouping of festively painted wooden dolls on the hall table, each one a mirror of the other but decreasing in size. He pulled a toothpick from the inside pocket of his suit jacket, stuck it in his mouth as he studied them.

"I've seen these before," he finally said. "They're... Russian, aren't they?"

She stared at him with a coolness that belied the rapid pulse visible in her neck. "Yes."

He gave a little nod, and then reached back into his pocket. *"My* card," he told her. "In case you remember something you think we should know."

Jillian took the card. "Good evening, Detective."

When he'd gone, she shut the door and then leaned heavily against it. After several tense moments, she met Jesse's gaze and, Jesse was sure, was about to thank him again for driving her home, which was a polite way of telling him to get lost. Jesse was trying to figure out a way to forestall her when the commotion outside surprised both of them.

Jillian whipped around to look out the sidelight, and Jesse came to stand behind her, peering over her head. The streetlight illuminated the two detectives, standing on opposite sides of their car. Gannon, one hand on the open passenger door, used the other to rub his balding head as he glared into the oak branch which hung over the sidewalk.

Below him, Jillian tried to suppress another laugh.

"Care to clue me in?" he asked as they watched the detectives' car pull away.

She froze, as if only now realizing that he was standing so close.

"It's this squirrel that lives in the tree." She shrugged as she turned around, fixed her gaze somewhere around the vicinity of his collarbone. "He throws acorns when I forget to feed him."

"Don't squirrels eat acorns?"

"Yes, but he's kind of… spoiled." She looked a little sheepish.

"So what does he eat?"

She finally looked up. "Trail mix."

Jesse nodded, as if that made perfect sense. "You didn't feed him today?"

"Actually, I did. Before the party. I'm not sure why Kil… why he threw an acorn at Detective Gannon."

"Wait a minute, wait a minute. Don't think I'm going to let that slide. What do you call it? The squirrel."

She hesitated a beat and then sighed. "Killer."

"You have an attack squirrel." His brows shot up. "A trained attack squirrel named Killer that you bribe with nuts and berries to do your bidding."

A smile tugged at the corners of her mouth. "Don't say that where my next door neighbor can hear you. He already thinks I'm the scourge of the neighborhood for feeding what he considers vermin."

"My lips are sealed."

When her gaze flicked toward his mouth and her cheeks colored again, Jesse had to force himself to take a step back. "Do you have any tea bags?"

She blinked. "You want tea?"

"No, but my mom swears by it for calming the nerves. And since this is the second time I've mentioned my mother this evening, you're going to think I have an Oedipal complex or live in her basement, which I can assure you I do not, on either count. But I thought maybe *you* could use a cup of tea after talking to the cops, given your… unpleasant experience. You're shaking."

"Am I?" She pulled her sleeves down, as if that could disguise the fact that she was trembling. "I didn't realize."

He reached out and touched her arm. "I'm not saying that to embarrass you," he said softly. "But I can't help but be concerned. If you don't drink tea, maybe warm milk, although I've always thought that was a little gross. But to be perfectly honest, I don't feel right leaving you like this."

She frowned up at him and Jesse figured she was about to decline. Probably tell him to take his thinly veiled ploy to stick around and go to hell. But she surprised him by nodding. "A cup of tea sounds fantastic, actually."

He hid his relief with an easy smile. "Great."

She smiled back, a little uncertainly. "The kitchen is this way."

"After you," he said and swept out his arm.

She preceded him down the hall, seemingly unaware that she was still clutching his shirt in her hands.

And Jesse didn't quite know why that struck him as significant.

CHAPTER FOUR

THUGS. And stupid thugs at that.

The man watched the two younger men stumble down their stairs, laughing uproariously at some private joke. Swimming in alcohol. And looking to cause more mischief.

They had the strong, upright carriage of youthful males, but he judged them to be soft. Pampered. And impaired by drink.

They wore all black, quieter now as they scuttled down a side street like cockroaches. Except that cockroaches had more survival skills than these two, their antennas always twitching, sensing the air of their surroundings.

The two in front of him hadn't even realized they were being followed.

One of them pulled a tire iron from where he'd hidden it inside his jacket. He slammed it against his open palm, chuckling softly at a comment made by his companion. The one with the tire iron made a playful gesture, feigning that he was hitting the other over the head with the iron. The damage they'd wrought so far was minimal, but he could see that they were getting bolder. Busting the window glass in the car was the worst they'd done. But he thought it might not be long before they ended up hurting someone, even if only by accident. They were cowards, but if an angry property owner chased after them, they would likely use the iron to bust more than a simple window.

Aside from that, he didn't want them drawing more police attention to the neighborhood. Attention was something he didn't need.

He would have to disable the man with the weapon first. And then they would have a …discussion.

The man smiled. It had been a long while since he'd felt this good.

DUE to the high water table, most homes in Savannah didn't really have basements, but a lot of the older townhomes featured a lower level that was partially underground and accessed by a recessed door beneath the outside staircase. Many homeowners had turned them into street level apartments, especially in the heart of the historic district where real estate was at a premium. Given the close nature of their friendship however, Jillian paid rent to live in the main part of the house and the lower level housed the washer and dryer, holiday decorations, unused furniture and some accumulated clutter from her grandparents that neither Katie nor her parents had yet gotten around to sorting.

It was the laundry facilities that Jillian sought. She'd read that table salt could be used to absorb red wine stains from fabric, followed by soaking in a vinegar mixture, so she'd left her dress and Jesse's shirt to soak overnight.

She opened the interior access door leading from the kitchen, flipped the light switch.

Nothing happened.

She tried again, with the same results. The light fixture in the stairwell must have burned out.

Jillian backtracked, grabbed a new lightbulb from the utility closet, along with the flashlight that was anchored into a wall unit for recharging. One thing she could say for Katie, her friend was a little anal about organization. Jillian suspected it came from being a chef, having to have all of her ingredients lined up and prepared. Considering Jillian suffered from what Katie called Right Brain Syndrome – a polite way of saying she tended to lose track of things – Jillian appreciated her housemate's OCD.

Switching on the flashlight, she went halfway down the stairs, unscrewed the burned out bulb, screwed in the new one, and then climbed back up to flip the switch again.

Nothing happened.

"You have to be kidding." The breaker must have tripped. Which meant she'd replaced the lightbulb for nothing. Sighing, Jillian turned the flashlight back on and braved the depths of the lower level. Luckily, some light came in from the windows at the front and rear of the space, but given the fact that it was an overcast morning in December, that light was murky at best.

She made her way toward the Freddy Krueger Room, as she thought of the space in the cellar that contained the water heater and the inner workings of the townhome's heating and cooling systems. Jillian was fairly handy with basic home repair – hence the reason she'd been the one nominated to fix the squeaking stairs – but something about the old pipes and bare brick walls in that part of the building really creeped her out. Sucking it up, she opened the door, shined her flashlight around the stygian depths of the windowless room.

No horror movie villains lurked in the corners, so she skirted the boxes and old tools and various assorted detritus, aiming for the breaker panel. Jillian was glad that Katie's grandparents had updated the system from the old style fuse box, because flipping a breaker was much easier than replacing a fuse.

She opened the panel, found the appropriate switch. "Let there be light."

But Jillian frowned at the lit room. Had she turned on the light switch when she'd entered? She honestly didn't remember. Switching off both her flashlight and the overhead light, she pulled the door closed, surprised by the brightness that greeted her.

Apparently the hall light had been left on, and light also shone from under the door to the storage room.

Well, no wonder the breaker tripped. Jillian thought she'd been the last one down here last night, and she certainly hadn't left the lights burning in any of the storage areas. She spotted the stack of red and green tubs, and thought maybe Katie had come down to see about the Christmas decorations. It was time they hauled them out.

Jillian dutifully turned off the light in the storage room, and then headed toward the laundry area.

The light switch was in the "on" position, but the room remained dark. She flicked the switch again, got nothing. Okay. Okay, so this lightbulb burned out because it was left on all night, along with the others. It was indeed odd, but there was nothing supernatural about it.

Luckily she had the lightbulb from the stairwell in her pocket. She got the ladder from the storage room, dragged it back to the laundry area and changed the bulb.

Now that she could see what she was doing, Jillian turned her attention to the laundry tub. Wrinkling her nose at the smell of vinegar, she lifted the dress out, examined it. The stain was almost entirely unnoticeable. Hopefully the final trip through the wash cycle would eliminate it completely.

Jillian wrung it out before dropping it into the washing machine, and then reached into the tub for Jesse's shirt.

It wasn't there.

Confused, Jillian looked around. It wasn't anywhere on the floor. It wasn't in the washer, nor in the dryer. It seemed to have disappeared.

"Okay," she said out loud this time, because she was feeling just a little freaked out. Maybe Katie came down here last night and left the lights burning, but why would she take Jesse's shirt out of the sink? It made no sense.

The knock on the front door caused Jillian to jump.

"Jesus," she said, laying a hand against her pounding heart. Uneasy now, she poked her head out of the laundry room, looked toward the lower level entrance. No one ever came to that door.

Jillian thought of the cops who'd been here last night, of the questions they'd asked her. Her throat felt dry and raw when she tried to swallow.

"Jillian?"

The voice was muffled, coming as it was through the door, but she thought she recognized it.

Only slightly less uneasy, Jillian dried her damp hands on her jeans and walked toward the front. He was a friend of Brian's, she reminded herself. Not a serial killer. They'd talked quite amiably over tea last night. He hadn't even given Katie's knife block a second glance, let alone attempted to grab one of the utensils and attack her.

Despite the pep talk, Jillian paused when she reached the door, glanced out the barred window to the side. Jesse stood there, huddled against the rain that had just started to come down. The porch overhead sheltered him from the worst of it, but the wind had also begun to blow.

She couldn't leave him standing out there. Especially not when he saw her looking at him through the window and gave a friendly wave.

Jillian unbolted the door.

"Hey," he said in greeting. "I hope I'm not disturbing you."

"No, no. Just startled me a little, because people don't generally come to this door."

"I did ring the doorbell, and when you didn't answer, I started to leave. But I saw the light through the window down here, and figured I'd give it a shot."

"Oh." That made sense. And it was rude of her to keep him outside. She considered her messy ponytail, the damp spots on her jeans that smelled like vinegar. Well. It wasn't like she'd made a stellar impression last night. "Won't you come in?"

He ducked a little as he came inside. The ceilings down here were only a little over seven feet, which wasn't too terribly far over his head.

"I try to tell myself it makes it cozy rather than claustrophobic," she told him.

He smiled, and she tried to figure out why he looked different. "You're not wearing your glasses."

"Contacts," he said. "I ran out of solution yesterday, which is why I was wearing my glasses."

"I like the glasses," she surprised herself by admitting.

"Oh yeah?" The smile he gave her bordered on cocky.

"Sure. If you *had* been a serial killer, I could have broken your glasses and run away while you were groping around, half-blind, trying to find me."

He laughed. "Do you always think in worst case scenarios?"

"I like to be prepared."

"In that case." He pulled something out of his pocket. "I found this on the floorboard of my Jeep. It must have fallen out of your purse when you bent over to pick up the shirt last night."

Jillian stared at the key. She'd taken her car key off her ring yesterday and dropped it off at the garage. Somehow, this one must have slipped off as well.

She accepted it from Jesse. It was the key to the lower level, which was separate from the main house key.

She stared.

"It is yours, isn't it? I haven't had anyone else in my car recently."

"What? Oh. Yes." She cleared her throat. She knew she risked sounding like an idiot, but the question had to be asked. "You, uh, didn't happen to let yourself in overnight and take your shirt back, did you?"

"Excuse me?"

She waved her hand. "Never mind."

"No, wait." He reached out and grabbed her wrist. "What happened?"

64

She glanced at his hand on her wrist and when he removed it, she finally met his eyes. His brows were drawn together. "Sorry. I'm just a little jumpy, I guess."

"Jillian. What happened?"

"It's nothing, I'm sure. Just… weird. I put your shirt into the sink with my dress, to soak them both overnight – I was planning to give it back to you – but the shirt is gone. Katie must have taken it for some reason when she came down here last night."

"Katie spent the night at Brian's."

"What?" This time Jillian's brows drew together. "No. I…" was sure she'd come home last night. Jillian had been surprised that she was already up and gone when she'd awakened this morning – she'd really wanted to talk to her friend about the visit from the cops – but figured Katie had gone into holiday panic mode and was trying to fit some shopping in before she had be at work. "How do you know that?"

"I talked to Brian this morning. Katie had too much to drink, so Brian wouldn't let her drive." Jesse hesitated, and then admitted with a wry lift of his lips. "And he wanted to make sure I hadn't made any untoward moves on his honorary little sister."

"Oh." One part of Jillian's brain considered that it was kind of a shame he hadn't, but a larger, much more vocal part suggested that maybe her earlier unease hadn't been for naught.

Jesse must have picked up on her concern. "Other than my shirt, was anything else missing?"

"I don't know," she admitted. "Nothing that I noticed off hand. But the breaker had tripped, and when I came down here to fix it, all of the lights were on. I know I didn't leave them on when I went back upstairs last night."

"You said you'd had some vandalism in the neighborhood. Any break-ins?"

"None that I'm aware of."

He considered that. "Do you mind if I have a look around?"

Jillian debated with herself, but finally shook her head. "I don't mind. Although the windows down here are barred, and we keep the door to the upstairs bolted – the bolt was still engaged when I woke up. Aside from that, we have an alarm. I texted Katie to tell her I was going to set it, and to be aware of that when she came in."

He glanced around. "Can you show me the breaker box?"

"Sure."

She took him into the mechanical room, flipped on the light. "It's right over there."

He stared at the old boiler. "That thing looks like it should be in a museum. Or a horror movie."

"I call this the Freddy Krueger room."

"I can understand why." The concrete in this room had never been painted, and parts of it were crumbling. Jesse frowned at the floor before moving across it. He opened the panel, examined the breakers. "It looks like the security system is on the breaker that tripped. But there should be a battery backup. Did the control panel say anything about a power outage? Or did you hear any loud beeping last night?"

Jillian opened her mouth but no sound came out for at least five seconds. "No. The alarm was off when I got up this morning, but I thought Katie must have turned it off when she left the house. But if she was never here…" she pressed her hand against her stomach. "Oh my God. What if we were robbed and I slept through the whole thing? I took a couple Tylenol PMs," she admitted. "After you left last night. I likely wouldn't have slept at all otherwise. I didn't think they were strong enough to keep me knocked out during something like that, but I need to look, see if anything is missing."

When she started to turn in a panic, Jesse took her arm. "Hey. There's no reason to believe you were robbed, okay? One missing shirt does not a robbery make. You said you didn't notice anything else out of place?"

She shook her head. "But I didn't go into Katie's bedroom. Or the office. Or the front parlor. There are some valuable antiques in there. Collectible things, I mean. Easily carried."

"You mentioned that your studio was in the garage. Is that on a separate alarm system?"

"It is. And I've already been out there this morning. Nothing seemed to have been disturbed."

"Okay." He ran his hand up and down her arm in a gesture meant to soothe. "Let's just have a look and see what we find."

Suddenly chilled, Jillian crossed her arms and nodded.

There were no signs of forced entry, either in the lower level or upstairs. No broken glass or unlatched windows. They examined every room, found the electronics and other valuables intact. And aside from Jesse's shirt, it didn't appear that anything was missing.

"You probably think I'm nuts," she said when they'd concluded their examination and were standing in the kitchen.

"Not at all. I do think you should call a technician from your alarm company and have them check out the battery, see if it's still functioning. Usually the system will let you know if it's on backup power or if your battery needs to be replaced, but since neither of those things appears to have happened, there could be a problem with your system. It wouldn't hurt to check."

Jillian nodded. "I'll do that right away."

"I'm also wondering if it's possible that you came downstairs again without remembering."

"You mean like sleepwalking?"

"You said you took a sleep aid. I've heard that can be a side effect."

"So, you think I turned off the alarm without remembering?"

"It's a possibility."

A scary one, Jillian thought. "Okay, turning off the alarm and turning on the lights, I can buy. I don't like the idea, but I can see where it would make sense. But why would I hide your shirt?"

"People do strange things when they're sleepwalking. I have a brother who used to wake up in the middle of the night and eat sticks of butter. In the morning, he didn't remember a thing."

"That's disgusting."

"And also pretty damn annoying when there's no butter for your toast."

Jillian wanted to tell him it wasn't possible, that she'd taken sleep aids before and never had a problem, but the fact was she couldn't say for sure.

"I don't know. Maybe. Maybe I did. And now I feel really stupid."

"A little paranoid, maybe, but not stupid. Cut yourself some slack."

She smiled in answer to his. "Gee, I feel so much better."

"That's what friends are for."

Friends. Somehow, over the course of the past twenty-four hours, she thought they might just have become friends, of a sort. There'd been an instant… connection, she guessed you would call it, from the moment she saw him.

The question was: were they going to become more.

His smile faded as he studied her face, and she studied his in return. She did like his glasses, but without them she could really see his eyes. Beautiful. It seemed a strange term to use on a man so inherently masculine, but they were beautiful, nonetheless.

Those beautiful eyes focused in on her mouth in that way he had of making everything else seem to fade into the background. She felt her lips soften in response, part in invitation. Jillian started to sway toward him just as the back door opened, and in spilled Katie.

"Hi," Katie said, her brows winging skyward as she divided a look between Jillian and Jesse, and then zeroed in on the latter. "I didn't realize you were still here."

"Not still," Jesse clarified, taking a casual step back. "Again. Jillian dropped her key in my car last night, so I stopped by to bring it back."

"Oh." Katie waggled her eyebrows at Jillian. "How convenient. Well, since you're here – again – would you care to stay for a late breakfast? I stopped by and picked up a couple baguettes on my way back from Brian's – and I was *not* drunk, despite what he says. He's just overcautious. Anyway, I'm going to make some French toast. There'll be plenty."

"If you don't stay," Jillian said when he glanced at her for direction "I'll be forced to eat an entire baguette myself. When Katie cooks, you eat. It's the law around here."

"I'm nothing if not law-abiding."

"Great." Jillian wasn't sure if the flutter in her stomach was nerves or... something else. "I'll set an extra place."

CHAPTER FIVE

STUFFED to the point that he was tempted to undo the top button of his jeans, Jesse's delighted stomach unfortunately had no mitigating effect on his temper. Instead of a pleasant carb-induced food coma, his knuckles were white ridges against the black leather of his steering wheel as he drove across town.

The rain had finally blown out to sea, but the access road he turned onto hadn't been very well maintained. Puddles the size of small golf course water features splashed muddy spray onto his windshield. Watching the wipers fling it away again was mildly cathartic, especially when he pictured himself as the wiper, and a certain, unnamed asshole as the mud.

The building at the end of the road was nondescript cinderblock construction, a little shabby around the edges. It had once been an automotive repair shop, now defunct. He pulled into one of the bays, hit a remote to lower the door behind him.

The garage had been part of a criminal syndicate that stole cars from dealer lots, re-painted them and then sold them on Craigslist. When they were busted, the garage ended up in Bureau possession. While Jesse had mixed feelings about asset forfeiture, as it tended to be abused by some unscrupulous law enforcement agencies – Georgia's forfeiture laws were some of the worst in the nation – he appreciated the inconspicuous meeting place. At this point, they were trying to keep the Bureau's presence in the investigation as little-known as possible.

Especially since it seemed that the SCMPD had a leak.

Jesse'd been around law enforcement long enough to know that an oath to serve and protect didn't always trump the lure of easy money. It was a reality of life, but one that pissed him off nonetheless.

Pocketing his keys as he headed toward the office, he then shoved his hands in after them. It was probably better for everyone involved if he didn't have them free to use as he might have liked.

He pushed open the door with his shoulder, strode into the room. Perched on the edge of the battered desk behind which Detective Axelrod was sitting, talking on his cell.

Axelrod flicked up a finger to indicate that he'd be finished with his call momentarily, and Jesse casually swung his leg back and forth.

Back.

And forth.

Detective Gannon strolled out of the adjacent restroom, cocky as ever, shaking his hands as if to dry them. He stuck a toothpick in his mouth and then shot Jesse an amused grin.

Jesse grinned back as he stood up.

Then his hand came out of his pocket and grabbed the detective's stylish shirtfront, seemingly of its own volition.

"Hey! Hey now," Axelrod called, ending his call even as Gannon sputtered "What the *fuck,* Wellington?" and pushed at Jesse's chest.

But Jesse had made himself a rock – he'd had plenty of practice, growing up with four rowdy brothers – and continued to stare at the other man from a distance of inches. Hostility radiated from Gannon, defiance and something else shining in his eyes. It was that something else that caught Jesse's attention. Embarrassment, maybe? Fear? Or a sly kind of satisfaction.

When Axelrod's hands landed on Jesse's shoulders none too gently, he let Gannon go. But he didn't look away.

Gannon glared back and then disguised the fact that he was the first to blink by looking down at his shirt, smoothing the wrinkles.

When he glanced back up, his expression was one of dispassionate irritation. "What the hell was that all about?"

Jesse shook off Axelrod, who was still hovering, obviously waiting for him to attack again. With one last glance at Gannon, he turned his attention to the man's partner. "First, I don't appreciate games, particularly not in this type of situation. An apparently innocent girl is dead, and that's on you. A not so innocent man is dead, and that's at least partially on me. Now the friend and housemate of my colleague's sister may potentially –"

Gannon snorted, but Jesse ignored him "– potentially," he continued, "be connected in some way that we have yet to determine, and given the swiftness and viciousness with which those other two were dispatched, I don't find it amusing to have Detective Gannon entertaining himself by playing *Don't I Know You* in front of that woman, who we're all aware has an aversion to law enforcement."

"Lots of people have an *aversion* to law enforcement," Gannon said, making air quotes. "But we don't handle them with kid gloves."

"We're not handling her with kid gloves. We're going on this little principle you may have heard of called innocent until proven guilty."

Gannon snorted. "If she didn't live with Parker's sister and he hadn't lost his shit, we'd already have hauled her ass in."

"On what grounds? The presence of her business card among Losevsky's effects is circumstantial at best. It gives us cause to interview her, which you did, last night."

"With you sitting on the sofa, all cozied up beside her."

Jesse let the implication slide. "And how far do you think you would have gotten if you had *hauled her ass in.*" He borrowed Gannon's air quotes. "You spook her, she's likely to lawyer up and make our jobs that much more difficult. Or worse, if it turns out she *is* connected somehow, you're painting a target on her back. I don't need to remind you what happened to the last witness you had in custody."

Gannon crossed his arms. "And the fact that she's Russian doesn't make you the least little bit suspicious?"

"She's American," Jesse corrected. "Her mother was Russian. She grew up in a little town north of Atlanta, raised by an aunt. She was a cheerleader, an honor roll student, and everything in her background is about as apple pie as you can get. She has no relatives of Russian descent that we've been able to uncover. She's had no contact with the Russian community here that we're aware of. Particularly not the criminal element of that community."

"Just because you're not aware of it," Axelrod joined the conversation "doesn't mean it ain't happening."

Jesse nodded to acknowledge the older detective's point. "And if we do turn up evidence to that effect, she'll be interviewed formally, at the Barracks, with an attorney present."

"Just whose side are you on, Wellington?"

Jesse turned, addressed Gannon in a tone that could turn the puddles outside to ice. "I'm on the side of the truth, Detective. And I'll conduct this investigation with that – and only that – objective in mind."

"The *truth* is that she was nervous as a cat in a room full of rocking chairs last night. We all saw it, and if you didn't, you're either blind or a liar. She's hiding something."

"That's a classic Othello error."

"What the hell does Shakespeare have to do with anything?"

"Points for knowing your English bards," Jesse said. "But Othello error means that we're conditioned to see what we expect to see. Interpreting as evidence of guilt the nervous behavior of someone who has a reason to be nervous – like a woman who's already had bad experiences with cops and finds them on her doorstep basically suggesting that she has knowledge of a heinous crime – says more about your need to confirm your bias than it does about her truthfulness."

"Please." Gannon snorted his derision. "Spare me the psychobabble."

"It's an elementary mistake in reading body language," Jesse said with a kindness that he knew would rub Gannon the wrong way. "Don't take it too hard."

"Speaking of taking it hard, maybe you see her behavior as proof of innocence because you have a boner for her."

When Jesse took a step toward him, Axelrod once again inserted his hefty bulk between them. "Hey. Hey now. Let's all just calm down."

Realizing that he'd allowed the other man to push his buttons, Jesse held up his hands in a conciliatory gesture. Stepped back.

Gannon stared at him for several tense moments. "I don't guess you heard about the two college kids who came into the ER early this morning, bruised and bloodied?"

Confused by the non-sequitur, Jesse frowned. "No. Should I have?"

"Seems these two – while having their various injuries tended and broken bones set – were real keen on admitting to getting drunk and performing some acts of vandalism in Ms. Montgomery's neighborhood. Including busting out the window in her car. Mostly for shits and giggles."

Jesse wasn't entirely sure where Gannon was going. "How helpful of them to confess."

"Wasn't it? From what I gathered after talking to the officer who took their statements, somebody beat the hell out of them and scared them into spilling their guts. They were apparently afraid that if they didn't confess and face the consequences, this guy might come back and do something even worse."

"Does your department have a suspect?"

"Nope. Because the two idiots insisted that their injuries were the result of an accident. A playful skirmish between the two of them that got out of hand. And that their consciences simply had gotten the best of them."

Which of course was a load of bullshit. Any law enforcement officer with even an ounce of seasoning wouldn't believe that.

"So someone who figured out that they were the guilty party decided to take justice into their own hands," Jesse said. "I can't support vigilantism, of course, since it's usually more about revenge than it is justice. But at least those two won't be causing any more property damage."

"I find it interesting that the vandalism has been going on for a couple of weeks now, but the day after Ms. Montgomery became a target, someone big and strong enough to kick two decent sized twenty-year-olds' asses put a stop to it. And made a threat frightening enough that confessing seemed preferable."

Jesse crossed his arms. "Exactly what are you suggesting, Detective?"

Gannon shrugged. "Nothing in particular. Although you may want to give Agent Parker's knuckles a glance if he ever decides to show up."

Jesse actually laughed. "You're kidding me, right?"

Gannon plucked the toothpick from his mouth, tossed it in the trash. "If this little meeting is adjourned, I've got some actual work to do. Like finding a killer."

He walked out the door, slammed it behind him, without waiting for a by-your-leave.

Axelrod dragged a hand down his jowly face. "He's a good cop," he said. "He's just a little… brash."

"If I was the type to throw my weight around, I'd point out that acting brash toward the person directly above you on the food chain is a good way to get your ass chewed. Not to mention that accusing a fellow task force member of criminal activity based on no evidence whatsoever is not exactly the best way to build rapport. "

Axelrod nodded, sending pockets of excess facial flesh quivering. "I know."

Jesse sighed. "I'm sure neither you nor Detective Gannon appreciates my casting stones at the inner workings of your department, but your superiors invited us in. And deflecting blame won't change the fact that somewhere along the line, you have a real problem. The guard at the jail mistakenly leaving Irena unattended with another inmate, an inmate who just happened to be carrying a shank. Somebody overlooking the fact that laundromat was built before current codes were in place, so instead of a solid firewall between it and the neighboring building, there was shared attic space that left a point of access to Losevsky's apartment unmonitored. Those are a lot of balls being dropped at exceptionally convenient times. And even if the preponderance of ball-dropping is in fact an unfortunate series of miscommunications – a problem in itself – the fact that Ghostbusters was playing on a loop in Losevsky's apartment should clear up any doubt that you have a leak. Somebody, somewhere along the line overheard someone on the original task force refer to this guy as The Ghost. And passed that information along."

Axelrod ran his hand over his face again. "I know. You've made your point there already. The autopsy on Losevsky is scheduled for today. You gonna be meeting us there?"

"Agent Parker will be." Unfortunately for Brian and his delicate stomach.

"Alright." More diplomatic than his partner, Axelrod stuck out his hand.

Jesse shook, and then watched the other man amble out. As soon as he heard their car start, he pulled a glove from his pocket, slipped it on.

Then retrieved Gannon's toothpick from the trash can.

He was just dropping it into an evidence bag when Brian came through the door.

"Hey," he said, shaking water off himself like a dog. "Made the mistake of walking under a tree when the wind blew." He stopped when he saw what Jesse was doing. "What's up?"

"That's the question." Jesse climbed to his feet, pulled another evidence bag, already labeled, from the pocket of his windbreaker. "I found this on the ground beneath the rear basement windows at your sister's place." He showed him the bag containing a toothpick. "And this is the one Gannon discarded about five minutes ago. I don't know if you've noticed that he has a habit."

"I have. Always chewing on wood like a damn beaver." Brian stared at the two bags. "You think he came back last night, snooped around?"

"I'm going to have the lab test the two, see if we have a match."

"Since you're not one to waste resources," Brian said "I'm guessing you have a reason for doing so aside from the fact that Gannon is kind of an asshole."

"I do."

"Judging by the look on your face, this can't be good."

Jesse sat the two bags on the battered and scarred desktop. "When I went over there this morning, Jillian was a little freaked out."

"I knew she would be. I told you she has that reaction to cops, especially the locals. That's one of the reasons I wanted one of us there when they talked to her."

Jesse nodded. "And I saw that firsthand." She'd been trembling like a damn leaf. Gannon thought it was a sign of guilt, but Jesse was withholding judgment until they had more information. And not because he wanted to have sex with her. He simply tried to examine the evidence with an impartial eye, and there was a large body of evidence which suggested that people telling the truth often acted far more jumpy and nervous than skilled liars, especially when they feared the consequences of their story – however true – not being believed.

"Aside from her interview with the detectives," he told Brian "there was a… situation this morning." He filled the other man in on the details.

"Shit." Brian's hands flew up, linked behind his head. "Shit. You don't think Gannon actually broke into the house, bypassed the security system?"

"At this point, I can't imagine why he would want to take that kind of risk. He certainly seems to want Jillian to be guilty of something, but going to that length would suggest some sort of personal stake. Do you have reason to believe it's personal?"

"He wasn't one of the cops she had the run in with, if that's what you mean. But there's bad blood there. You know how it is. Maybe Gannon knew one of the guys, or maybe he's just the type to take issue with anyone who's gone against a fellow officer."

"I'll check him out."

Brian paced back and forth. "If he did break into my sister's house to snoop around, I'll kill him."

"Let's not leap to any conclusions. I saw no evidence of a break-in, and Jillian says that nothing was disturbed as far as she could tell, aside from my missing shirt."

"So it was a breaker trip and a battery failure, happening simultaneously? No. No, that's stretching coincidence a little too far. And that stuff about Jillian sleepwalking, turning off the alarm and hiding your shirt someplace – you don't really buy that, do you?"

"Not really. But no one was home with her last night, so we can't know what did happen. I told her and Katie both to call a technician, have them come out and check the alarm system. But since you're more familiar with the house, you may want to swing by before the autopsy, have a look and see if there's anything I missed."

Brian's head dropped back on his shoulders. "Why do I have to witness the autopsy? Why me, God?"

"Just be thankful you're not full of your sister's French toast. You'd probably lose it."

He leveled a disgusted look at Jesse. "You got French toast? You got to eat my sister's famous French toast, and *I* have to go to an autopsy?"

"Some days suck like that."

"You're such an asshole. On second thought, I kind of hope it was Gannon snooping around. I hope he broke in and took your shirt so that he could make a giant voodoo doll with it."

"If I start to feel strange stabbing sensations or my hair catches on fire, I'll let you know."

Brian looked at the bags on the desktop. "This is too close to home," he said with no trace of levity. "Finding Jillian's card among Losevsky's possessions? That was like finding a bomb in the middle of your living room."

"I know. But like I told Mateyo," their boss "it's too early to tell. Everything so far is circumstantial. We need to collect some solid evidence before we can determine the best course of action."

"You went to bat for me," Brian said, still staring at the desk. "With Mateyo. He wanted to yank me off the case."

"Well, you did kind of lose it there for a little while."

"After seeing what we saw that morning in Losevsky's apartment, wouldn't you?"

"I don't even like that it happened in the same city as my family. So yeah. If I thought my little sister's housemate might be connected, I'd lose it, too. If I had a little sister. Which I'm feeling pretty thankful that I don't. Having three younger brothers is bad enough."

"It's hell man, sometimes, worrying about her. Them. Because you know Jillian's like my sister, too. I don't care if that sounds sexist or whatever. It's in the DNA when you're the big brother."

"You must have put Katie's boyfriend through the wringer."

A look of tolerant disgust overtook Brian's face. "His record is pretty squeaky. Guy's nice enough. But I still want to punch him every time I go over there and he's... there. Making himself at home. Like hey, want a cup of coffee? But what he really means is *I'm banging your sister.*"

"Yet another benefit of brothers," Jesse considered. "When I stop by to see one of them and they have a woman over, I'm delighted if she offers me a beverage. And if she intimated that she's banging him, I'd probably give her a high five."

"You're really trying to make me hate you today."

"Buck up, Buttercup." Jesse glanced at his watch as he grabbed the bags. "I have to take these to the lab. And you've got an –"

"Yeah, yeah. Don't remind me."

Jesse chuckled at Brian's back as he walked out, but quickly sobered when he looked at the bags. He didn't particularly relish the idea of going behind Gannon's back, despite the fact that the guy was a dick. But he needed to know what they were dealing with here.

And though he tried to stick with evidence-based assessments as much as possible, sometimes he got a feeling in his gut.

And this time his gut said that a whole boatload of trouble had just sailed into port.

CHAPTER SIX

JILLIAN smiled at the receptionist as she handed the woman the signed credit card slip. It had been a while since she'd taken a self-defense class, and though she liked to think that she would know what to do if she were attacked, she had to admit that her skills were probably rusty. She'd begun to... relax over the past couple years, she guessed you could say, and while she wouldn't complain about her life becoming calm enough that she'd been able to let down her guard, she also didn't want to be lulled into complacency.

Especially given the events of the past few days.

It was entirely possible that it was an unfortunate coincidence that she'd once again pinged on the Savannah law enforcement radar. It was also possible that in her subsequent nervousness she'd taken too many Tylenol, sleepwalked, visited the basement, turned off the alarm and then went back to bed.

But it made her uneasy. It made her *very* uneasy. And because she believed in being proactive rather than curling into a ball and hiding – a reaction with which she was all too familiar – Jillian had done an internet search for a self-defense refresher course and then walked over to the West Broad Street YMCA to sign up and pay. It didn't start until after the holidays, but at least it was something.

The receptionist glanced at her information as she handed Jillian the receipt. "Oh. You're going to be taking the class with the new instructor."

From the tone of her voice, that was significant. "Is that a good thing or a bad thing?"

The woman looked at Jillian over the top of her glasses, ebony eyes dancing. "It's about six feet plus of good thing, if you know what I'm sayin'."

Jillian couldn't help but smile. "Sounds like a lot to take to the mat."

"Honey, if it were me and him on a mat, he wouldn't have to toss me over his shoulder. I'd just lay right down."

It felt good to laugh. "Not quite the skill I was hoping to refresh, at least not in a public classroom." She glanced at the information sheet again. The instructor's name was listed as Jordan W. "Well, I'm looking forward to class even more than I was before. Thank you."

"My pleasure, believe me. You have a nice day, y'hear?"

"Same to you."

Feeling lighter, Jillian stuffed the paperwork into her bag as she turned the corner. She bumped right into someone coming from the opposite way.

"Oh, I'm so sorry. I wasn't looking... Jesse," she said, when she realized whose hands were grasping her arms. She looked up, up into those beautiful eyes. The receptionist's description of six plus feet of good thing came to mind.

Jillian was tempted to find the nearest mat.

"You might not want to get too close," he said, stepping back just a bit and wiping his forehead with the towel around his neck. "I'm sweaty."

So he was. Which made Jillian even more tempted to look for unoccupied rooms.

And okay. Maybe her libidinous drought was finally coming to an end.

"If I say *do you come here often,* does that put us right back where we started?"

"I'm afraid I don't have any wine to spill at the moment."

His gaze drifted down, lingered briefly on her chest, and then flirted with hers when it snapped back up. "A shame."

Really, a utility closet would do.

"So what *are* you doing here?" he asked. "I don't think I've seen you around before."

"Oh." Jillian hefted her mind out of the gutter. "I just signed up for a self-defense refresher course."

"A self... really." He looked slightly disconcerted, possibly because she was wearing the red striped dress and high-heeled boots she'd worn to her earlier meeting with clients, and looked more like a holiday confection than someone who knew her way around a wrist hold. But then he smiled. "Good for you."

"I'm not always the blubbering mess you've been witness to the past several days."

"I'd hardly say you were blubbering." He grabbed hold of the edges of his towel. "So what did the security technician say?"

"No problem with the system and the backup battery appears to be functioning. User error was his diagnosis. Either I thought I'd set the alarm and didn't, or turned it off and don't remember. Which still seems really unlikely to me, but..." She shrugged. "I can't be too upset, because nothing was missing."

"Except my shirt."

"Except your shirt," she agreed. "I still haven't found it."

"Strange," he said, frowning. "Can I walk you to your car?"

"I appreciate the offer, but my car is still in the shop. I walked here."

He cast a dubious look at her boots. "In those?"

"Walking in heels doesn't bother me," she said. "Although I usually choose more sensible footwear. But I had a meeting with clients – they're getting married this weekend – and this wasn't too far out of the way."

"Give me five minutes to hit the shower and change and I'll drive you home."

"That's not necessary."

"I insist."

She studied him a moment. "Okay, but at least partly because I want to see if you can really shower and change in five minutes."

"If I take longer, I'll buy you a drink."

"It's ten a.m."

"I'll buy you coffee."

The corners of her mouth twitched. "Deal."

He bolted off toward the locker rooms, and Jillian tried not to feel too guilty about watching him go. His rearview was just as enjoyable as his front.

"Might want to take that down a notch," she murmured to herself as she leaned against the wall.

Jillian pulled her phone from her bag and shot off a text to Katie.

Guess who I bumped into – literally – at the Y.

It only took a moment or two for Katie to answer.

Is he tall, dark and bespectacled?

Jillian smiled.

The very one. We're going out for coffee. So you can have your 'I told you so' speech all ready for when you get home this evening.

"Ready?"

At the sound of Jesse's deep voice right beside her, Jillian dropped her phone.

"I've got it," Jesse said, stooping down.

"No, no." The messages were still displayed. Jillian all but elbowed him out of the way. "That's okay."

She snatched the phone, shoving it into her purse as she stood back up. When she glanced at Jesse, his tongue was stuck in his cheek.

"I, um, wasn't expecting you so quickly."

"I told you I'd be ready in five."

"Yeah, but I didn't *believe* you." She took in his damp, clean hair, the jeans and soft blue sweater that had replaced the athletic shorts and T-shirt. "How do you do that?"

"Another benefit of growing up with four brothers and limited hot water. You learn to shower quickly."

"Well. Looks like you don't owe me a coffee."

"Yes, except that bet was what we call a ruse. I was planning on taking you out for coffee either way." He tilted his head in the direction of the door. "Shall we?"

They drove to a shop a few blocks over, a quirky little place near the park which had great coffee and terrible parking. Jesse circled the block once, and then whipped into a spot right behind the minivan which vacated it.

They placed their orders, found a relatively quiet spot next to a display of decorative mugs and holiday blend coffees tied up with silver bows. Jesse grimaced when he looked at them.

"You don't like Christmas?"

"What? Oh. Yeah. Sure I do. I just don't like Christmas *shopping*."

"Coming from such a large family, I imagine you have a lot of presents to buy."

"Luckily my brothers and I came to an agreement. We go in on our parents' gift and we don't bother with presents for each other. No one's produced any offspring yet – much to my mother's dismay – so no nieces or nephews to worry about. But I somehow still always seem to have a list." He took a sip of coffee, eyed her over the rim. "What about you? Do you have a lot of relatives?"

"No." Jillian shook her head. "I was raised by my aunt, but she passed away a few years ago. I have a couple cousins, but they're a good bit older. A card usually suffices. My parents died when I was five. Rip current. My mom got sucked under and my dad went in to try and save her. They both drowned."

"I'm sorry. That's awful."

"It was a long time ago."

"That doesn't make it any less awful."

"No," she agreed. "It doesn't. It sounds strange to say, but I wish I could remember something about that day. I was on the beach, saw it happen, and some Good Samaritan took care of me until the authorities could get there. But I don't recall any of it. I guess I blocked it out."

"That's pretty common after such a traumatic event, especially in children."

"So the therapist assured me."

"Your cousins, they don't live around here?"

She shook her head.

"No other relatives?"

Jillian hesitated. "No."

"I'm sorry." He sat down his coffee. "I don't mean to pry. I guess, considering that my own clan is legion, I just have a difficult time imagining what it's like."

"It can be difficult at times," she admitted. "But Katie, Brian, their parents, they've become my surrogate family." The bell over the door jangled, and three uniformed cops came in.

She glanced up when Jesse's hand closed over hers, guiding her mug back onto the saucer.

"It was sloshing over the rim," he said quietly.

She looked down. There was a small puddle of coffee on the table.

Embarrassed, she reached over to grab some napkins, wipe it up.

"Hey." His hand closed over hers again, clenched on the wadded napkins. "It's okay. They're leaving."

She looked over. The officers, complimentary coffees in hand, were heading back out the door.

Her shoulders slumped a little. "You must think I'm crazy."

"No. But I think that the 'unpleasant experience' you alluded to the other night was probably more of a traumatic event. One that you haven't blocked out." His jaw got tight.

"One that causes your hand to shake when you so much as see a cop."

"It's not that bad. At least not usually." She looked up, met his skeptical gaze. "I mean my reaction to the cops, not the... event. I won't downplay that. But I'm not so traumatized that I can't distinguish that not all law enforcement personnel are evil. I don't think that all of them are out to get me. It's just that the other night stirred up some bad memories. I guess I'm still a little shaky."

He studied her face for several moments, and then squeezed her hand before releasing it. "Can you talk about it?"

"I..." prefer not to, she started to say. But he'd sat there with her the other night while the detectives asked their questions. She hadn't had to face them alone – doubted she *would* have faced them alone, which would only serve to antagonize them and make them more suspicious. And he'd made her tea afterward.

"I can," she said instead. "If you really want to hear it."

"I believe I've mentioned that I don't make offers I don't want to make, and don't ask questions if I'm not interested in the answer."

Something in her chest fluttered at that way he had of zeroing in. "Okay. But after this, maybe we could talk about the weather."

He smiled. "Deal."

Jillian took a sip of her coffee to soothe her throat. "My senior year at SCAD I shared an apartment with Katie and another girl. Charlotte. Charlotte became involved with a Savannah cop. Everything was great at first. We all felt safer having Mike – that was his name. Mike McGrath. Anyway, we all felt safer having him around. But Charlotte was a beautiful girl, just stunning really, and Mike was a possessive guy. Despite the fact that Charlotte was crazy about him, he slowly became convinced that she was cheating. A girl that beautiful *had* to be receptive to the advances of other men. Especially men who made more money than a cop, or so Mike's own insecurities caused him to believe. Anyway, he became abusive. Charlotte tried to cover it up at first, to hide the abuse from us, but it got bad enough that Katie and I staged an intervention of sorts. We convinced Charlotte to pursue a restraining order – not an easy thing to do when the order is against a police officer. Needless to say, Mike was furious."

The coffee turned bitter in her throat, so she sat the mug back down. When she glanced up Jesse was watching her steadily. Patiently.

Jillian pressed on. "As I'm sure you can imagine, Mike blamed us. Me and Katie. But especially me, as I was the one who turned him away from the door one night when he showed up, drunk and enraged and demanding to see Charlotte. I'm the one who called nine-one-one. Who embarrassed him in front of his colleagues. And I'm the one who had my camera with me when he came back days later, when he caught Charlotte alone outside the apartment building, when he had her pinned to the wall, choking her even as he sobbed and begged her to take him back."

Many people had questioned her on this next part. On why she didn't immediately cry out or run to Charlotte's aid. But Jillian had known without a doubt that it would once more end up being her word or Charlotte's word against his. That even the bruises would be explained away as the blue wall closed in to protect one of its own. So she'd done what had come instinctively. She'd snapped off several photos even as she'd used her cell phone to again call nine-one-one.

And then she'd jumped on Mike's back.

"The photos were finally evidence that was irrefutable enough to get Mike put on leave," Jillian explained "while they conducted an internal investigation. But somehow during that time – and I still don't know how – Mike got to Charlotte. He scared her, I think, into withdrawing her statement. She said that I'd misunderstood. That it was consensual. That she liked it *rough*."

"Christ," Jesse muttered.

Jillian swallowed the bitterness that never quite went away. "Katie and I tried to talk to her, but she was adamant. It got to the point that she couldn't live with us, with our judgment, and so she moved out." She closed her eyes. "She moved in with Mike."

She felt Jesse's hand close over hers again. "You know that there's a psychological aspect to abuse. To why women – and sometimes men – stay with their abusers. That they have to be ready to help themselves before you can help them."

Jillian nodded. She knew. But it didn't make it any easier. "I did all I could, but like you said, Charlotte had to be the one. Anyway, I went about my business, heavier of heart, but minding my own. But things started… happening. I got pulled over for doing only a mile or two over the speed limit, more than once. Cops followed me for no reason. Katie and I had our apartment raided because *someone* called in a tip that we were selling drugs. We both spent the night in jail, despite the fact that there were no drugs on the premises. I'm only surprised that they didn't plant them."

"You were the target of a harassment campaign."

"Payback. Mike got his friends on board. *He* was never involved himself, so I couldn't accuse him of abusing his position to seek revenge. Brian found out about the raid and came down here – he was at Quantico at the time – and raised holy hell. The cops backed off."

Sharp blue eyes searched her face. "There's more."

"There's more," she agreed. And it was the more that still caused her to wake up occasionally in the night, sweating, a scream trapped in her throat. It was the more that caused her hands to shake when she spotted a blue uniform.

"They left Katie alone after that. I think they didn't want to risk pissing off a federal agent, especially one of Brian's size and disposition. Plus, Katie's family has some connections in this town. She became too risky as a target."

"But not you."

"I don't have connections. I'm an orphan who was raised by my aunt. Aside from that, I was the one who really pushed. The one who took the photos. The one who dug my fingers into Mike's eyes so that he'd release his grip on Charlotte's throat."

A fierce smile broke free like the sun emerging from a passing cloud. "Good for you."

"I would have liked to have kicked him in the balls, but I was coming at him from the wrong side."

The smile faded, and Jesse gave her hand another squeeze. "Let's hear the rest of it."

A fine tremor wanted to start in her legs, but Jillian refused to allow it. She distanced herself from the story, became the narrator, not the protagonist. It was something that had happened to someone else. "There were a few more incidents – my car being broken into, my camera stolen."

"That's what you were referring to the other night."

She nodded. "But I couldn't specifically pin them on Mike, because things like that do happen. Then weeks passed without any sort of event," she said slowly "and it seemed like Mike was through. Brian's threats had done the trick. I let my guard down. I was on River Street one night, down toward the end, away from the hotels, because there was a full moon. A spectacular full moon over the water. I wanted to get some photos – with my new camera. Our apartment wasn't too far away, so I started to walk back, full of the thrill of knowing I'd really nailed a few of the shots. You can tell sometimes, you know? Even before you see the results, you can tell that they're going to be good. So I was sort of bouncing along, buoyant with that creative power, not paying all that much attention, when... someone grabbed me. Pulled me into an alley."

Jillian closed her eyes, tried not to feel the impact of fists against bone, of rough hands on tender flesh, of her hair being pulled from the root as they dragged her by it. "There were three of them. All in black. Masks covering their faces. They beat me. Had me down on the ground behind a dumpster, kicking and punching. Groping. The dumpster smelled of old frying oil and rotting fish. There was a puddle – it had rained the day before, and there was a muddy puddle in the middle of the alley – and my head was in it. It wasn't terribly deep, but every time I turned my head to the side to try to... get away, the water choked me. I thought that I might drown. But it seemed better than being raped by Mike and his friends. Because I'd seen his eyes through the hole in the mask, and I knew that it was him, knew what he had planned. He wanted me to know. And he laughed, knowing that I couldn't do anything to stop him."

She winced when Jesse's hand tightened on hers, almost painfully this time, and he immediately released her. "I'm sorry." He looked at her hand. At his. Back into her eyes. "I'm so damn sorry."

She knew that he meant more than just the fact that he'd squeezed her hand a little too tightly. "It's okay. Really. Unbeknownst to me, Brian had asked one of his friends, a cop in a different division from Mike, to keep an eye out. I still don't know whether he somehow got wind of what Mike was planning or just happened to be in the right place at the right time that night, but he came to my aid. The other two who were with Mike ran off, but Mike and the other officer grappled. The officer – his name is Sam Herrera – was shot in the arm. Finally realizing what he'd done, Mike took off too, but backup had arrived by that point and they were able to apprehend him a few blocks over. Mike and his cohorts went to jail – more, I think, because another police officer was shot during the course of their attack than for the attack itself – but… anyway, they went to jail. Mike is still there, although the other two have since been paroled. Thankfully, they no longer live in the area. But Officer Herrera was forced to accept a desk job after his gun arm was ruined. He isn't bitter, though. At least he didn't seem so the last time I saw him. I photographed his two daughters as a birthday gift for his wife."

Jesse stared at her for several long moments and then leaned back against his chair.

"I don't know what to say," he admitted. "Offering to kill the bastards who hurt you doesn't seem very productive, but it would sure as hell make me feel better."

She smiled. "That's very chivalrous of you. Some people don't... believe me. That it happened in quite the way I claimed, I mean. There's a culture in this country of hero-worship when it comes to public servants. For a lot of people, anyway. They don't want to believe that not everyone who pins on a badge is filled with integrity and the desire to serve and protect. Charlotte," this was the most difficult part for her "Charlotte convinced herself that I was jealous of her relationship with Mike, that I wanted him for myself. That that's why I kept after her to break things off, and that I somehow... enticed him, chased after him, leaving him no choice but to put me in my place."

"She's delusional."

Jillian nodded. "I know. It took me a while to come around to that in my heart. I knew it, logically, but the heart's more stubborn. And I also know, logically, that there are lots of good people in law enforcement. Sam and Brian are proof of that. But that wariness – and yes, fear – doesn't always respond to logic. So... now you know."

He was quiet for several beats. "Now I know. I don't blame you for feeling wary, though the fear... I hate that you're still afraid. But the self-defense class makes even more sense now."

"I won't be helpless." She lifted her chin. "Never again."

Their eyes met, held, until Jillian's chin slowly lowered. The air between them seemed to stir. To heat.

He finally broke contact, glanced at the clock positioned on the wall behind the counter. "I should take you home."

She followed his gaze toward the clock. They'd been talking for nearly two hours.

When she looked back, he was watching her in that way of his. But this time the flutter it caused was considerably lower.

"Thank you for the coffee."

He watched her for another heartbeat. "Any time."

CHAPTER SEVEN

"*SHOULD* I be alarmed," Brian said as Jesse pulled the knit beanie onto his head "that you dig this disguise stuff as much as you do?"

"I don't know that this qualifies as a disguise." Jesse checked the rearview mirror, satisfied that he'd completely obscured his hair. "And besides, why should you be alarmed?" He adjusted the plaid shirt he wore over a paint-splattered vintage T-shirt, and then angled around the steering wheel to roll up his jeans.

"Because it's so out of character."

Jesse glanced up at him through his thick black-framed glasses. "Exactly."

"You should talk to Davis. Katie's boyfriend," he clarified when Jesse arched an inquiring eyebrow. "He does theater stuff. Maybe he'd offer you a summer job."

"The problem with you, Parker, is that you fail to take advantage of the fun side of law enforcement."

"Fun."

"Technology is great," Jesse explained, "but all of the digital age tools have diminished what I like to think of as the Columbo appeal."

"The dude with the rumpled raincoat?"

"The very one. Now Columbo, he didn't have GPS tracking and long range microphones and camera-equipped drones. He had his wits."

"And a script writer."

"That too. But Columbo, he wasn't hiding behind a laptop. He was out there in the trenches, digging up evidence, pitting himself against the criminal masterminds who thought he was no match for their genius."

Even in the dim interior of the car, Brian's skepticism radiated like the sun. "You're crazy, you know that?"

"It's been suggested from time to time." Jesse looked out the window. The night was brisk and clear, with stars scattered like diamond chips across the black velvet sky. Down here on earth, the scenery was considerably less poetic. They were parked a couple of blocks away from The Shady Lady, a bar whose origins dated back to the days when Savannah's waterfront was rife with shady characters doing even shadier business, though it had changed names, owners and incarnations dozens of times since then.

Most recently it had been purchased by the same dummy corporation which also controlled the Fluff and Fold where Losevsky's body had been found.

Seafarers still frequented it, as Savannah was a busy international port. It was likewise popular with adventurous tourists, as the building was rumored to harbor the ghosts of the pirates who'd once used the underground tunnels to shanghai unsuspecting patrons.

SCAD students and denizens of the local counter culture also congregated here, hence Jesse's transformation into a stereotypical hipster. The bar had a reputation for being an outlet for drugs – particularly hallucinogens – but much to the frustration of the Counter Narcotics Unit, they never could seem to find the evidence they needed to make a major bust.

Jesse wasn't interested so much in the drugs as he was in the person responsible for cooking and peddling the stuff, primarily because he was a stone cold killer. Losevsky was far from upstanding, but the image of his brutalized corpse was permanently imprinted on Jesse's brain. And he couldn't stop thinking about the girl – Irena. Taken away from everyone and everything she knew, forced to perform degrading and dehumanizing acts for someone's sick enjoyment and someone else's profit. Failed by those who should have been protecting her.

For Irena, if for nothing else, he wanted to take this bastard down.

"I don't know what you think we'll find," Brian muttered. "The undercover narcs haven't been able to score any deals recently, let alone any information on the distributor. After Irena escaped and brought the organization to the cops' attention, they seem to have locked things down pretty tight. Nobody knows nothing about nothing. And after what happened to Losevsky, I doubt that any of his employees, however peripheral, will even fart in the direction of someone who looks like a cop."

"Luckily for us we don't look like cops."

"You know what I mean. I don't think we can expect anyone to roll over, no matter how dire our threats or how tempting our incentives."

"Consider this a fishing expedition," Jesse said. "We don't know if they're biting, but we know they're here. You can't expect to catch anything if you never venture near the water."

"Waste of time," Brian muttered.

"Maybe. But interviewing the laundromat employees and neighbors got us nowhere. Forensics is still processing the evidence from the scene, but I'm not really counting on a stray hair. The car washes are self-serve, so there's no one to talk to. We've got Bristol working on following the money, but digging through all those layers is going to take a while. I have no doubt the massage parlor will relocate and reopen under a different name, but so far the business permit applications I've sorted through haven't sent up any red flags. This is the last 'legitimate' business that falls under the umbrella of the dummy corporation." He paused. "And it's the one that Losevsky referenced on the back of Jillian's business card."

Brian's jaw tightened as he stared out the window. "You haven't found anything connecting her to any of this."

"No, I haven't. And I've dug pretty hard to compensate for what Mateyo and the SCMPD detectives see as your bias. Whatever the reason for Losevsky having her card, I don't think she was lying when she claimed not to know him."

Brian's gaze shifted toward Jesse. "I feel like shit deceiving her. Not telling her straight up that I'm involved in this case. That you are, too."

"The alternative would have been to agree to let Axelrod and Gannon take the lead with her. Gannon would have been his asshole self, she would have lawyered up, and you would have been sidelined because you have a relationship with someone who is now seen as a hostile witness, or possibly a suspect. Handling it this way wasn't as… straightforward as it could have been, but I got to be present at the interview, observe her behavior, without her realizing I was part of the process."

Brian continued to stare. "Are you going to try to start something with her now that she's no longer a person of interest?"

Jesse snorted. *"Oh hey, and by the way, I'm actually an FBI agent.* I'm sure that would go over well."

"You're attracted to her."

More than he wanted to admit. "I have eyes, don't I?"

Brian shook his head. "Katie'll kill me if you just ditch her. She called me the other day, all excited over the fact that you two were having coffee. Which I don't recall being part of the plan."

"I bumped into her. She was planning to walk several blocks in high heels. Offering her a ride seemed like the polite thing to do."

"Polite. Is that what they're calling it these days."

More than finished with the topic, Jesse made sure the overhead light was turned off before he opened the door. "I'll take the bar. You can crush some poor fools' egos at the pool table in the back room. Anything comes up, text me. Otherwise I'll meet you back here."

Jesse took one route, Brian another. He moved purposefully until he passed by an alley, found himself stopping. Backing up.

He glanced at the street signs just to be sure, but this was the place. The alley Jillian had been dragged into, beaten, nearly raped.

The dumpster from a nearby seafood restaurant leaned against one wall, the smell coming from it just as Jillian had described: old frying oil and rotting fish. There was no puddle in the alley but he could picture one there, in the depression in the pavement. Picture Jillian's beautiful hair, delicate face in the filthy water.

He'd read the reports. He'd known what happened to her, because he'd made it his business to know everything he could, to try to find some sort of link to Losevsky or the organization he'd worked for.

But hearing it from her lips made it so much more personal. So much worse.

And him so much angrier than he really had a right to be. After all, justice had been served. The perpetrators convicted, and either doing or had done time.

And he still wanted to track each of them down and rip them limb from limb.

"Definitely better to stay away," he muttered to himself, recognizing that in the few times they'd been together, it had somehow become more than a simple attraction. There'd been a click, almost audible, the first time he'd laid eyes on her, standing on Brian's back porch, looking charmingly uncertain.

And a click was not something he needed or wanted right now. Especially not with this woman.

Putting Jillian out of his head, Jesse finished making his way toward the Shady Lady. The building was old – parts of it still boasted the wavy glass typical of the eighteenth century. The unassuming wood and tabby construction looked like what it had been then and now: a den for both pirates and criminals of the landlubbing variety.

Jesse opened the heavy wooden door, strolled in.

The bar area occupied the oldest part of the structure, and as such consisted of low, beamed ceilings and thick plaster walls. Smoking was prohibited in enclosed public spaces in Georgia, but the stain from years when that law had not been in effect darkened the walls. The scent of stale tobacco still clung to the wooden ceiling. In the corner stood a statue of a female pirate complete with corset and ample cleavage rising above it as a nod –albeit a slightly sexist one – to the history of the place.

But judging by the skimpy costumes on the female wait staff, Jesse didn't think that political correctness was high on the management's priority list.

He ambled over to the bar, took the vacant stool near the end. A blonde waitress lifted her chin in acknowledgement of his presence as she poured a draft for another customer, and then popped up in front of him a couple minutes later.

"Hi," she said, looking him over. "What'll it be, handsome?"

It was faint, very faint, but Jesse thought he detected a hint of an Eastern European accent. "What's good?"

Her lips twitched and she leaned on the bar, showing off cleavage to rival the make-believe female pirate's. "That depends on what you're in the mood for."

Jesse allowed his gaze to dip lower while he considered the best course of action. He'd likely lose her if he tried to garner any information up front, so instead he'd wait and see how far he could get after flirting with her for a while.

"I'm in the mood for a lot of things," he said "but I'll start off with a beer." He named his choice, watched her shake her hips as she strolled off to fill his order. He glanced over his shoulder when the door opened again, saw Brian walk in, looking big and mean and far more like a street thug than a federal agent.

Jesse turned back around, feigning disinterest, and smiled when the bartender slid his beer in front of him. "Thanks."

"You need anything, you just call me. My name's Yuliya."

"Yuliya. I won't forget it."

Especially since Yuliya had been Jillian's mother's name. Jillian was an English derivative. The coincidence jarred him a little, causing his brain to swerve into the corner where he'd shoved all thoughts of his attraction for the time-being. Since mental detours weren't productive, he forced his attention back to the matter at hand.

He studied the bartender while she wasn't looking. A very attractive woman with her ample assets on display, he wondered if the flirtation was an act. He thought of Irena, of the other women like her who'd been forced into a life of sexual slavery in a country far from their own. Despite the hint of accent, Yuliya's English was as good as his own, and she didn't have the haunted, vacant look in her eyes that he'd seen previously with victims of human trafficking. And there'd been no indication from any of the other local law enforcement agencies that sex was an item on the Shady Lady's menu, despite the provocative costumes. Maybe she was encouraged to flirt with the clientele, maybe she did it because it earned her bigger tips, or maybe she did it because she wanted to. But he didn't get the impression that she was acting against her will. But then he didn't think the man they were after was dumb enough to put sex slaves who spoke English well enough to ask for help in a position of communicating with the general public.

He'd come back to Yuliya later.

Jesse turned around on his stool, surveyed the other patrons in the bar. An eclectic mix, with the majority of the crowd involved in the pursuit of nothing more than having a good time, or perhaps drowning their sorrows. Gannon and Axelrod had already interviewed the staff about Losevsky, whom all of them claimed not to know. The bar – conveniently – had no security cameras, and none of the man's credit card statements placed him here.

But the handwriting on the back of Jillian's card was his. And given who he'd worked for, Jesse had no doubt that Losevsky'd been here multiple times. So someone here had to know something.

The sound of groans coming from the back room indicated that Brian had just cleaned up at the billiard table. He'd win a few games, establish himself as someone to beat, and hopefully draw the attention of the regular sharks. He'd win again or maybe throw a game, depending on the temperament of the people he was playing. Offer to buy a round of beers, start shooting the breeze instead of pool. If they were people who hung out here often enough, they were bound to have seen something.

It was a thin hope, but until they had the forensic results and the money trail untangled, Jesse figured it was more productive to chum the waters a little.

He brought the bottle to his mouth, took a drink as he scoped out a trio of men in a nearby booth. Then the door opened again, and Jesse choked on his beer.

Jillian stood in the doorway, wearing the same expression of uncertainty she'd had on Brian's back porch.

Then she squared her shoulders, walked purposefully toward the bar.

And all Jesse could think was: *Fuck.*

CHAPTER EIGHT

JILLIAN'S heart kicked like a mule against her ribcage, but she forced herself to move. The bar was crowded, the light dim, both of which served to make her feel less conspicuous but also less secure.

She was crazy to do this, but she hadn't been able to stop thinking about it since the detectives' visit the other night. *Why did that man, Losevsky, have her card?*

If his surname hadn't been Russian she probably could have – would have – brushed it off as exactly what she'd claimed it was: a coincidence.

But what if it wasn't?

What if… well, she was here to see about the *what ifs,* wasn't she?

All of the barstools were taken, so she squeezed through the crowd, made her way over to the very edge of the bar top.

It took several minutes, but one of the bartenders – a blonde female in a ridiculously small corset that made Jillian's own breasts ache in sympathy – finally appeared in front of her.

"What can I get you?"

Jillian hesitated. The woman had a hint of an accent, which both relieved and frightened her. She hadn't been sure what to expect. But this was what she'd come for, so she laid her hand on the bar with the twenty dollar bill visible beneath it. She risked offending the woman, having her laugh in her face or – more likely – losing the money because she wouldn't know what the hell Jillian was talking about or wouldn't tell her even if she did.

"What I'd really like is a little information."

The woman stared at her out of blue eyes much shrewder than the platinum blonde hair and corset might have suggested.

She took the twenty, slipped it into her pocket in a move so quick and subtle that Jillian would have missed it if she hadn't been looking.

"Make it quick. We're slammed tonight."

Jillian glanced around. Most of the bar's patrons were locals at this time of year, and the conversation was being conducted primarily in English. Her Russian wasn't great, and she took yet another risk in using it, but she really didn't want to be overheard.

I'd like to know if there's been anyone in here... asking about me. My name is Jillian Montgomery.

Something flared in the woman's eyes, whether surprise at the fact that Jillian had spoken in Russian or recognition of the name, Jillian couldn't say. Or maybe Jillian had misjudged and the woman didn't speak the language. Or maybe she did and Jillian had flubbed it up, despite practicing it before she came here. Or –

Two Savannah detectives, the woman answered. *I don't remember their names. They showed your photo, wanted to know if you'd been in here, if you'd been with a man named Losevsky.* She paused, and then said something that Jillian didn't quite understand.

I'm sorry. I didn't understand the last thing you said. My Russian isn't very good.

The woman smiled a little. *It's not bad, though your pronunciation needs work.* "I called them pig dung," she explained in English. "Which is probably something you wouldn't have learned in a language course." *And I told them that I had never seen you before.*

Jillian released the breath she hadn't realized she'd been holding. "Thank you." She hesitated again, but figured while she was here and had the woman's attention she might as well go for broke. *Has there been... anyone else? Asking about me?*

The bartender's expression went from mildly friendly to guarded. "No." *And better for you that way.* "Now if you'll excuse me, I have to get back to work."

Jillian watched her walk away and then simply stood, staring blindly at the wall behind the bar. When her gaze refocused, she realized she was looking at her own reflection in a mirror. She looked startled, frozen. Richard Adams, in his book *Watership Down,* coined the term *tharn* to describe a rabbit that was made immobile by shock or terror.

If she'd been a rabbit, *tharn* would be an accurate word to describe her at the moment.

And she didn't like it. She didn't like it at all.

Feeling suddenly claustrophobic, Jillian pushed her way back past the other patrons who were waiting their turn for drinks, shoved open the door, practically ran into the cold, clear night. She needed to clear her head, needed to think through the implications of what the bartender had meant by that, if anything.

A warning? Against what? Whom?

Or maybe it was just a toss away comment, like *no worries.* But she'd spoken in Russian, when the rest of her sentence had been in English. Surely that was significant.

Maybe she should go back in, try asking her what she'd meant, but somehow Jillian didn't think she'd talk to her again. There'd been a sort of finality in her tone before walking away.

Which meant Jillian was both relieved and disturbed by the brief conversation. She'd expected the detectives to ask about her – sensed that Gannon in particular wanted her to be guilty. Of lying, and therefore obstructing an investigation, if nothing else. It made her feel oddly better to have her suspicions confirmed, to hear what the bartender told them. There were other employees, and Jillian had no doubt the detectives had also talked to them and possibly even to regular patrons, but she couldn't track down every one of them and ask them. Talking to one would have to be good enough.

But regarding the other... *And better for you that way.* Was she reading too much into things to feel like that was some kind of warning?

"Jillian."

Jillian's hand went automatically to the canister of pepper spray on her wrist, but a strong hand clamped over hers, preventing her from releasing it. "Hey," said a familiar voice. "It's me."

"Jesse." Her heart was so far into her throat that his name emerged on a croak. "Jesus, you scared me."

"Sorry." His eyes were unreadable above the plaid shirt he wore buttoned up against the cold, but his voice held rebuke. "You didn't honestly walk here, did you?"

"What? Oh, no." She glanced around, realized she'd walked a little further away from the bar than she'd intended. She was outside the range of the security lights in the parking lot, standing in the shadows of a darkened commercial building. "Oh, God." She realized that she wasn't too far away from the street where she'd been assaulted, and that she hadn't even been paying attention. "I can't believe I did that."

The line of Jesse's mouth turned even grimmer. "Where's your car?"

She squeezed her eyes shut, blocked out the memories that wanted to assault her yet again. She'd forced herself to come this way numerous times over the years, but it was generally in daylight, and when she was mentally prepared. She'd been so caught up in analyzing her conversation that she'd allowed herself to become distracted.

Dumb, dumb, dumb...

"Hey." She found herself being shaken, not entirely gently, by the shoulders. "You're safe. You're okay. Just tell me where you parked your car so that I can walk you to it."

She drew in a deep, stuttering breath that burned as if she'd been sucking in sulfur instead of oxygen. "I don't have my car back yet," she told him. "I took a cab. I was planning to call one when I left the bar, but I… I was distracted." She glanced up, suddenly putting two and two together. "Were you there? The Shady Lady, I mean."

He hesitated, and then nodded. "I saw you walking out, so came after you."

She considered that. "I don't mean this to sound offensive, but I wouldn't really have tagged that as the kind of place you hang out."

"It isn't." He hesitated again. "Brian's in the back room, playing pool. I think he's already scared off everyone at the sports bars and billiard halls in town, so he's looking for new victims."

The corners of her mouth lifted slightly. "He's a terrible winner, too. Rubs your face in it."

"I learned not to play against him after about three times." He studied her face a moment, and Jillian hoped that the shadows were deep enough that he couldn't see the residue of anxiety, of fear. "I have to say that I'm equally surprised to see you here. You sounded... disdainful the other night when the detectives asked you about it."

She detected a note of censure in his voice. Or maybe it was her own... she couldn't exactly call it a guilty conscience, but maybe she was projecting. "I am disdainful," she said, a little sharper than she intended. "That place is like Hooters for pirate fetishists."

Jesse coughed into his hand, and when he spoke again, his voice unmistakably held traces of suppressed humor. "So why were you there?"

Jillian wavered on what exactly to tell him. The truth. Or most of it, anyway. "I wanted to know if those detectives have been in there asking about me. I don't know if I mentioned it, but my mother was Russian. Her name was Yulia. The man who had my card, the one who was killed, his name was Russian, too. I looked up stories online, and apparently he came here originally from Novosibirsk. I think, because he had my card, because he'd written the Shady Lady and a date and time on the back of it, that they assume I have some sort of connection, to either the man or the bar. I told you what I've been through with the Savannah police previously, so... let's just say that I like to know what I'm up against."

He stared at her for several long moments before rubbing his hand across his jaw. "That makes sense. But at the risk of coming across as high-handed, I'm going to suggest that inserting yourself into the investigation probably isn't the best idea."

Her own jaw set. "I'm not going to be blindsided again. Or sit back and wait for them to concoct some sort of... fabricated story."

"What makes you think they would do that?"

It wasn't exactly ladylike, but Jillian snorted. "Better question is what makes me think they wouldn't? Mike McGrath still has plenty of friends on the force," she told him. "I'm sure that they wouldn't hesitate to, let's say *interpret the evidence* in a way that isn't favorable toward me."

Jesse stabbed his fingers into his hair, which already looked like he'd been running them through it regularly. "Fair enough. But if you have concerns, you can always tell Brian. Or even an attorney. Taking this into your own hands isn't safe or particularly smart."

Her spine became a steel rod. "Are you implying that I'm stupid?"

"No, I'm stating flat out that this wasn't the smartest decision. Even if you had good intentions, it will look bad should the detectives get wind of it. They might claim you were interfering with an investigation, and to some degree they have a point."

"I'm not interfering," she said, outraged. "I'm defending myself."

"Preemptively."

"Because it's better to wait until *after* someone has cooked up charges against you to figure out how to handle them?"

"That's not what I'm saying."

"It sure sounded that way to me."

Jesse drew in a breath that conveyed pure masculine frustration. "Let me drive you home," he said, changing the subject. "We can talk about this in the car."

Jillian considered telling him what he could do with his car and his discussion, but realized that would be childish. She *liked* Jesse, even if he was being a bit of a high-handed ass at the moment. "Fine. Thank you."

He looked at her sideways.

"What?"

He shook his head. "It's just that when my mom uses that ultra-polite tone, I've learned to duck and run."

"You know, I think you just might be a mama's boy after all."

He stared at her and then laughed, muttering something that sounded like *trouble*.

"Let me tell Brian I'm leaving. You want to wait inside while I go get my Jeep? I parked a couple blocks away. It'll be a brisk walk."

"I'll be fine." She didn't want to set foot inside the bar again. Now, more than ever, it seemed repulsive to her.

"I'll text him." Jesse started to pull out his phone and then hesitated, unbuttoning the heavy flannel he wore over a T-shirt. He draped it over her shoulders.

"Oh. That's not necessary." But it was sweet. She felt her ire melting into something considerably warmer. "Thank you."

The moonlight was just strong enough that she could see his eyes flash with some unreadable emotion. "You're welcome."

He turned away from her and pulled out his phone.

CHAPTER NINE

THE air inside the closed Jeep churned with tension, to the point that Jesse thought you could scoop it up and spread it on toast.

Jillian stared out the window and Jesse kept his eyes on the road so that he wasn't tempted to stop the car, grab her by the shoulders and ask her just exactly what the hell she was up to.

She'd spoken Russian. She didn't realize that he'd overheard her conversation – bits and pieces of it, anyway – as he'd turned away as soon as she'd come in. There'd been a few people on stools between them, which was good in that it helped keep her from recognizing him and bad in that their voices obscured whatever Jillian and the bartender were discussing. Not that he could have followed anyway, since he didn't speak the language. But that fact that she did was a revelation.

Nowhere in the information he had on her did it indicate she was bilingual. Her mom had died when Jillian was still very young, and though she may have picked up on the language during her toddler years, chances were she would have lost most of it without regular practice.

Maybe she'd taken a course or learned via language tapes or something, but Jesse wanted to know *why*. And as much as he didn't like to admit it, it sent up a red flag. Especially since she'd chosen to speak with the bartender at the Shady Lady in that language.

Wanting to know if the cops had been asking about her was understandable, especially given her previous experience. But going there, conversing in Russian…

His hands tightened on the wheel.

"Do you paint?"

Her voice sliced through the wall of tension, and he looked at her in confusion. "What?"

"Your T-shirt," she explained. "It looks like the ones my friends in the fine arts classes always wore, with the…" she gestured with her fingers across her chest "smeared paint."

"Oh." He'd unrolled his jeans, removed the hat and the clear-lensed glasses he'd worn over his contacts before following her outside. He didn't want her to wonder why he was suddenly dressed like an art student.

But he'd forgotten about the T-shirt.

"I think it's one of my younger brother's that got mixed up with my stuff. He went through a phase where he thought he was going to be the next Picasso, but luckily came to his senses. Mostly, I think he took the art courses because of some girl he was interested in at the time."

"What does he do now?"

"He's, ah," shit "an assistant district attorney."

"Really?" It sounded like she was going to ask him more questions – something Jesse hoped to avoid – but luckily they'd reached her townhouse. He pulled to the curb.

When he turned off the ignition she looked at him, and he said, in a tone brooking no argument, "I'll walk you to the door."

Because he was a gentleman, damn it. Even if he was torn between wanting to throttle her for her potential deception and wanting to follow her straight upstairs.

He opened her door, averted his eyes from her legs as she climbed from the seat. She was wearing those damn boots again, and they inspired very unprofessional thoughts. Very human thoughts.

Very *male* thoughts.

She handed him his flannel.

"Thanks for loaning me your shirt. Again. I'll give it back to you now, since I seem to have a bad habit of losing them."

"No problem." He shut the door.

"Really, you don't have to –" She stopped when she saw his expression. "Okay," she said, pausing at the bottom of the steps "would you care to explain why you've been in a pissy mood ever since I bumped into you? Or since you bumped into me, to be more accurate. You didn't have to come out after me, you know."

She shook her head. "Never mind. I have the feeling it will involve you calling my judgment into question again, and quite frankly, it's none of your business. Thank you for the ride."

She started up the stairs.

"Jillian. Wait."

He practically ran over her, because she'd stopped midway up. Having the advantage of height despite the fact that she was standing on the step above him, Jesse noted the cellophane-wrapped basket sitting on the porch.

"Early Christmas gift?" he inquired.

"I don't know. I guess. It must be from Katie's parents." She climbed the last two steps, bent down to examine the card.

"Problem?" Jesse said when she only stared.

"It's addressed to me."

"Secret admirer?"

The look she sent him was droll. "Why yes. I have random men leaving fruit baskets on my porch on a regular basis. It's surprising I can even make it through them to get to the door."

He glanced at the boots. "I can believe it."

When she drew in a breath, probably in preparation to tell him to take a hike, Jesse bent down and picked up the basket. "I'll carry it in for you."

She pursed her lips. "Has anyone ever told you that you have a way of using impeccable manners to disguise the fact that you're a human bulldozer?"

Jesse considered that for a moment. "It might be a family trait."

Jillian shook her head, but took out her key, opened the door. "Thank you," she said, finality in her voice. "You can just sit it there." She gestured toward the hall table.

Jesse sat it on the table, next to the collection of nesting dolls that Gannon had noticed the other night. Seeing them there reminded him of who she was. Of what she might be hiding.

And yet he still wanted her as much as he wanted his next breath.

He looked her in the eye as he put his palm flat against the door, slowly closed it. With him still on this side of it.

Jillian's chest began to rise and fall more rapidly.

Jesse knew what he was doing was wrong. But he was going to do it anyway. He didn't know yet, not positively, that she was guilty of anything other than – as she'd mentioned – slightly questionable judgment. However, once

133

he discovered she was connected to Losevsky – *if* she was connected to Losevsky – she would be on the other side of a line that Jesse ethically could not cross.

Would not cross.

But he didn't know. And until he knew, he wasn't going to pass up the chance to touch her. Just once. And maybe that made him a bastard, but he decided he could live with that. Because if he didn't touch her, he was pretty sure he was going to spontaneously combust.

They stood there, staring at each other in the dim light of the front hall. The porch light shone in through the sidelights, but Jillian hadn't bothered turning on the overhead light. Probably because she didn't want to encourage him to stay.

Well, too bad.

He reached out a hand, slowly enough to give her a chance to tell him that she really did want him to leave, but she didn't. And he could tell by the way her eyes widened, her lips parted, that she wasn't going to.

He took hold of a thick lock of her hair, the hair that had practically struck him blind when he'd seen the sun hitting it on Brian's back porch, twirled it slowly around his hand. Never taking his gaze from hers.

He drew her toward him.

When they were mere inches from each other he simply stood there. Waiting. It had to be her move. That was the condition he gave himself, the admittedly flimsy means of assuaging his guilt.

But this was as far as he was willing to push it.

Realizing, after several moments, that he'd dropped the ball in her court, Jillian's gaze drifted toward his mouth, her own lips parting further, and Jesse's groin tightened in response.

Rising onto her toes, she brought her lips to his, sweet, slow. He tasted her, just a little. He'd known she'd be sweet. Suspected that they would... fit.

What he hadn't expected was the burst of uncontrolled possessiveness that raged through him when she made a little whimpering noise in the back of her throat.

He wasn't sure how it happened. One minute his hand was wrapped in her hair, his lips lightly pressing against hers.

The next he'd yanked her forward, lifting her up on her toes before backing her into the wall beside the door.

They fit together well – oh hell yes, they did – and she tasted even sweeter when he worked his tongue into her mouth, changed the level of the kiss from taste to devour.

She made the noise again and his brain shorted out completely, the few remaining cells that suggested this was a bad idea exploding in a fiery death.

He grabbed her ass and boosted her up so that her legs in those fuck-me boots wrapped around him. Then he pressed himself between them.

It was madness, no doubt about it, but the pain from his zipper digging into his arousal wasn't sufficient to bring him to his senses.

Her fingers tangled in his hair this time, pulling just a little, and he nipped the corner of her lip in retaliation. She gasped, her eyes flying open, staring into his. They stayed that way, simply breathing heavily, for the space of several heartbeats.

And then she pulled his mouth back to hers.

He wanted to carry her into the parlor, bend her over one of those very uncomfortable chairs and then bury himself inside her.

Again. And again. And again and again and again.

He ground himself against her and the skirt she wore, a sort of stretchy thing, rode up on her thighs. She wore some kind of heavy hosiery – tights, or whatever you called them – but he could rip those away. With his teeth if necessary.

Something fell over, crashed to the floor – he thought they'd bumped into the table – but neither of them paid much attention. His entire world centered where their mouths fused, where their bodies tried desperately to join despite the barrier of cloth and zipper.

Not much cloth on her part. He slid the fingers of one hand under the tights, encountered the scrap of lace that covered her ass.

She whimpered. Jesse growled.

"Jesse." His name was a mere breath against his ear, and the sound of it was twin torture. He wanted to hear her say it again, to hear her scream it as he tossed her over that chair, as he took what she so obviously wanted to give.

But it also reminded him who he was. Who she was.

And why they couldn't do this.

In a move that should earn him a medal for physical restraint, Jesse pulled back, laid his head against hers for several long, pain-filled moments. Shit. Just shit.

He slowly lowered her to the floor.

Her eyes, when he looked down at her, were glazed with a kind of sexual wonder.

He wanted to stomp his own ass for letting things go this far. He wanted to beat his head against the wall.

And above all he wanted to finish what they'd started.

Because he did, Jesse stepped back, accidentally kicking something on the floor. He glanced down. The fruit basket. They'd knocked it off the table, along with several of the nesting dolls.

"What's wrong?"

So many things, he thought. But he chose the less problematic answer. "We knocked over your fruit basket."

The cellophane must not have been secured terribly well, or else it had torn when it fell, because oranges and apples were scattered on the floor amidst sparkly shreds of paper.

"Oh." It was obvious that Jillian was still coming back from that kiss, and while part of Jesse appreciated immensely the effect he'd had on her, the more rational, ethical part of him demanded that he get the hell out of there.

But not before cleaning up the mess. The literal one, anyway. The metaphorical one wasn't something that could be handled with a broom.

He leaned over, slapped his hand on the light switch next to the table. "If you'll get something to sweep up this confetti, I'll pick up the big stuff."

She continued to stare at him for another moment, uncomprehending. "You want to clean. Right now."

He glanced up. Her skirt was still up around her hips, her hair a tangled cloud surrounding her head, and he had to restrain himself from giving his very last fuck a little backpack and sack lunch and sending it out the door. "Yeah."

She gave the kind of half laugh that suggested she thought he was crazy. He couldn't say he disagreed.

Noticing the position of her skirt for the first time, she smoothed it down over her legs with a kind of embarrassed dignity that made Jesse feel even worse. He started picking up oranges, returning them to the basket.

Jillian started to walk past him, presumably to get a broom, although at this point he thought she was probably as likely to beat him with it as she was to sweep up. He wouldn't have blamed her.

But she stopped, looking at the turned over basket. Jesse followed her gaze.

There was a box inside, maybe the size of a child's shoe box, the kind that petit-fours and other little holiday confections tended to come in. It was covered in festive foil paper, but the separately wrapped lid had come askew. An inch or so of some kind of fabric or something hung out of it.

Transfixed, Jillian slowly reached down, lifted the lid aside.

Jesse shot out his arm, but wasn't quick enough to catch her before she fell.

"*JILLIAN.* Jillian."

Her eyes fluttered open. Jesse's face was immediately above hers.

"There you are. She's coming around," he said into his cell phone.

Jillian looked past him, saw the fancy chandelier in the front hall blinking in and out of focus. Was she lying on the floor?

"I don't know," Jesse was saying, even as his hand shifted under her. He seemed to be holding her head. "Yeah, she cracked it pretty good. I couldn't catch her. Now would be good. No, *now.*"

He looked down at her, saw her watching him. He tucked his phone between his shoulder and his ear. "How many fingers am I holding up?"

"What?"

"How many fingers?"

"Three. Though I would appreciate it if you'd stop wiggling them in front of my face."

His frown deepened. "Yeah, I think so," he said into the phone "but I'll keep her immobilized until the EMTs get here, just in case. Don't move," he said to Jillian.

"You seem to be laboring under the delusion that you're the boss of me."

"The fact that you can put together that sentence encourages me some, but for the moment, I am the boss of you. I said don't move."

She scowled at him, and he scowled back.

"Why am I lying on the floor?"

"You fainted."

"I didn't faint." Had she? "I've never fainted."

"There's a first time for everything. And you cracked your head pretty hard on the edge of the marble-topped table as you were going down. Are you in pain?"

"I wasn't until you mentioned it."

He leaned even closer. "Your pupils are even at least."

"How kind of you to notice."

"Can you move your arms and legs?"

"Didn't you just tell me not to move?"

"I meant your head. We have to make sure you haven't injured your spine. But I want to know if you can move your extremities."

"Does my middle finger count?" Agitated for reasons she couldn't explain, Jillian shifted her gaze to the side. And saw the red cellophane on the floor. "Oh God," she said, memory flooding back.

"Don't move your head," Jesse repeated.

"I have to," she said. "Because I'm pretty sure I'm going to throw up."

"Shit."

Jillian tried to get up, to get herself to the powder room, but Jesse basically held her in place. He rolled her over, careful to keep her head, neck and body aligned, and she ended up vomiting on the floor.

It wasn't much, thank goodness, mostly just liquid. But now she was embarrassed in addition to her head hurting and... "Oh God."

"Are you going to be sick again?"

Jillian fought back tears. "No."

Jesse took the shirt she'd handed back to him earlier, used it to wipe up the mess and then tossed it aside, all the while holding her head steady with his other hand.

Jillian couldn't see what was lying on the floor behind her, but the image was burned into her brain. "It's Killer."

Jesse hesitated. "Are you sure? I don't know how to distinguish one squirrel from the other."

"I'm sure." Jillian fought past the lump in her throat. "He has a reddish spot on his back hind leg." She'd taken enough photographs of him to recognize the marking.

A tear slipped out of the corner of her eye, and Jillian squeezed her lids shut. Jesse muttered a curse. A moment later, she felt his thumb brush over her cheek.

When she heard the sound of sirens, her eyes popped open again. "You called the police?"

"I called an ambulance."

Panic began to set in. She didn't do well with hospitals. "I don't need an ambulance. I'm fine."

"Let's let the paramedics be the judge of that. You hit your head awfully damn hard."

"I'm fine," she repeated.

"You just threw up on the floor."

"That's because..." she'd been horrified to see an animal she had grown to love, to think of almost as a personal mascot, dead and wrapped up like a holiday treat. Left on her doorstep.

"I know it was a shock," Jesse murmured. "And I can understand why it would make you sick. But that's a worrying sign in conjunction with a head injury. So just let the EMTs check you out."

Considering she could already hear them outside and that Jesse was like a ton of bricks holding her in place, Jillian didn't see that she had much choice. "Fine."

"I'm going to let go of you for just a minute so that I can go let them in," he told her. "I asked them to come to the back door, since we want to disturb the basket as little as possible." He hesitated again. "Brian is on his way. I figured you'd be more comfortable if I contacted him than the cops."

He eased her onto her back again, his face hovering right above hers, and when their eyes met, some dangerous emotion flickered in his. Anger, she thought. Bright and hot.

But it was gone just as quickly as it had appeared. "Don't move," he reiterated as he stood up, strode down the hall toward the kitchen and the back door.

Jillian didn't, but not because she was worried about her head or her spine. She didn't want to look to the side. Didn't want to see... that again. It was bad enough that she could smell it. Her own vomit on one side of her, and the odor of death on the other.

There'd been blood matting the fur on his head.

Jillian closed her eyes and breathed through her mouth, determined not to be sick again. Or to cry. That she would do when she was alone.

She always cried alone.

She heard Jesse leading the paramedics back down the hall, instructing them to be careful not to touch the basket, the cellophane, any of the fruit that still littered the floor. He reminded her of Brian in that moment. No wonder the two of them were friends.

The EMTs came in, did their thing, a nice woman named Nicki taking her vital signs and shining her penlight in Jillian's eyes, asking her where she'd gotten her boots to keep Jillian's mind off the horror on the floor beside her. After a series of evaluations, Jillian was given permission to move. She did, with help, to the sofa in the parlor. Jillian felt slightly disoriented, but thought it was more a product of the situation than of banging her head.

Nicki recommended that she go to the hospital and get checked out by a doctor just to be sure she didn't have a concussion. Jillian declined.

Nicki frowned at her, but packed up her bag. "Stubborn," she said. "Should have known that a woman with boots like that wouldn't be a pushover." She went on to warn Jillian that signs of a concussion occasionally took hours to develop. "Over the next twenty-four hours," she said, including Jesse in the conversation, "you're going to want to watch out for any more vomiting, worsening headache, neck pain, seizures, blurred vision, slurred speech or numbness."

"Does she need to be awakened every two hours overnight?" he asked from his position leaning against the parlor doorframe.

"That was the next item on my agenda. Sorry sweetie," she said to Jillian. "Don't plan on getting a good night's sleep tonight."

"I'll be right back," Jesse said, pulling away from the doorframe to show the EMTs out.

When he came back, Brian was with him. Jillian could see him, from her position on the sofa, bending down to examine the remains of the fruit basket scattered across the floor. He and Jesse spoke to each other in low voices, but Jillian couldn't hear what they were saying. Until Brian looked up sharply at Jesse, and let forth with a heartfelt curse.

Jillian's shoulders curled in, her heart rate picking up a little. Brian very rarely got visibly angry, hardly ever cursed. At least not within Jillian's hearing.

Brian climbed to his feet, shaking his head as he left Jesse in the hall and walked into the parlor. He hesitated, and then sat on the table directly in front of Jillian, hands hanging between his knees. When he finally spoke, he kept his voice low. "Are you okay?"

Jillian studied his face. Brian was always so open, so affable with her, joking and teasing just like he did with Katie. She hadn't seen him look this solemn, this closed, since he'd watched her testify at Mike McGrath's trial.

"I will be. Brian," she started to say she was sorry, but didn't see how this could be her fault. "I hate that you're being dragged into this again."

"Into what?"

Her eyes widened at the question. "This." She gestured toward the hall. "It... it has to be Mike. One of his friends. He put them up to this."

"Did he?"

Jillian drew back. "Who else could it have been? I... I posted photos of him. Of Killer. On my website. On social media." And for that, she *was* sorry. In letting her affection be known, she'd inadvertently made him a target. "I've done a few blog posts about him. The squirrel, I mean. And you know I testified, when Mike was up for parole last month. On why it shouldn't be granted. And it wasn't. This is payback."

Brian rubbed a hand over his face. "It's possible."

"Possible?" Her heart rate picked up again. "Brian, I don't understand."

"Is there anyone else you can think of who might want to... upset you?"

"Because I'm such a horrible person that I can provide you with a whole list?"

"That's not what I meant."

"I know, but that's the way it *feels*." She touched a hand to her head, which was throbbing.

"I'm sorry," Brian said softly. "I know this is hard, but it's a question that has to be asked."

Jillian lifted her shoulders. "Mr. Pratt next door – the younger one, Adam – he's not shy about letting it be known that he thinks the squirrels are vermin. They eat the seed from his bird feeders. He's crotchety and cranky, but I can't imagine him doing something like…" she glanced toward the hall and swallowed. "That."

"Okay," he said after drawing a deep breath. "I'm going to bag all the evidence, get it to the lab. We'll find out who's behind this." He reached out, took her hand, icy cold, between both of his.

And lowered his voice even further. "You know I love you like a sister, right?"

"The feeling is mutual."

He nodded. "I know. And that's why I'm going to say that if there is anything, anything at all, going on with you that you have maybe been afraid to talk about, you can tell me."

There was some sort of subtext here that Jillian didn't fully understand. "Do you think I'm hiding something from you?"

Brian stared at her. "Are you?"

At first Jillian couldn't answer past the lump in her throat. "No. *No*. Does this… surely you're not asking me this because those detectives questioned me the other night, are you? You don't actually believe I had anything to do with that man's death."

"No," he said after a moment. "I don't. But Jillian, showing up at the Shady Lady tonight…" he shook his head. "Look, don't do anything like that again. It's throwing fuel on the flames of suspicion."

Basically what Jesse had said. "I just wanted to know what I might be up against," she said in her own defense. She hated being scolded like a child who'd made a bad decision, even if the logic behind that decision sounded flimsier every time she said it. But she'd had to do *something*.

"I understand that," Brian said. "But Jillian, these are people you do not want to mess with. Period. You understand?"

"The cops," she asked "or the people… at the bar?"

"At this point? Both." He squeezed her hand. "Katie's on her way home. She'll be checking on you through the night. I'm going to gather up the evidence, and then Jesse's my ride." He paused, and then leaned in to kiss her cheek. "Take care of your head. And make sure that alarm stays set tonight."

"Don't worry about that. If Katie's waking me up every two hours, I certainly won't be doing any sleepwalking." Not that she was entirely convinced that was what had happened before. But the alternative was... what?

She still didn't have an answer.

Jillian watched him walk out, anxiety and grief and anger and fear mixing inside her until she felt nauseated again.

She almost called Brian back, but Katie came bustling in, a bundle of concern and outrage, and by the time she'd filled her friend in on the details, she realized Brian had gone.

As had Jesse. And he hadn't even said goodbye.

CHAPTER TEN

JESSE opened his laptop, pulled up the video he'd uploaded last night. He then turned the machine around so that the screen was visible to the other people gathered around the table.

"Our sound guru is working on this, seeing if she can separate out more of the conversation in question from the background noises that obscure it. But I wanted to make sure everyone was up to speed while we're waiting."

"Thoughtful of you to include us," Gannon chimed in, the slightly nasal tone of his voice sounding more pronounced than usual. "Hours after the fact. Although I can't help but notice that you conveniently left us out of the loop during that little incident at Ms. Montgomery's house last night."

Brian started to protest, but Jesse held up a hand. "At this point there's no evidence connecting that incident with the current investigation. In the event that evidence should arise, you'll be fully informed of any developments."

"Seems to me that any incidents out of the ordinary that involve Ms. Montgomery – particularly ones that could be deemed... threats – should be approached as connected to the current investigation."

"Generally speaking," Jesse told him "I like to have at least a shred of concrete evidence on which to base assumptions. You were informed of the occurrence. Unless and until we have that shred of evidence, you can count yourself lucky that I told you that much."

Leaning back in his chair, Gannon grinned around his toothpick. "I know Parker here has a personal stake, but are you the lady's lawyer now? I thought it was your brother that got off – or maybe just got rich – defending scum."

"Nick," Axelrod said with a weary glance at his partner. "That's enough."

But Jesse returned Gannon's gaze. "My brother may be a criminal defense attorney, but at least he's never had to ask me to send him soap on a rope."

Gannon's front chair legs hit the floor with a bang just as the door opened, admitting the translator. "I'm sorry," she said, tucking a strand of dark hair behind her ear. "I got held up in traffic."

"No problem," Jesse said, pulling out a chair and ignoring the heat of Gannon's glare. He explained that their technician was working her magic to try and clarify the recording, but wasn't promising anything. "So in the meantime, we need a basic idea of the content of the conversation."

It had taken everything he had last night not to run the video through a translation program so that he knew what they were dealing with, allowing both Brian and himself time to mentally prepare if it turned out that Jillian had been lying. But that was putting his personal feelings in front of his professional ethics. Something he couldn't allow himself to do – at least not to a greater extent than he already had.

And though it pained him greatly, Brian had agreed. Jesse glanced at his friend's bruised knuckles, recalling the wall that had taken the brunt of his frustration last night.

If he'd told Brian exactly how the fruit basket had been knocked to the floor, he was pretty sure his face would have suffered the same fate.

The translator settled into the chair. "Let's hear it," she said.

Jesse played the video, which he'd shot with his cell phone by placing it on the bar. A couple drink glasses, people moving their hands or leaning on the bar obscured the picture, but at least part of Jillian's conversation with the bartender was relatively clear.

He played it one time through, then again, stopping it at various points as the translator requested to hear certain parts while she jotted down notes.

Finally she sat back. "The woman who is asking the questions, Russian is not her first language. Her phrasing is too formal, her accent too stilted. I can't hear exactly what she says at first, but the bartender, she distinctly answers '*meen-tih,*' which is slang for cops. The other woman must not understand the slang term, because the bartender then explains it in English, but with the much harsher 'pig dung.'" She cast an apologetic look around the table. "Sorry."

"We've heard worse," Axelrod assured her.

"I lost most of the conversation after that," she continued, "but I can tell you that the other woman says 'anyone else.' I can't hear the bartender's response, as someone next to the phone's microphone started laughing really loudly." She lifted her shoulders. "Unless your sound technician can clear it up, I'm afraid that's the best I can do."

They thanked her for her time, and Jesse waited until she'd gone to discuss what they'd learned. "We can put it through the digital translator," he said "see if we get anything different, or can get a little more, but based on what she said it coincides with Ms. Montgomery's explanation. She went there to find out if someone from the police department had been in there asking about her."

Gannon snorted. "And she just happened to speak Russian? I interviewed that bartender. She speaks perfectly good English. Why would the Montgomery woman choose to talk to her in Russian unless she had something to hide?"

"The bar was crowded," Brian said. "Maybe she didn't want people to know she was asking about a police matter."

"So why not go when the bar's less crowded? Why bother asking at all, unless you're worried that one of your buddies might have contradicted your story, revealing that hey, yeah, this chick was in the bar after all. Meeting her boyfriend or her whatever, Losevsky."

"Losevsky wasn't her boyfriend," Brian said tightly.

Gannon shifted his gaze Brian's direction, raised his brows. "And you know that positively? You didn't even know she could speak Russian. I doubt she's gonna broadcast to an FBI agent that she's fucking a criminal."

Brian's bruised hand clenched in his lap, and despite the fact that Jesse wanted to smash his own fist in Gannon's face, he had to acknowledge that the man had a point. "So we investigate further."

"How about we just ask her?"

"You did," Jesse reminded the other man. "She said she didn't know him."

"So we ask her again in a more formal setting. Like down at the Barracks. In an interview room."

Brian spoke up. "There's no evidence to support the supposition that she was lying about knowing Losevsky."

"Except for the fact that she was at the Shady Lady – an establishment she claimed not to frequent – talking to the bartender in freaking *Russian* in an attempt to cover her sweet ass!"

"Nick," Axelrod said, grabbing his partner's arm to pull him back down into his chair. "Calm down."

"Calm down?" the other man shot some disbelief at this partner. "While we let these two derail the investigation because one of them has a previous relationship with the suspect and one of them wants to get in her pants."

Brian shoved to his feet, and Jesse stifled the urge to do the same. "I'd like to remind you," he addressed Gannon "that I am the lead in this investigation. A position which both your boss and mine agreed upon. As such, I'm going to make the call if and when Ms. Montgomery needs to be brought in for formal questioning. Detective Axelrod, if you and Agent Parker will excuse me, I'd like to speak with Detective Gannon alone for just a moment."

Gannon stared at Jesse across the table, ignoring the murmured words from his partner before he filed out in front of Brian. Brian shot Jesse a look as he closed the door, but Jesse ignored it in much the same fashion.

"If you've got something to say, spit it out," Gannon said.

"I have several things to say, and I'll get to them in good time. First, you may want to reconsider casting stones at Agent Parker when your own house is one big plate glass window."

"What the hell are you talking about?"

"I'm talking about Mike McGrath, in case my prison metaphor sailed over your head earlier. Which I don't think it did. Otherwise you wouldn't have reacted so strongly to the crack about soap on a rope."

Gannon's eyes narrowed. "You think the idea of a cop getting raped in prison is funny?"

"No, but nor do I think the idea of that same cop attempting to rape a woman is amusing. You complain about Parker's bias, but a little digging was all it took for me to find out that you and McGrath used to be fast friends."

"So?"

"So, you've seemed to have it in for Jillian Montgomery since the moment her card was discovered among Losevsky's effects. I thought maybe I was imagining it at first, or that you were simply a bit overzealous, given the gruesome and dramatic nature of the man's death, but then I began to suspect there was something more to it. Namely your friendship with Mike McGrath."

"That has no bearing on this investigation."

Jesse slowly nodded. "You know, I'd like to believe that. I'd like to believe that you are, in fact, a professional, capable of separating your personal feelings from the job at hand. Or at least separating them enough so that they don't cloud your judgment. It's not always easy to do, and if you feel that you can't be objective with regards to Ms. Montgomery, I'll understand if you want to ask your lieutenant to reassign you."

Gannon snorted, and then leaned across the table. "Are you threatening me?"

"No, see, threatening was what happened to Ms. Montgomery when she attempted to report your friend McGrath for domestic violence. In fact, it went well beyond threats to harassment, assault, attempted gang rape – egregious acts of petty revenge by a violent, sociopathic bully."

When Gannon remained silent, his reddening face the only indication of his rising anger, Jesse continued. "Surely you don't think she *had it coming,* do you?"

"She was a nosy bitch. Tried to ruin his relationship, his career."

"It seems to me that he ruined his own relationship, his own career by beating up on women and then shooting another cop."

"That was an accident."

"Did his fists also accidentally connect with his girlfriend's face? With Ms. Montgomery's? That's some piss poor motor control."

"You know nothing about it."

"Sadly, I know all too much about it. And what I know sickens me. You know what else sickens me? Seeing an innocent animal butchered, wrapped up like a fruit cake and left on a woman's porch. A woman who just happens to have earned the ire of your friend McGrath. And an animal, interestingly enough, that hit you in the head just the other night."

Much like Brian had done, Gannon shoved away from the table. Made himself large. "Are you implying that I had something to do with that?"

"I don't know." Jesse paused. "Did you?"

"You're an asshole, Wellington."

"Maybe," Jesse admitted. "But one thing I'm not is a dirty cop."

"Fuck you," he said in a tight voice.

"Not even if you bought me a steak dinner." Jesse tossed a paper onto the table, and Gannon glared at him before picking it up.

"What's this?"

"It's the lab results from the toothpick I found behind Ms. Montgomery's house the other day, beneath her basement window."

Gannon's head jerked up.

"Seems like the DNA matches that from the toothpick I pulled from the trashcan at the garage last week."

Seeing that he'd made his point, Jesse leaned across the table. "You'd better hope that you don't have one speck of filth clinging to you, Detective. Because if I find out you had anything to do with that threat against Ms. Montgomery, I will personally take you down."

CHAPTER ELEVEN

JILLIAN reduced the color saturation in the background of the photograph she was currently editing. Her subject – a vibrant high school senior named Bethany – perched on the tailgate of an old blue pickup truck surrounded by a field of high grass. Since the girl was obviously the focal point, the hue of the grass needed to fade out so as not to draw your eye and detract. Jillian toggled the targeted adjustment tool slider to the left and leaned back, considered. Then toggled it a little more.

There. Perfect. Bethany's crisp white dress, honey blonde hair stood out like spots of sunshine against the dark truck, the faded grass. The red cowboy boots gave the image a sort of patriotic, vintage feel, which suited this daughter of an Air Force colonel right down to the ground.

Jillian closed her eyes. If only real life were so easy to edit. To basically flip a switch and create the picture you wanted.

Or erase the one you didn't.

"Hey."

Startled, her heart skipped a beat as she looked up. "Oh."

Jesse tucked his tongue in his cheek. "About as enthusiastic a greeting as I expected. May I?" he nodded to the seat across from Jillian.

Jillian was tempted to tell him that he could just take his kiss-you-against-the-wall-and-then-bail-without-saying-goodbye-or calling-for two-days ass right back out the door, but didn't want to be petty.

Or to let him know that his behavior had affected her in the least.

"Be my guest."

He slid onto the bench seat, glanced around at the high wooden walls surrounding the booth, which was tucked next to the bar in the manner of an Irish snug. "Looks like a nice quiet place to work."

She'd come to Parker's on the Park – Katie's restaurant – as she had for the past two days. She couldn't stand to be home, or even in her studio in the converted garage. The space felt... tainted. It was something she was going to have to get over, but she knew from experience that it would take time.

"It is quiet at this time of year, as long as I come between the lunch and dinner rush. The restaurant is getting so popular though, that I probably won't be able to use it as my backup office for too much longer."

"I know Brian is pretty proud."

Brian. Who'd been very... guarded in his communication with her since the other night, as if a gulf of mistrust had formed between them. It made her both nervous and sad.

"How's your head?"

"A little tender," she admitted. "Though no more signs of brain injury. I... look, this is embarrassing, but I'm just going to say it. Thank you for taking care of me the other night. I'm sorry I threw up on you."

One corner of his mouth tugged up. "As I recall, you threw up on the floor, not me."

"And you wiped it up with your shirt. So that's two I owe you."

His smile faded. "You don't owe me anything. In fact," he rested his forearms on the table, leaned in. "I'd like to apologize. My behavior was... more aggressive than it should have been. I was out of line."

"Oh." Jillian wasn't quite sure how to take that. Yes, he'd taken her by surprise when he'd pinned her to the wall and...

She cleared her throat. "It's not like I was resisting."

Something hot, possessive flared in his eyes just as a basket of warm cheese straws with spicy avocado dip appeared on the table between them.

Jillian looked up to see Katie, beaming at Jesse.

"How nice to see you again," she said. "This is your first time here, isn't it?"

"Ah, Katie. Hi. I've been meaning to get over this way since Brian mentioned you opened, but yeah, this is the first time I've managed it."

"Well, then please accept this with my compliments. Our signature appetizer."

"I would say that's not necessary, but I never turn down food, especially if it's half as good as your French toast."

"Oh, it's better than half. What's your poison? It's almost happy hour," she reminded him. "We have some excellent craft beers. You look like a dark lager type."

He smiled. "Should I be concerned that I'm so easily read?"

"No, I'm just damn good. Bo," she called out over her shoulder. "Bring this gentleman a pilsner of the Black, please." She finally turned her attention to Jillian. "You're still on pain meds, so you'll have to stick with your tea. And eat some of those cheese straws so that I don't have to keep hovering over you. Having you pass out in the middle of my restaurant is bad for business. I do hope y'all will consider staying for dinner," she smiled guilelessly as she returned her attention to Jesse.

"Ah…" he glanced at Jillian. "Sounds good?"

"Of course it does," Katie agreed, taking the pilsner that the bartender slid toward her and placing it in front of Jesse. "Enjoy. And just let Bo here know when you're ready to eat."

She sailed away, and Jillian waited several beats before meeting Jesse's gaze. He raised his eyebrows. "I don't recall her being so…"

"Dictatorial?" Jillian filled in. "She's usually not, unless it involves food and what she feels you should be eating, how much you should be eating, or who you should be eating *with*. She's the real life soup nazi, except instead of *no soup for you*, it's *eat these cheese straws*."

He grinned, and then picked up a cheese straw, bit in. "Good," he concluded. "Very good. As far as dictatorial edicts go, I have to say that *eat these cheese straws* is better than *off with their heads."*

"That would be completely counterproductive to her dietary agenda," Jillian explained as she bit into her own cheese straw. "Headless people can't eat."

"Excellent point."

Jesse took a drink of his beer, studying her over the rim. "We've covered your physical well-being, but how are you doing, emotionally? I know it was a pretty bad shock."

Jillian started to say that she was fine, but the fact was, she wasn't. "I think the worst part is the guilt," she admitted. "Someone killed that poor animal as a means of hurting me. It's difficult to get past that."

"I would tell you the blame lies with the perpetrator, not you, but I think you already know that. You told Brian you think it was McGrath. That he put one of his friends up to it."

"He had a parole hearing last month. I testified. It seems obvious to me that it's payback."

Jesse nodded. "It makes sense. But for the sake of argument, can you think of anyone else who would possibly want to hurt you? Or threaten you?"

Her heartbeat picked up. "Like who?"

"Exes are always good candidates for that sort of thing."

"Brian told you I was married."

Jesse tilted his head. "Is that something you'd prefer I didn't know?"

"No. It's not like it's a secret. A mistake, yes, but not something I'm going to hide. It was after... Mike's trial," she admitted. "I just wanted to get out of Savannah. I went home – which is a small town in the North Georgia Mountains, called Ellijay. I stayed with my aunt for a while. I also bumped into Cooper Montgomery, who was a friend from high school. We dated a few times, and though there was no real spark there for me, he seemed safe. I craved safety at that point."

"So you married him."

She sighed. "I knew it was a mistake, even as I was saying 'I do.' My aunt knew it was a mistake, Katie – I think even Cooper knew it, too. But he'd had a crush on me when we were seniors, and so he thought I was what he wanted. Turns out we were both wrong. I wasn't what he wanted, and he wasn't safe."

Jesse's gaze sharpened. "He hurt you?"

"No, nothing like that. So if you're thinking he had something to do with, with the package the other night, you're wrong. He's not vindictive, or mean. But safety... I'm learning that it's mostly an illusion. That's why you can't live your life hiding in your comfort zone, or not taking risks. Because even when you do, bad things still happen."

"True. Although sometimes you can take the kind of risk that almost guarantees something bad will happen. Jillian." He paused, seeming to gather his thoughts. "When you went to the Shady Lady, was there... anyone else there who you feel might have some reason to want to hurt you?"

Jillian froze, completely unable to form a credible answer, but then something caught Jesse's attention. He muttered a heartfelt *"Shit."*

Jillian followed his gaze, saw a tall, dapper and extraordinarily handsome man leaning on the bar, aiming a sexy smile at an expensive-looking blonde.

Then he glanced their direction and his smile changed. "Jesse," he said, face alight with recognition.

He strolled over to the table, clapped Jesse on the shoulder, and then turned his attention to Jillian. "Jack Wellington." He offered his hand, eyes narrowing thoughtfully when Jillian took it.

"You look familiar," he said. "Were you in my law office today?"

"*AND* how," Jack said, while pouring three fingers of whisky into his glass. "Was I supposed to know that you were working rather than simply on a date? With a very attractive woman I might add. Naturally I was delighted by the prospect of the end of your recent dry spell."

Jesse turned away from Jack's office window to glare at his older brother, whose stone gray eyes danced with amusement.

"It's not like she can Google you now that she knows I'm your brother and have your federal ID pop up. You keep your information locked down. But I'm curious as to how you managed to get that cozy with her – and the two of you looked *awfully* cozy – all without her figuring out who you actually are. Rather devious of you, Agent Wellington. You have skills, little brother, of which I was previously unaware."

"Knock it off with that little brother bullshit."

"You *are* younger." Jack lifted his glass of whisky. "And it works so well to get a rise out of you."

Restless, Jesse crossed the room and dropped into the chair across from Jack's mammoth desk, pinching the bridge of his nose. His head felt like an army of elves was mining his skull with pickaxes.

He'd been forced to forgo Katie's suggestion of dinner because there was no way to graciously tell Jack to get lost without looking like an asshole. Probably for the best.

No, definitely for the best. He'd been pushing his luck anyway, tracking Jillian down, using his need to apologize for his unprofessional conduct as – let's be honest – an excuse to see her again. And she didn't even know he'd been unprofessional. Because she didn't know what he actually did for a living.

It had taken some fancy footwork to get himself and his brother out of there without Jack revealing that tidbit of information.

Jesse tried not to examine all of the reasons he wasn't ready for her to know. It had made sense at first to avoid telling her who he worked for, given her feelings about law enforcement. He'd acted as a sort of referee between Brian and Detective Gannon in particular, trying to make sure that the case moved forward without traumatizing Jillian unnecessarily, since Losevsky's possession of her business card was flimsy grounds on which to base an investigation. But questions *did* need to be asked. So they'd come up with a plan – meant to only be in effect temporarily – which met everyone's needs.

The detectives had conducted their interview, Jesse'd listened in and made sure they didn't cross any lines, and Jillian hadn't been the wiser. Meanwhile, he'd investigated her background thoroughly and found nothing in her conduct, finances or connections to arouse suspicion.

Until she'd walked into the Shady Lady the other night.

"At least you hadn't given her an alias. That would have been really awkward. And don't look at me like that," Jack said. "If you want me to pretend like I don't know you when I see you out in public, we're going to have to come up with some kind of code word or secret hand signal."

"How's this?" Jesse lifted a middle finger.

"You'll blend right in with the rest of my fan club."

Jesse leaned over, snagged the glass at Jack's elbow.

"You said you didn't want any," Jack pointed out as Jesse tossed it back. "And I'll have you know that's 18-year-old Macallan you're swilling like a frat boy with a bottle of Budweiser."

Jesse coughed, eyes watering as his throat burned with fire. "Not my fault you waste a hundred bucks on a bottle of whisky."

"Two hundred. And it's not a waste if you savor it. Jesus. It's confounding to think we come from the same gene pool." He took the glass back, added another finger. "Here.

That's all you're getting because you're driving and I don't want to have to bail you out of jail. Now how about you cut the bullshit and tell me what's really up."

Jesse looked at Jack across the desk. Yeah, they liked to rag on each other, but the fact was his older brother knew him better than just about anyone else.

"Look, Jack." He leaned forward, forearms resting on his knees "this isn't the first time that you and I have been on opposite sides of a legal issue, but it's the first time we've ended up in a position to butt heads during an investigation. We knew it would probably happen eventually, but... shit." He shook his head. He was the one who suggested that Jillian get an attorney, and now it was coming back to bite him in the ass. "I can't believe she retained a lawyer from your firm."

"She didn't."

Jesse's head came up. "You said she was here today."

"And she was. She spoke with Ainsley."

Jesse nearly groaned. Ainsley Tidwell. Jack's underling. And Jesse's ex-girlfriend. Not to mention the legal equivalent of a barracuda. "This just gets better."

"I don't know what they discussed, and I wouldn't tell you even if I did. That pesky code of ethics. But either she's shopping around for an attorney who's more reasonably priced or a better fit personality-wise, or Ainsley didn't feel that your... let's just call her a person of interest, since I don't know the whole story. Anyway, maybe Ainsley didn't feel that she needed her services." He studied Jesse over the rim of his glass. "But from the look on your face, I'm wondering if maybe Ainsley didn't misjudge the situation."

Jesse sat there, torn. He really shouldn't tell his brother anything. He should probably get up and walk out of the office.

But he and Jack had always been close. And he wanted his brother's... not advice, precisely. Maybe he just wanted to use him as a sounding board.

"Anything I tell you is between you and me. If... anything develops that causes Ms. Montgomery to decide she does in fact require the services of your firm, this discussion never happened."

Jack swirled the liquid in his glass. "What discussion?"

Jesse's shoulders relaxed a little. "You called her a person of interest, and that's a good description." On so many levels. "But she's extremely wary of law enforcement, and with good reason. And she lives with Brian Parker's younger sister."

Jack sipped his whisky. "That sounds like a clusterfuck. I'm surprised your SAC hasn't pulled Parker off the investigation for conflict of interest."

"He's mostly operating on the periphery at this point, but if they tried to pull him completely, he'd probably lose it. Or quit."

"So you're the lead investigator."

"With a task force of Savannah's finest."

Jack grinned. "And to think it wasn't that long ago, after that little incident in South Carolina, that you were in the professional dog house."

"I'm still in the dog house. They just lengthened my chain. Anyway, do you remember a case about five years back, three local cops busted for assault, attempted rape, one of them shot the officer who stepped in to break it up?"

Jack tipped his head back, sorted through his mental files, which Jesse knew from experience were scarily accurate.

"I think Andrew Blevins defended the shooter," he said after a moment. "The other two plea bargained, but Blevins isn't the type to miss an opportunity to put himself in front of a jury or a camera. Pompous windbag," was Jack's assessment.

"I would make a comment about pots and kettles, but it would deflect off your ego in the manner of asteroids bouncing off a force field."

"You read too much science fiction as a kid, and not enough girly magazines. It stunted your development. This woman – Jillian. She was the one they assaulted."

"Yeah. You remember?"

"I didn't until you brought it up."

"Well, several Savannah cops still have a hard on for her. When her name came up in the course of an investigation, one of the detectives involved all but blew his load."

"Which is why she was here today."

"Yeah." Jesse considered what, and how much else to say. "I'd like to say that's the worst of it, because that's certainly enough. But this case in which she's a person of interest? If it turns out she is connected, what she went through before will be child's play in comparison."

Jack studied Jesse's face. "You're worried for her."

"These are bad people we're dealing with. And the fact that she lives with the sister of a federal agent adds another whole layer of cluster to the fuck. What?" he said when he noticed Jack's expression.

Jack leaned back in his massive leather chair. "You can, and likely will, tell me to mind my business."

"When has that ever stopped you before?"

Ignoring that, Jack went on. "I know you Jesse. And while what I'm hearing is cause for concern, it's what I'm seeing that really worries me."

"And what's that?"

"A man who's walking a fine line between sound professional judgment and... emotional entanglement. And the fact that you didn't immediately contradict me means you're at least being honest enough with yourself to recognize the danger."

Jesse stared into the glass of whisky. "I know how to do my job."

"Of that I have no doubt. I don't think you're careless or rash. Despite what your bosses think about your occasional... rogue behavior. That's simply because you know how to recognize bullshit when you smell it and prefer to go around it rather than sit there mired in it just because some bureaucrat said you should. And I don't think you're a sucker for a pretty face. At least not enough to get you in trouble."

"Okay," Jesse said, sitting the empty glass on the desk. "Then what am I a sucker for? Because you obviously think I am."

"The wounded," Jack said. "The vulnerable. The huddled masses yearning to be free. You have a strong sense of justice, and a protective streak a mile wide. I'd say this woman – this pretty, wounded, vulnerable woman who is a person of interest in what sounds like an already dangerous investigation – has already gotten under your skin."

Jesse wanted to protest, just on principle. Jack made him sound like a pushover for whatever sob story people spewed.

But he knew that on some level, his brother wasn't wrong. He wasn't a pushover, but he did have a protective streak.

And Jillian Montgomery had managed to rouse it.

"Fuck," Jesse muttered.

"Probably not the best idea under the circumstances."

"You should have been a comedian instead of an ambulance chaser."

"I don't have to chase the ambulances. They come to me." He took the glass back from Jesse, and studied him with his cool gray gaze. "Acknowledging that you have a problematic attraction is the first step. The second step, of course, being to keep your pants firmly zipped so that the little head doesn't have a chance to convince the big head that the pretty, wounded vulnerable woman who is a person of interest in a dangerous investigation will be best served by screwing her six ways from Sunday."

"I'm not an idiot," Jesse said. "And anyway, you're one to talk about keeping your pants zipped."

"But you'll notice that my pants always remain zipped around clients, witnesses, colleagues and opposing counsel. Pissing in your own pool is bad form."

Jesse shook his head. He couldn't believe they were even having this discussion. He wasn't going to have sex with a potential suspect, or a potential witness, or a potential whatever the hell Jillian was.

And the fact was he didn't *know* what she was. He'd been caught completely off guard by her appearance at the Shady Lady, and still, despite the translator mostly confirming Jillian's version of events, wasn't completely convinced that she was telling the whole truth.

Anyone else…

It could mean anything, including Jillian believing that someone else might have been asking about her at the bar.

Who? And why?

Those were questions that needed to be answered. He'd been making some progress that direction before Jack showed up, which in hindsight was probably fortuitous. He had to do this right. If he had any lingering uncertainties, any suspicions at all, he should address them in a formal interview. He had been walking a fine line, and it was time he planted his feet firmly on the side of professional ethics. He'd never be able to live with himself otherwise. When they'd had the meeting with the translator, it hadn't seemed like there was enough evidence to question Jillian's story. And maybe there wasn't. But he also had to make sure he wasn't allowing his personal feelings to influence the way he looked at her potential involvement in the case.

"I have to go," he told his brother. He needed to talk to Brian.

"Not that I won't see you beforehand, but you'll be at Mom and Dad's for Christmas Eve dinner, right?"

"Like I'd miss Mom's ham?"

"Silly question."

Jesse put his hand on the door knob, glanced back over his shoulder. "Thanks for the whisky. And the conversation."

"Any time," Jack said, his expression softening. "You know that."

He did. As big a pain as his brother could be, Jesse knew he always had his back.

Jesse mulled things over as he walked down the steps, through the nearly deserted building. A Christmas tree stood in the lobby, its lights reflecting on the marble floor like a cache of diamonds.

It reminded him of the tree in the laundromat, Losevsky's blood staining the angel's white dress. Which took him right back to the beginning of this mess.

The way he saw it, there were a couple of possibilities. One: Jillian lied and was somehow connected to Losevsky, or maybe to the person who'd ordered his death. He'd watched her closely for any signs of deceit during the original interview, and thought she was being forthright. At least as far as Losevsky was concerned. But someone associated with that organization? That was another matter. The tremor he'd detected in her hands could have been the result of general nerves about being questioned by the police, but he wasn't willing to rule some sort of duplicity out completely.

And that shamed him. Shamed him that he'd given in to his baser urges, kissing her the way he had. All but having sex with her against the wall of her foyer, even while harboring uncertainties. Regardless of her guilt or innocence, she deserved better from him. And his employer certainly deserved better from an agent in which they'd entrusted a badge.

If he looked at it from that angle, the dead squirrel looked less likely to be a form of payback from Mike McGrath than a warning from an unknown party.

Don't cooperate with the police or you'll be next.

If that was the case, her very real fear when she'd seen Axelrod and Gannon might have less to do with her previous experience and more to do with a current threat. It also suggested, by the fact that she hadn't already been eliminated, that either the information she might be able to impart was less damning than that of the other two victims – Losevsky and Irena – or that the opportunity to silence her simply hadn't presented itself yet.

Or as a third possibility, perhaps she... meant more, on a personal level, to whomever was calling the shots.

Jesse couldn't stop his jaw from clenching at the thought.

"Thanks Dawson," he said to the guard who held the door open for him.

"No problem, Mr. Wellington. Looks like we're about to get more rain. You stay dry now."

"I'll do my best."

The brisk night air slid over him, cooling the heat the whisky and his own guilt and anger had kindled beneath his skin. He stopped in the light of the flickering gas flame lanterns that flanked either side of the entrance. The breeze picked up, bringing with it the smell of the approaching rain and of the pine from the wreath on the door behind him. Both familiar smells, but for some reason the entire nightscape struck Jesse as alien. He felt separated not only from his surroundings, but from his normal good judgment.

He wasn't used to feeling tangled by his own fishing line. Caught in a trap of his own making.

Shaking off the self-recrimination for the time being, Jesse admitted it was not unfeasible that someone in the Savannah Chatham Metropolitan Police Department *had* seized the opportunity for payback, starting when they'd discovered her card. He couldn't ignore the toothpick belonging to Gannon he'd found under Jillian's window.

So maybe she was telling the truth about that. About everything.

And maybe he'd become so… entangled that he couldn't judge any of this objectively.

"Hell," he muttered to himself. Jesse started down the front steps when his cell phone started to vibrate. He pulled it from his pocket, checked the readout. "Hey. I was just about to call you."

Brian rattled off a residential address. "You need to get over here. Now."

"Whose apartment?" Jesse asked, clicking the remote to unlock his Jeep.

"Gannon's." Brian said, just as the first raindrops started to fall. "He's dead."

CHAPTER TWELVE

AS many dead bodies as Jesse'd seen during his career, it never got any easier visiting a scene. Especially when the deceased was someone you knew.

Knew, and didn't like all that much. Jesse wasn't going to pretend otherwise. But that didn't mean he was happy about the situation. In fact, it both sickened him and pissed him off.

"First apartment on your left when you step off the elevator," the uniformed officer said after Jesse flashed his badge at the door to the building. Rain dripped off the man's hat, which was covered by a plastic poncho. "And wear these."

Jesse took the shoe covers the man handed him, meant to help preserve any evidence that would be compromised by people trudging in and out of the wet. He took the elevator, happy to find himself alone in the car, and slipped the booties over his sneakers before approaching the apartment. Another uniformed cop greeted him, checked his identification, and then allowed him to pass.

Taking a deep breath, Jesse entered the apartment.

His first impression was that it was neat as a pin. Gannon was either anal retentive, or hadn't spent much time here. Or maybe, judging by the scent of pine cleaner, his maid service had paid a recent visit.

The forensics team was already busy collecting evidence, and Jesse sidestepped them, following the voices toward what he presumed was the dining area.

His heart skipped a beat when he approached the doorway. The table had been pushed to the corner of the room, and one of the chairs – currently on its side – was positioned beneath the chandelier.

Gannon hung from it.

His eyes were open, protruding in the manner typical of hanging victims, and seemed to accuse Jesse. Of course, Jesse was probably just reading that last part into it.

He dragged his hand over the lower half of his face.

Brian spotted him, and made his way past a couple of plain clothes detectives, who were taking notes while a photographer documented the scene from every conceivable angle.

"His ex-wife found him," Brian said in a low voice, giving him the rundown. "Was supposed to pick up their kid after school, never showed. She was pissed at first, assumed he'd forgotten, tried calling and texting to chew him out. She got worried when he didn't respond after several hours. Tried contacting him through the station, thought maybe he'd gotten called out on a case, but it turns out he'd phoned in sick earlier in the day. There's some over the counter cold medicine – the knock you out kind – on the vanity in the bathroom, used tissues piled on the nightstand, and the bed had been slept in recently. Looks like he was legitimately ill. Anyway, she has a key – I guess they're still on decent terms – and stopped by to check on him." He glanced at Gannon's body. "Not a very pleasant thing to discover."

Jesse continued to stare. "Was the kid with her?"

"What?"

"When she stopped by, was their kid with her?"

"Oh. No. Dropped him off at the grandparents' house first. Didn't want him to get sick, or so she explained. She's back in the spare bedroom, talking to Axelrod. She's pretty shaken up. They both are."

"No wonder." Jesse was pretty shaken up himself. Then he frowned. "Did he purchase the cold medicine today?"

"It's a new box. Plastic bag in the trash can contained the receipt. Paid cash early this morning, right after he called in. Still need to confirm it was actually him that purchased it. I'm sure they'll be requesting video from the drug store."

Jesse looked at Brian, recognized that his thoughts were tracking along the same lines. "Yeah," Brian said in answer to Jesse's silent question. "If you're planning on killing yourself that day, why bother treating your cold symptoms, right? That suggests a desire to get well."

"Or maybe just a desire to stop coughing."

"True. But it strikes me as odd, and it seems to strike you that way, too. Maybe he wasn't planning on killing himself."

"Any signs of a struggle?"

"None that I've seen," Brian said. "Aside from the bedroom and the table here being shoved out of the way, nothing in the apartment is out of place. Has a cleaning service, the building manager said, that was here yesterday afternoon. The forensics crew said they must do a good job, because they're not finding a lot of fingerprints."

"So if it is indeed suicide, the question is what happened between this morning and afternoon that made him decide to kill himself." Jesse stared with frustrated resignation at the detective's corpse. "He's wearing my shirt."

"What? Who?"

"Gannon," Jesse explained. Then he pulled Brian slightly out of the doorway, and continued in an undertone. "That's the shirt I took off and loaned to Jillian the night of your party. The one that disappeared from the laundry room in the basement."

Brian opened his mouth. Closed it. And then his face drained of all color. "Jesus. Are you sure?"

"It was from one of my fraternity events in college. I've had it forever. I'm sure."

"How did Gannon get a hold of it? And why the *hell* would he choose to wear it when he hung himself?"

"I don't know. As a final *up yours?*" Jesse suggested. Then he heaved a big sigh. "I confronted him the other day. After the meeting. Regarding the DNA match on the toothpick I found beneath your sister and Jillian's basement window."

"And you think that's enough for him to decide that swinging from a rope is his only option? Proof that he was poking around?"

"Maybe if the poking around were connected to breaking and entering. Or leaving a dead animal on the doorstep."

Brian's hand shook when he lifted it to rub over his bald head, but his voice remained steady. "The squirrel I can maybe understand. Like Jillian said, payback for her testifying in McGrath's parole hearing, making sure he stayed behind bars. But why the hell would he break into the house? Why would he take your shirt?"

"Those are questions we need to answer." Jesse considered. "Did he leave a note?"

"Not that anyone has located so far. They're waiting on one of the tech people to get into his laptop, see if he typed out a draft or maybe composed an email that he didn't send. But shit, Jesse."

"We need to check the soles of his shoes. All of them."

"I'm guessing you have a reason."

"I don't know if you've noticed that the floor in the boiler room at your sister's place is crumbling. The old concrete grit was stuck in my shoe tread after I left that morning. I noticed some of it on the floorboard of my Jeep. If he was there, if he did somehow bypass the alarm – or maybe Jillian was mistaken and she actually forgot to set it. Anyway, if he was there and messed around in the basement, took the shirt – whatever his reasons – he'd possibly still have some concrete dust in the soles of his shoes."

"Unless he tossed them. Or cleaned them. Or wore freaking booties." Brian gestured significantly to their covered feet.

"Yeah, yeah, I know. But if we can put him in that basement, it's a place to start. We need to find out how he came to be in possession of that shirt." Jesse felt like there was a bigger picture here, something more than just a cop who might have committed a felony or two and was afraid of being found out. The truth was that cops did far worse than that and, with a good union representative, faced seriously reduced charges.

Unless the breaking and entering and the dead squirrel were only the proverbial tip of the iceberg. Maybe Gannon had far more damaging secrets.

Jesse looked past Brian, into the dining room. "We're going to have to have a talk with Axelrod and the other detectives. I need to tell them about the toothpick and the shirt, as well as our conversation. But first I want to have a look at the scene."

They went back into the dining room, where Jesse introduced himself to the detective who'd been assigned to the case – at least the one who was still in the room – a woman by the name of Portman. "Has the photographer documented everything?"

"Yes," she answered. "And we've got the sketch and measurements, too. As soon as the ME gets here, we'll start the examination of the bod…" she stopped herself, flushed.

"Of Detective Gannon, I mean. I sort of shut out the fact that he's one of ours."

"Sometimes shutting down your emotions is the only way to do the job until you can process it all later." Jesse pulled on gloves. "Do you mind if I take a closer look?"

She shook her head. "You know the drill. Knock yourself out."

"Thank you." Jesse approached the middle of the room, walked around the macabre centerpiece. His nostrils flared at the unpleasant stench of violent death and he couldn't stop the brief flare of anger when he got close enough to see the date printed on the shirt. It seemed like the deliberate sullying of one of Jesse's fonder memories.

But like the detective, he shut out – as much as he could – his more human, visceral reactions and tried to observe with an objective eye. There didn't appear to be any signs of violence on the body, apart from the obvious injuries associated with the ligature around his neck. Jesse stared. It hadn't been readily apparent from a distance, or maybe he'd simply been too stunned by the presence of his shirt to fully comprehend what he was seeing. But up close the nature of the ligature was apparent.

He turned to the detective. "Christmas lights?"

She winced. "Yes."

Jesse glanced around. "He doesn't have a tree. No decorations. Do you know if he had a problem with the holiday? Seasonal disorder, or whatever that's called."

"Not that I know of. The ex-wife said that this was his weekend to keep their son, and he planned to take him to see Santa and maybe do some decorating then, although she says he wasn't much into decking the halls."

Warning bells went off in Jesse's head. "Did they have a close relationship? He and his son?"

She shrugged. "Close enough, I think. To be honest, I didn't know Detective Gannon very well. I only recently moved into the department. I think that's one of the reasons I got this assignment – the hope that I could stay objective."

"Have you found any decorations? Storage tubs or whatever?"

"Not yet. But there's a room on the first floor of the building where tenants can rent additional storage space. We'll be checking that out next."

Jesse turned back toward Gannon's body. The Christmas lights, even more than the presence of his T-shirt, made him uneasy. Rather than simply an expedient means of hanging oneself – especially if the lights hadn't been handy and the sick, medicated man had had to trudge to the storage room to get them – seemed like a statement.

A statement of what was the question.

Jesse continued his examination as best he could without actually touching the body. That would have to wait for the ME. Gannons's hands hung limp in front of the pockets of his jeans, which remained unbuttoned. His feet were bare.

Jesse leaned in, squinted at what appeared to be something sticking out of one of the pockets. He froze, and then glanced over his shoulder.

"Agent Parker?" he called out. "You want to come take a look at this?"

Brian abandoned his conversation with the uniformed cop at the door and returned to the dining room. "What?"

"Does that look like what I think it does?"

Brian grimaced as he leaned in closer. And then stood up and cursed.

Sensing that she was missing something of importance, Detective Portman came over. "What's up?"

With a sinking feeling, Jesse turned to address her. "The little plastic bag in his pocket? I'm pretty sure it contains LSD."

CHAPTER THIRTEEN

JILLIAN anchored the length of fresh garland on the end of the porch rail. The air was crisp, but not so cold that she couldn't enjoy what she was doing. In fact, it was a perfect December morning. Last night's rain had moved off, leaving a sky washed clear and blue as…

As Jesse's eyes was the first thought that popped into her mind, but she frowned. He'd acted very oddly after his brother appeared at their table and pointed out that he'd seen Jillian in his law office that day. Almost as if he was uncomfortable with the two of them talking. She wondered if he were… embarrassed somehow by the fact that she'd consulted with a criminal defense attorney, despite the fact that he'd suggested that very course of action. Which she would have done anyway. She had too much experience to have faith in the system to protect her best interests.

Or maybe he simply didn't like his brother knowing that she'd been in need of those services.

She supposed she should have recognized the name Wellington on the door along with several others, but she'd had more important things on her mind. Like protecting herself legally. Ever since those detectives had shown up, she'd felt like there was a safe perched somewhere above her, and even though she couldn't see it, the slightest move in the wrong direction would send it crashing down on her head.

Because she was decorating for Christmas – one of her favorite things to do – Jillian refused to allow her thoughts to be dragged down into that particular morass. The fruit basket had already tainted her holiday association enough, and she wasn't going to let it go any further. She had a holiday-themed wedding to photograph later this afternoon – *the* holiday-themed wedding of the year, as the bride's sweet but very socially connected mother had pointed out on more than one occasion – and she needed to be in good spirits.

She tucked her earbuds into place and pulled up the Christmas playlist on her phone.

Having already dragged the ladder out of the basement, Jillian set it up in front of the porch so that she could wind red ribbon through the pine and magnolia leaf garland. *Rockin' Around the Christmas Tree* played in her ears and she swayed her hips slightly as she worked. The song had just segued into *Jingle Bell Rock* when she felt a hand on her leg.

"Oh!" Jillian lost her balance, falling backwards. She found herself in Jesse's arms with the ribbon still clutched in her hand.

Definitely as clear and blue as a rain-washed sky, she thought as she looked at him from a distance of inches. Although at the moment they were a little red around the edges.

He studied her a moment, his gaze drifting down from her eyes toward her mouth, but then his jaw clenched and he set her back on her feet.

"Sorry. I didn't mean to scare you."

"It's okay." She turned off her playlist, removed the buds from her ears. "I probably had the music too loud."

They continued to stare at each other for several heartbeats, and Jillian began to see that it wasn't just his eyes. His whole body seemed to radiate exhaustion. "Are you okay?"

"That depends on your definition. Look, I know I'm intruding again, but do you have a few minutes?"

"Sure." Realizing she was still holding onto the ribbon, she sat the coil on the ladder. "Would you like a cup of coffee?"

"As much as I'd like to finally land a blue marlin."

"I'll take that as a yes."

"A very large one."

He followed her up the steps, and Jillian shoved aside the tubs of decorations she'd left littering the entryway.

"Excuse the mess. Katie's been so busy that I just decided to haul everything out and get started without her. Not that her participation usually extends much beyond her drinking egg nog or wine and telling me how great it looks. She cooks a mean Christmas dinner, but decorating is not particularly her thing. I... is something wrong?"

She noticed that Jesse was standing just inside the doorway, staring into one of the tubs. "Your decorations are very organized."

"Oh. That's Katie. I should have added that she's far better at taking down than she is at putting up, as she labels everything and – as you can see – even wraps the lights around special clothes hangers to store them. If I didn't love her so much, I'd probably have to kill her."

Jesse glanced up.

"I'm kidding, of course."

Jesse nodded, and then lifted his glasses to rub his bloodshot eyes. "Yeah. Sorry. I'm just sort of fried." Then his head came up in the manner of an animal sniffing the wind. "Is Katie here? Something smells delicious."

"No, Katie and Davis went out to do some shopping before the crowds got too crazy. I'm making *pryaniki*."

"I'm not going to pretend that I know what that is, but I'm pretty sure I want the recipe."

"You bake?"

Jesse scratched behind his ear, looking uncomfortable. "At the risk of sounding even more like the mama's boy you accused me of being, my mom made all five of us learn how to cook. Baking isn't my forte, but I could probably figure out how to measure ingredients if it made my kitchen smell like that. When I get a kitchen again, that is. Or you can go into business with Katie and then all of my dietary needs will be covered in one place. I'll never have to touch a stove again."

Jillian laughed. "The *pryaniki* I can make with unfailing success, but I think I'll leave the cooking to Katie. Come on." She tilted her head. "You can have some with your coffee."

He entered the kitchen behind her, pulling up short in the doorway. "Holy shit. It looks like the Keebler elves have been here."

Jillian looked around at the multiple racks of cooling cookies. "Tis the season. I made enough for the neighbors because we did a cookie swap thing last year and everyone seemed to love them. Here." She took a few off the nearest rack, slid them onto a plate. "Go ahead and sit down. I'll get the coffee."

"Thanks." He dropped heavily onto one of the stools at the counter, took a bite, and then closed his eyes in apparent bliss. "Oh my God."

Jillian smiled as she poured coffee into a mug hand-painted with holly leaves. "It's an old family recipe. Handed down to my mother from her mother who got it from her mother and so on."

"Are you still in contact with any of your relatives in Russia?"

Jillian hesitated. "No. My mother's father abandoned the family when she was a young girl, and she spent most of her childhood training for the ballet. Her mother died when she was just a teen."

"Rough."

Jillian glanced up. "She wasn't fortunate, like I was, to have an aunt to step in, love her like her own daughter. It was difficult, losing both my parents, but my aunt and my cousins made me feel a rightful part of their family. In that I was very lucky."

"You mentioned that your cousins don't live nearby."

"No, and that's a hardship for me, even though they're a good bit older. One is career military and he's been stationed all over the world. The other lives in Alaska."

He used one of the napkins from a holder beside him to wipe the stickiness from his fingers. "Alaska. I hear the salmon fishing there is fantastic."

"Do you relate everything back to fishing?" she said as she sat the mug in front of him.

"If at all possible."

"Must be a professional hazard," she said as she poured hot water over an herbal teabag, since she'd already consumed several cups of coffee while she was baking. "Kind of like I'm always framing photographs in my mind."

She turned to find Jesse staring at her, an odd look on his face. "What?" She rubbed her fingers beside her mouth. "Do I have cookie glaze on my face or something?"

"Jillian." The tone of his voice made her slowly lower her hand. "Sit down. Please."

"That doesn't sound good."

He pulled out the stool cattycorner to his. "Please."

"Okay." She slid onto the tractor-style seat and assessed the funereal look in his eyes. Her throat seemed to constrict. "Is it… Brian or…"

She left the question open-ended. In response, Jesse lifted his hip, pulled something that looked like a thin wallet from his pocket and slid it across the table.

"What's this?"

"It's pulling the bandage off in one quick yank."

Her heart began to knock in her chest like a caged animal that senses a storm approaching. Knowing that it's trapped and can do nothing to avoid the elements. Keeping her eyes on his, she reached out, flipped the leather bi-fold open.

And then stared down at his ID. His federal ID.

"You're an FBI agent." She didn't even recognize her own voice. It sounded hollow. Like it was coming back to her across a vast, empty distance.

"Yes."

Something began to percolate inside her at the blasé nature of his reply. Like *oh, hey, by the way*... That, she did recognize. It was betrayal and disbelief, coated with a fine layer of rage.

She'd felt it before, when Charlotte had accused her of acting out of jealousy.

"Are you here to arrest me?"

"Generally speaking, I don't ask people whom I'm about to arrest to have a spot of tea with me before I break out the handcuffs."

She nodded, still outwardly calm except for that odd sense that she was like a tea kettle perched on a burner. Rapidly approaching a boil. "Then I'd like for you to leave."

"Jillian –"

She jerked her gaze away from his identification and actually felt her eyes flash fire. "Leave."

His jaw clenched, but he shook his head. "Not yet."

She pushed away from the counter. "If you don't get out of this kitchen right now, I'll –"

"You'll what? Call the police?"

Her head drew back as if he'd slapped her. "You… bastard."

"Yeah. Yeah, I probably am. I fully admit that I've done you wrong. But regardless of that, I'm not leaving until I tell you what I came to tell you. If you'll sit back down and listen, I'll be out of your hair in ten minutes. Fifteen, tops."

She laughed. Cackled, really. It was a sound of disbelief. "You *lied* to me. And yet you expect me to sit and listen to whatever you have to say?"

"I didn't lie."

A strangled noise emerged from her throat. "Let me guess: you simply *omitted* a few things."

He at least had the grace to look slightly shamefaced. "That's right."

"That's right. That's *right.*" Rigid with fury, Jillian gave a sharp nod. "Okay then. If you won't leave, I will."

She marched out of the kitchen.

Jesse caught up with her in the hallway, his hand clamping down on her shoulder. "Jillian, wait."

"Don't touch me."

He lifted both hands.

She stalked toward the front door.

"Damn it, Jillian."

He grabbed her again, and she shook off his hand before whirling around and raising her own. She saw that he was braced for the slap she'd been about to deliver, so she lowered her arm. "I won't be a cliché."

"I'm glad to hear it, especially since I was prepared to let you get in one shot."

"Oh, you were going to *let* me, were you? How chivalrous."

"You have a right to be angry."

"I also have a right as an individual to be free from being harassed by federal agents inside my home, but yet here you still are."

"I'm trying to be reasonable here," he retorted "and handle this professionally, but that's difficult when you're acting like a child."

She ignored the aspersions he cast on her maturity in favor of addressing the more salient point. "Professional? You call lying to someone – and omission is lying, however much you want to believe otherwise – pretending to be something you're not and then kissing them blind while shoving your *hand* under their *skirt* to be *professional?"*

He hesitated. "No. And I'm sorry."

"Oh, you're *sorry.* Well then, that makes everything better."

"Look, if we could just sit down and discuss this like rational human beings –"

"Rational." She nodded. "Yes, let's be rational. In fact, if you had been *rational* from the beginning – because in retrospect, meeting you at Brian's party *was* a set-up, wasn't it?" And she swallowed the hurt of that. She'd have to deal with Brian later. "Anyway, if you both had treated me as a *rational* human being rather than someone that you had to, to *trick* because… what? I'm too emotionally unstable to handle the questions that needed to be asked? You…" she stopped. Drew a breath. "The questions that detectives Axelrod and Gannon asked that night. You're part of that investigation. That's what this is all about."

She hadn't phrased it as a question, but he nodded anyway. "Yes. And I hope you can appreciate how difficult it was for Brian when we discovered your card."

"Right. How difficult for Brian. So difficult, in fact, that he lost all of his mental faculties and decided that this elaborate…" she waved a hand around "*production* was a more reasonable approach than simply telling me what had happened and giving me an opportunity to answer any questions that arose without all the subterfuge."

"And you wouldn't have panicked if the cops had simply shown up at your door, right? Because that's probably what would have happened if Brian hadn't lobbied to keep you from being treated as a hostile potential witness. Given your history with the Savannah PD, I don't think they would have been inclined to handle you gently."

He had a point, but she wasn't ready to acknowledge it. "He could have simply *told* me –"

"No," Jesse interrupted, his voice tight with frustration. "No, he couldn't. Because one of the hard and fast rules of an investigation is that you don't warn witnesses or suspects ahead of time so that they can prepare their response. You want them off guard. He could not say anything to you ahead of time. And if he'd tried, our SAC would have benched him so fast his head would have resembled a scene from The Exorcist. What we did was unorthodox, yes. And not entirely what you might call honest. But it was the only solution all parties could agree upon. The questions were asked and you also had a… let's just describe my role that night as a buffer."

"That night. So you didn't intend to have any contact with me afterward?"

"Not after I returned your key, no. Bumping into you at the Y was purely an accident."

"And I guess you *accidentally* asked me out for coffee as well."

He hesitated, and then shook his head. "That was a deliberate decision."

"Because you wanted to interrogate me?"

"Because I wanted to be with you. I tried to tell myself that I was just being a nice guy or conversely, that I could take the opportunity to dig a little more deeply. But that's bullshit. I would have done just about anything – *anything* – to keep you from walking out that door without me."

She stood there, raw breaths tearing in and out of her lungs, her heart trembling on a precipice that she was afraid to peer into. "Fine. Fine, I understand. And now that you've explained everything, I would like you to leave."

"I haven't explained everything."

She threw up her hands. "I don't want to hear anymore, okay? Whatever you have to say about… what happened between us, I'm not interested. It's over. And it won't be happening again."

"Jillian," he called after her when she rounded the newel post and started up the stairs. The tread squeaked, reminding her that she'd forgotten again to tighten the screws. That just pissed her off even further.

"Do *not* touch me!" Her voice went shrill when he impeded her progress up the stairs.

"I'll stop touching you when you stop running away." He pulled on her shoulder until her back was to the wall. She glared up at him. He glared back.

But then his expression changed fraction by fraction from one of intense frustration to… something else. His gaze landed on her mouth.

"Jesus," he said, the word sounding like it had been ripped from his throat. "You're beautiful."

"No need to pretend to be attracted to me any longer," she spit back. "You've already accomplished your plan."

His head jerked up. "That wasn't part of the plan," he said. "And I wasn't pretending."

Her breasts rose and fell in a rapid pulse beneath her sweater. "It doesn't matter."

"Yeah," he said softly. "Actually, it does."

He leaned closer, inch by tortuous inch, giving her plenty of time to stop him. And she should. She *should*. But

God help her, despite everything she'd just learned, she still didn't want to.

"I hate you."

"No, you don't." He placed his hands on the wall on either side of her head. "You probably wish you did, but you don't. I kind of wish you did, too, because that would make this a hell of a lot easier." He leaned in, close enough for their breath to mingle, and murmured in her ear. "The first time we met? Something clicked. I looked at you and everything else fell away, until you were the only thing I could see. And I'm still seeing you. It's damned inconvenient."

Despite everything, the corners of her mouth trembled into the tiniest of smirks. "Well then. Serves you right."

"Probably." He pulled back a bare inch. "I want to kiss you right now. I want to put you over my shoulder and continue right on upstairs and toss you onto your bed. And do… everything."

Jillian's bones began to melt and she was on the verge of saying "Why don't you?" but she could see it in his eyes. "But you can't."

He paused, and then gave a slight shake of his head. "I can't. Not yet. There's some very bad stuff going on and somehow, Jillian, you're connected to it. Damn it."

"What?" her heart began to pound again, this time with anxiety. "I'm *not*. I told Brian and the detectives and *you*, repeatedly. I did not know that man Losevsky. I don't know why he had my card."

Jesse pulled back even further, and studied her face. "Maybe not. But maybe you do know who killed him."

"What?"

Jesse sighed. "Sit down, will you? I haven't slept in over twenty-four hours. I'm tired."

Because she'd noticed previously that he was in fact exhausted – and because she wasn't sure her own legs would hold her – Jillian slid down the wall to sit on the step. Jesse sat down on the one beneath her, and leaned against the rail, hands dangling between his knees.

"You were in Katie's restaurant all afternoon yesterday. And there are plenty of witnesses to that fact."

Jillian didn't like the sound of that. "Why should I need witnesses as to my whereabouts?"

"Gannon's dead."

She didn't fully process what he was saying. "What?"

"Detective Gannon. I can't go into too many details," he said, visibly measuring his words. "But suffice it to say that he did not die of natural causes."

"Oh my God." Her hand flew to her mouth, and then dropped away, boneless. "And you think I had something to do with it?"

"No. If I thought that, I wouldn't be sitting here. And you'd likely be down at the Barracks, being interrogated by some very angry detectives from the Savannah PD."

"Then why did you say that about my whereabouts yesterday?"

Jesse dragged his hand down his face. "I can't tell you. I'm sorry," he said when she started to protest. "I can't. I can't – won't – compromise an ongoing investigation by leaking information."

"Then why did you bring this up? To scare me to death?"

"Not to death, no. But I don't mind if you're scared. If you're scared, you'll be extra cautious. Jillian." He measured his words again. "Were you acquainted with Detective Gannon prior to the night he interviewed you in your living room?"

"What? No!"

Jesse nodded. "And you'd never been to the Shady Lady before the other night?"

"Never." She shook her head for emphasis. "Never. Jesse, you *are* scaring me."

"Have you ever had any involvement with illegal drugs, using or selling?"

Jillian stared to climb to her feet. "I'm not going to keep answering questions that I've already answered. Especially not without an attorney.

"Jillian, wait. *Please.*"

It was the utter exhaustion in his tone that caused her to reconsider. She slowly sat back down. "Fine. But I'm not so naïve that I'll allow you to soften me up with some flattery and forget that you're an agent."

"Is that really what you think I was doing?"

She studied his face, his tired, beard-roughened face, and wasn't sure if her answer was what her gut told her or merely what she wanted to believe. "No. But damn it Jesse, you *lied.* It's difficult to trust you after that."

"And I understand. And I promise to be as straightforward with you as I can be from this point forward – if you promise to be straightforward with me."

She considered, and then nodded. "Okay."

He hesitated, and then reached out and took her hand. "I have one more question, and I want you to be completely honest with me. If there's something you're... afraid to reveal because you think it will put either yourself or Katie or anyone else that you care about in danger, I can promise you that the Bureau will do everything within its power to keep you safe. *I* will do everything in my power to keep you safe."

"I appreciate that. I do. But there's nothing like that. I didn't know Losevsky, and the only time I've ever been to the Shady Lady is the night I bumped into you. Working, I guess you were," she said with a note of reproach in her voice. "And I'd never even seen or heard of Detective Gannon until I saw him standing on the sidewalk in front of the house. And as to your last question, I have never sold, manufactured or used illegal drugs. Growing up I feared disappointing my aunt too much to experiment, and then after the incident with the raid on Katie and I's apartment, I feared the police. And now, well, I just don't have much interest. You have to believe me."

She could see that he wanted to. Eventually, he nodded. "I can't say any more. If my boss knew I'd come to talk to you like this, he'd probably chew my ass. But I needed to come clean with you because… well, because. And more than that, I needed to tell you to be careful. I know you said you don't know anything, but if you think of anything – anything at all – that you think might somehow be pertinent, I want you to call me or Brian. Maybe a conversation you overheard in Russian, whatever. But call."

She realized what that meant. "You heard me speaking Russian to the bartender the other night."

"Yeah, I did."

"I can tell you what I –"

"I know what you said."

"You speak... oh," she said when she understood what he was getting at. Someone had translated it for him. Maybe even the bartender herself. Maybe she was an undercover agent, since the Shady Lady seemed to be playing a large role in their investigation. "I see."

Jesse studied her another long moment, and then gave her hand a squeeze before climbing to his feet. He stretched, and then looked down at her. "Be careful. Please."

His expression was unguarded, allowing her to see the depth of his attraction. His... concern.

"You, too."

He nodded. "I'll show myself out."

Jillian watched him walk down the steps and out the front door. He didn't look back.

She let her head rest against the wall, studied the plaster medallion on the ceiling.

And wondered if she'd somehow made a terrible mistake.

JESSE cut the crime scene tape from the doorway, and then stepped aside so that the building manager could unlock the apartment.

"Terrible thing," the man said, though there was a sort of avidness in his eyes that Jesse recognized. Sure enough, he peered inside after opening the door, no doubt hoping to catch sight of something which he could later describe to his friends.

Violent death was exciting when it didn't happen to you or one of your loved ones.

"Thank you," Jesse said, stepping in front of him to block his view. Not that there was much to see. No blood spatter or broken furniture. Gannon's death had caused little disturbance to the physical environment of the apartment.

"Do you, uh, know when the investigation might be finished? I've got a waiting list," the man explained. "This building is pretty popular thanks to the location."

"I'm sure the SCMPD will let you know just as soon as possible."

"Yeah. Well, okay. Just call me when you're ready to leave and I'll lock up again."

"Will do."

He waited for the man to toddle off before going in and shutting the door. He'd spent the entire evening and most of the night here, and wasn't keen on being back again.

But there was something he had to check out.

He glanced around at the remnants of the forensic investigation, the finger print powder laying like comic book shadows over various surfaces – artificially dark and designed to imply something sinister around every corner.

Shaking off the maudlin thoughts, Jesse located the coat closet first and inspected it from top to bottom. Having no luck – depending upon how you looked at it – he closed that door and then went toward Gannon's bedroom. The sheets and mattress pad had been stripped to check for any evidence that the man might not have been alone in the apartment yesterday. Jesse doubted he'd invited a woman over when he was sick enough to call in, to douse himself with cold medicine, but you never knew. And if there had been a woman – or hell, a man – then maybe they knew something about what had caused Gannon to hang himself.

If he'd hanged himself.

Until there was conclusive evidence that that was indeed the case, the detectives would pursue this like any other suspicious death – as a potential homicide.

And it was that which had Jesse concerned.

He opened up Gannon's closet – pretty good sized, he noted objectively. Gannon had it filled. The man had been something of a clothes horse, a little vain about his appearance. Jesse wondered if he dressed sharply to disguise the fact that his hair was thinning, his gut starting to paunch. And felt a pang of sympathy for the man whom he hadn't liked very much.

Glancing down, Jesse noted that Gannons's shoe rack was gone. He'd provided a sample of the concrete dust from Jillian's basement for the lab to make a comparison against whatever they found on the soles of the detective's shoes. If this particular expedition confirmed his suspicions, having evidence that Gannon had indeed been inside Jillian's house would be of particular importance.

Jesse pushed aside hanger after hanger, occasionally removing an article of clothing so that he could have a better look. He found nothing that matched what he was looking for.

He closed the closet doors and considered if there was any place else to look. Almost anywhere, if one had been attempting to conceal the evidence.

But Jesse didn't think that was the case. Given the fact that Gannon had been wearing Jesse's shirt, had a baggie of what appeared to be the Russian's LSD in his pocket, subterfuge didn't seem to be the name of the game.

He stood there for several moments and then on a hunch, went into the bathroom. He partially closed the door, found a robe hanging from a hook on the back of the door.

And noted the sparkly red hanger.

His professional satisfaction over the fact that his hunch had been correct was overshadowed by a personal crisis. But after the barest hesitation, he yanked his phone from his pocket.

Brian answered on the second ring.

"I'm about to call Detective Portman," Jesse said, "but I wanted to fill you in first. I stopped by to talk to Jillian this morning."

There was a significant pause. "And?"

"*And* I told her the truth. As much as I could anyway."

He could practically hear Brian rubbing his head. "She's gonna kill me. And then Katie will grill my liver and serve it with a nice chianti."

"For doing everything you could to protect them? I don't think so. And besides, I took most of the heat." As he should. Brian wasn't the one who'd kissed a person of interest in an ongoing investigation.

But Brian didn't need to know about that.

"That's not why I called though."

"Why do I have the feeling I'm not going to like this?"

"Because you're not. You know how we all looked yesterday to try to find Gannon's Christmas decorations?" Which the man apparently didn't actually have. Axelrod said his partner had talked about buying one of those little artificial trees, fully decorated, and calling it a day. "Well I think I know where the string of lights came from."

"Don't say it. Please don't say you think they came from Katie's house."

"Sorry, man," Jesse said, meaning it. "But I'm in Gannon's bathroom staring at the sparkly red hanger labeled *Christmas Lights* right now."

CHAPTER FOURTEEN

"I feel like Cindy Lou Who," Katie said.

Shivering against the chilly air, Jillian slid a hand into Katie's, too upset to formulate a verbal response. They sat on the bench in the back courtyard, waiting for members of the SCMPD to finish poking around in the basement. The cops had also hauled away several of their Christmas decorations, leading to Katie's comment.

"This is bullshit," Davis said from beside the bench, where he stood with arms tightly crossed and his expression radiating hostility. "I don't know what makes them think they can just take your stuff."

"A warrant," Katie replied sourly. "But at least it was very specific as to the areas of the house they could search and what they could remove as possible evidence. Brian got us that much."

"I'm sorry," Jillian said quietly, and had Katie turning toward her.

"For what?"

"This is the second time that we've had our home invaded by the police. And both times have been my fault."

"How do you get that this is your fault?" Davis demanded.

"I pushed the issue with Charlotte and Mike," she told him. "I made enemies of a number of the cops. This is connected to that, somehow. Detective Gannon was friends with Mike." She glanced at Katie. "I asked Sam. He said he was pretty sure the two of them had been tight. Plus, I let Jesse – Agent Wellington – in today. He had a really weird look on his face when he spotted the tub of Christmas lights. I don't know why they're important, but they obviously are.

And now the house is full of cops who are stealing our roast beast."

Katie laughed, but quickly sobered. "They're not stealing our roast beast. If they try removing anything from my kitchen, there will be hell to pay. And it's not your fault." She gave Jillian's hand a squeeze. "You did what was right. What I wish I'd had the courage to do, honestly. But I didn't want to get involved in Charlotte's business. As far as letting Jesse in today, I have to think that whatever evidence they're looking for here would have come to light eventually – no pun intended." She paused, her expression softening. "And thank you for believing me when I told you I had no idea that he worked with Brian."

"How long have I known you? You can't keep a secret worth a damn. There's no way you could have – or would have – lied to me about that." Jillian sighed. "Plus, you've been so busy getting your restaurant up and running over the past couple years that you can't be expected to know all of your brother's colleagues."

Katie's face returned to mutinous lines. "I'm going to kill Brian."

"No, don't." Jillian had had time to think about everything, and she did understand what a difficult position Brian must have been in. He had to have been worried for

Katie – and her. She'd seen him only briefly when he'd shown up with the cops, and the look on his face spoke volumes. She'd known him long enough to recognize that he was miserable but resigned to his duty. "We can't fault him for doing his job."

"Oh, fine," Katie said, sounding like a child who'd just been told they can't eat a cookie because it will spoil their dinner. "Have it your way."

Jillian was trying not to fault Jesse, but was having a more difficult time being magnanimous. The fact that he'd eaten her cookies, revealed that he'd been lying to her, talked about carrying her upstairs and ravishing her and then calmly walked out and filed – or whatever the right term was – for a warrant for the cops to search her house was a bitter pill to swallow.

She couldn't deny the attraction, but she also couldn't completely set aside the feeling of betrayal. Especially since he wasn't even here to face her ire.

A movement to the side caught her eye, and Jillian glanced over and saw the plantation shutters in the kitchen window next door opening a little.

"Great," she said, crossing her arms as she turned back around. "Mr. Pratt is over there spying on us again. Probably has the binoculars out so that he can delight in my downfall."

"Old fart," was Davis's opinion. "He's like a caricature in a bad play. *Grumpy Old Man.* He even wears a cardigan."

"At least he doesn't have a huge social circle like Mrs. Franklin," Katie said. "I bet she's burned through the data plan on her cell phone just this morning. We'll be the talk of the Baptist Church bingo room. And don't say you're sorry again," she snapped at Jillian. "It might bring people in to the restaurant to gawk. You know how southerners love their scandals. Hell, the story of that antiques dealer who killed his male prostitute lover created an entire cottage industry."

Jillian kissed Katie on the cheek, because her friend always made her smile. "I hope they're finished soon," she said afterward. "I have to get ready for the wedding."

"Shit, this nonsense makes me wish I had a cigarette," Davis muttered.

"You quit," Katie reminded him.

"Yeah, yeah. I know. But that doesn't mean I don't still crave them from time to time. Here comes Brian," Davis said, nodding toward the back door, through which Brian was emerging.

"Good," Katie mumbled. "Maybe I won't kill him," she continued "but I didn't say anything about maiming him a little."

THE bell over the door jangled when Jesse walked through. The shop was filled with – to his mind, at least – some really bizarre pieces of modern art that were nonetheless all the rage of a certain set in Savannah.

A certain very wealthy set, he amended, as he checked out the price tag on a painting that looked basically like a Twister mat stuck on the wall.

He didn't get it, but then he'd never been particularly concerned with what Jack referred to as *culture*. From where Jesse stood, what a lot of people considered culture was a bunch of overpriced nonsense.

"Can I help you?"

Jesse turned, and the eager smile on the face of the clerk melted instantly into an expression of distress.

"What are you doing here?" the outrageously blond, immaculately coifed, entirely effeminate man hissed.

"I'm not allowed to shop?"

He made a sound caught between panic and derision. "Your idea of great art generally involves canines and black velvet."

"Now that's not true. Even I know that black velvet is tacky. Oil on canvas is the only adequate medium to capture the brilliance that is dogs playing poker."

"You…" Feathers ruffled, the smaller man started to opine, but then glanced quickly around. Luckily it was almost closing time and they were the only two in the gallery at the moment. Jesse'd waited until he'd seen the last patrons leave. "Won't you please step into my office?"

Amused by the officiousness despite the fact that no one was around to hear it, Jesse smiled as he followed the other man toward a frosted glass door etched with something that resembled a child's monochromatic crayon drawing.

"I'll never understand how you managed to convince people to pay good money for this stuff, LeRoy."

LeRoy – whose real name was Buster Leonard Royce, but he refused to answer to that – sniffed as he flicked a hand toward a chair that looked like a spiny sea urchin.

"Are these… melted plastic pipes?" Jesse asked. "Like, for plumbing?"

"I wouldn't expect you to understand."

"I hope you don't expect me to sit, either. Some of us don't care to have our rotos rootered."

LeRoy stared at Jesse over the top of his bright green cat's eye glasses, which Jesse knew were fashion choice rather than necessity. "You really haven't evolved since adolescence, have you?"

"Just remember that I was the one who repeatedly saved your adolescent ass."

"Fine, fine." LeRoy sighed dramatically. "Sit there." He pointed at a far more normal looking chair, albeit one that appeared constructed from matchsticks. Jesse sat, tentatively, not entirely convinced that it wasn't another piece of "art" that would crumble into kindling under his weight.

It held, and he turned his attention to LeRoy, who pulled a bottle of fancy water from the mini-fridge under the bar. "Beverage? No? Well I hope you don't mind if I have one." He splashed some of the water into a glass, followed with a healthy shot of chilled vodka. "My nerves are positively shot."

"Well, I did warn you that long-term psychedelic use could have that effect."

LeRoy sat his glass down, very carefully. "Luckily I don't indulge in that habit anymore."

Jesse snorted, and carefully shifted his weight forward. "LeRoy, as I told you the time I caught you indulging in that habit, I don't particularly care what you put in your own body. I might be a federal cop now, but low-hanging fruit like non-violent drug users are not worth my time. If your drug use causes you to bring harm to another person or their property, or to steal to feed your habit, *then* you and I will have a problem."

"I would never harm anyone," LeRoy insisted vehemently as he dropped into the pipe chair. "And I certainly don't need to *steal.* As *I* told *you* before, most of the great artists throughout history have engaged in experimentation with altered states. Certain substances open the mind, blocking out all of the *noise* of society, allowing us to communicate freely with the universal flow of creativity." He crossed his legs, showing off socks the same hue as his glasses. "They put us in touch with our *muse.*"

"Is your muse a big fan of Milton Bradley?"

"Excuse me?"

Jesse waved a hand to signify it wasn't important. "LeRoy, I'm not here to bust your chops. I actually need a favor."

Sensing a shift in the power dynamic, the other man sat up like a meerkat sniffing the air for the scent of a tasty bug. "Oh?"

"I've been straight with you, haven't I?"

He sniffed again. "Disappointingly so at times."

Jesse grinned. "I'm flattered, LeRoy, but I'm afraid that's the way I'm wired. But back to my point. I haven't lied to you. I'm not here on some secret mission to entrap you or to blackmail you now that you've made the big time on the local art circuit. And I'll just say that I'm hurt that you even considered it."

LeRoy looked shocked. "I didn't –"

"Now, now. Let's not let a little paranoia stand between us. We have history, you and I, based on the fact that you were an easy target for bullies in high school, and I don't much like bullies."

"And I appreciate all that you've done for me in the past. But I don't –"

"What I need you to tell me," Jesse said, talking right over him "is what you know about a drug that appears to be real popular right now. It usually comes on tabs with friendly looking little brown bears on them."

LeRoy crossed his legs, looking guarded. "What about it?"

"The local narcs made a bust at a bar called The Shady Lady. The dealer went down but he refused to roll over on his supplier." Probably because he would have ended up bleeding out from several holes in his person if he had. "Since then, the owners of The Shady Lady have become considerably more cautious. Not that drug deals aren't still taking place on their property – the narcs are almost certain that they are – but the staff there seems to have developed radar where the cops are concerned. Either that or there's a mole in the department, somebody's palm being greased to look the other way. Regardless, the outcome is the same in that the trail to the supplier has dried up, so I have to approach this from another angle."

He gave LeRoy a meaningful look, causing the other man to go a little pale. "You're asking me to be an informant."

Pausing, Jesse studied LeRoy's face, now drained of color. "I'm not looking to make a bust," he admitted. "All I need is information."

"I can't help you."

"You know something."

"I know I can't help you. Can you imagine a man like me in a place like The Shady Lady? The very idea." He laughed, though the sound was tinged with a note of hysteria.

"This isn't a situation in which I'm asking you to wear a wire or testify in court. I'm not asking you to put yourself in a compromising position. Pretend we're talking hypothetically."

"Hypothetically speaking, if I wanted to purchase a psychedelic – and I'm not saying that I do – there are alternative, and more reputable, outlets than anyone associated with that establishment."

"Word on the street is that the other more 'reputable' outlets have been run out of town. The brown bear has the market cornered on LSD, 25i, all the related derivatives. If you want a psychedelic, you get it from the Russian."

"Really? Well that just proves how little I know regarding the subject. Now, if that's all, it's time for me to close up shop." The other man rose.

"Sit down, LeRoy."

"I'm not going to allow you to bully –"

"Sit. Down."

LeRoy considered refusing – Jesse could see it in his eyes – but apparently he recognized that Jesse wasn't playing. He lowered himself back into the chair, his wariness telegraphed by his stiff posture and rapid blinking.

"A cop is dead, LeRoy."

"I don't know anything about that. You can't think that I –"

Jesse held up a hand. "I'm not accusing you of killing anyone. But I am telling you that the death of a police officer who was working an investigation related to this particular drug is going to bring the full attention of local law enforcement down on anyone known to be associated."

"I don't have any sort of criminal record." LeRoy hesitated. "The only law enforcement officer who would associate me with drugs is *you.* And I've already told you that I don't do that anymore." He gestured around him, indicating the gallery. "I have too much at stake to risk indulging in illegal pastimes."

Jesse studied his… well, he couldn't exactly call LeRoy his friend. But he was someone for whom Jesse'd always had a soft spot, and he'd hate to see him hurt. "I strongly suspect you're lying to me, LeRoy."

"Barring evidence to bear out those suspicions, I'm afraid you'll have to take me at my word."

"If you are lying to me, the police are the least of your worries."

LeRoy's lips formed an astonished pout. "Are you threatening me?"

"No, I'm just telling you plain. The people who manufacture this drug are extremely dangerous. That's putting it lightly."

"Well then." LeRoy visibly swallowed. "How fortunate for me that I don't have any cause for interaction with them."

Recognizing the underlying apprehension – and the fact that he wasn't going to get any more out of LeRoy at the moment – Jesse reluctantly stood.

"If you change your mind," he told the other man "you have my number. Or you can find me at the marina. I'm staying on my boat temporarily."

"How positively rugged. I'm all aflutter."

Jesse smiled, but it faded quickly. "The bullies in the high school bathroom are nothing compared to this organization, LeRoy. And if you refuse to tell me anything, this time I won't be around to help you."

LeRoy's lips tightened. "Have a nice evening, Jesse."

Jesse walked out, more frustrated than ever. He felt sure that LeRoy not only still used drugs – and probably passed them out like candy at his numerous parties – but that he also had information. A name, a number. Something.

But something – or someone – had scared him enough that even his long-standing debt to Jesse couldn't sway him. Jesse could apply more pressure if it came to that. But he didn't want to go that route unless he had to. For one thing, LeRoy was right in that Jesse had no evidence. It had been years since he'd caught the man tripping on LSD. He also didn't want to ruin LeRoy's career, despite the fact that he didn't understand it. And – more importantly – he didn't want to endanger his life. At this point, he didn't have a whole lot of faith in the effectiveness of protective custody for informants in this case.

Jesse walked along River Street, the cold air whipping off the river sending his hands into his jacket pockets. Seagulls gave their harsh cry as they flew in circles overhead. Jesse could relate. He felt like he was circling, circling around this case, but still too far removed to detect exactly what was lurking beneath the surface.

Gannon's death disturbed him, in more ways than one. While there'd been no indication of foul play at the scene, for a man of Gannon's ego and disposition to kill himself when he'd exhibited no indication of depression or suicidal tendencies, it indicated that the alternative was something far more horrendous than death.

A threat to his son, his family?

The presence of the LSD tabs was another concern.

Gannon's medical records indicated he wasn't taking any prescription drugs, including antidepressants – some of which were known to cause suicidal thoughts. They'd have to wait for the results of the autopsy to see if he had anything stronger than cold medicine in his system. Psychedelics could cause vivid hallucinations, some of which might cause a person to do something extremely dangerous or commit self-harm, although usually it was more along the lines of leaping off a balcony because they suddenly thought they could fly than hanging themselves from the chandelier.

If Gannon had been using, it could possibly add another layer to why he'd gone after Jillian with such gusto. Not only was it payback for his friend Mike, but it might also direct attention away from any involvement he himself had.

However, Axelrod had vehemently denied that his partner had been involved in the drug scene. He claimed that Gannon had been acting funny over the past few days, saying that he might be on to something but that he wanted a little more time to mull it over before he shared it with his partner. Apparently that was a normal part of their working relationship. Gannon liked to think through things independently before putting their heads together.

That opened up other possibilities. Exactly what was it that Gannon thought he was on to? And the presence of the LSD tabs coupled with the string of Christmas lights harkened back to the scene of Losevsky's murder – the very theatrical scene. Complete with the sort of dark satire feel of the blood dripping on the Christmas tree topper.

The fact that the lights had almost certainly come from Jillian's basement caused Jesse's stomach to do a slow roll. It was possible that it was somehow an *up yours* to Jesse, if Gannon in fact committed suicide.

If he hadn't, the presence of the lights took on another meaning entirely. And forged another link to the scene of Losevsky's murder, considering they'd found Jillian's card.

The upside of that was that it made it more likely that Jillian was in fact their best lead. Somehow, somewhere, she likely had a connection to the Russian's organization.

The downside was that somehow, somewhere Jillian likely had a connection to the Russian's organization.

"Shit," Jesse muttered.

Jillian. There was something there, something that she either knew, or perhaps didn't know she knew. Either way, they were going to have to have a come to Jesus talk in the near future. He didn't particularly relish the idea, considering he probably wasn't on her favorite person list right now anyway. But there was no help for it.

Wanting out of his own head for a few moments, Jesse looked around for a distraction. The tourists weren't thick as clouds of gnats this time of year, but despite the bite in the air, River Street was still bustling. Only twelve shopping days left 'til Christmas, as he'd been advised by a sign in the window of one of the historic candy kitchens.

Jesse winced. He and his brothers had gone in together to send his parents away for a weekend in Napa Valley, so that item was ticked off his list, but he still had to pick up gifts for a few people in the office. They had a party coming up.

He stopped, eying the tower of boxed chocolates in the window display. The size and pattern on the bottom box looked like the one that had contained the dead squirrel, putting Jesse right back into the pattern of thought he'd tried to break out of.

The delivery of the dead squirrel in the fruit basket was another time that… let's just call it the holiday spirit had been subverted. Jesse frowned. Maybe there was something more to that than he'd previously considered.

Someone bumped into him from behind.

"Apologies," said a man when Jesse whipped around. He looked up from the phone he held in both hands. His eyes were moss green in a face dominated by high, Slavic cheekbones beneath shaggy light brown hair. He spoke in a voice deeply accented. "I was not paying attention."

"No problem."

The man stared at him, and then smiled a little, bobbing his head. "Have a pleasant day."

Jesse watched him walk away, the man's attention once again on his phone. As if sensing Jesse's gaze on him he glanced briefly over his shoulder, but turned quickly away.

Savannah was a popular tourist destination. The city drew visitors from all over the world. It was also an international seaport, bringing container ships and their foreign crews into their waters daily.

Hearing accents of all sorts wasn't uncommon.

But the hair on Jesse's neck stood up.

He started off after the man, but the door to the candy shop opened, disgorging a gaggle of holiday shoppers. They blocked his view, and by the time he'd maneuvered around them, the man was gone.

Disappeared into one of the shops or restaurants maybe, or up one of the cobblestone ramps that led to East Bay Street.

Jesse walked briskly that direction, glanced into windows and up stairwells. But whoever the man had been – tourist or something far less benign – he'd disappeared into one of River Street's many crevices.

Like a rat, Jesse couldn't help thinking.

Turning in a slow circle, Jesse looked around one last time. And though the wind blustering over the water continued to bite, he didn't put his hands back in his pockets.

He thought it best to retain easy access to his gun.

CHAPTER FIFTEEN

JILLIAN shoved the gnawing anxiety over the morning's events to the back of her mind, as she refused to let it taint the festive, joyous atmosphere of the wedding. No snow fell outside the windows, but white lights sparkled among boughs of evergreen, frosted pinecones and sprays of red roses, turning the interior of the Gingerbread House – a steamboat gothic mansion and famous historical landmark – into a winter wonderland.

Jillian moved among the bride and groom and their celebratory guests, shooting photo after photo, changing lenses, memory cards. She grabbed a handful of hors d'oeuvres and called it dinner. Remaining as unobtrusive as possible, she captured candid moments interspersed with a few more formally posed portraits. This couple was full of life and fun and the promise of family, and Jillian knew that the candids would be the shots which would most satisfy them as clients.

They cut the cake – designed to look like a collection of gaily wrapped presents – enjoyed their dances with their respective parents and for their first time as man and wife. By the time the reception wound down – Jillian got one last shot of the bride winking over the groom's shoulder as he carried her over the threshold – her feet throbbed and the back of her neck ached like a bad tooth. She was exhausted, physically and emotionally.

Standing off to the side, she rolled her head, closing her eyes as some of the tension eased out of her shoulders.

A deep voice spoke beside her. "You look like you could use this."

Jillian glanced at the waiter who held a tray containing a single glass of champagne. He smiled at her with sympathy.

"I've seen you running around here all evening," he said in an easy drawl "carrying that big camera. Since the bride and groom are gone, I figured it wouldn't hurt you to have a drink. Unless you don't drink. In which case we'll just pretend this never happened."

She smiled her gratitude. "I would love a glass. Thank you."

"No problem. I've worked enough of these things that I know how exhausting the behind-the-scenes stuff can be. A bit like being part of a stage crew for a theater production. All of the work, none of the glory."

"Well, weddings certainly do have many of the same elements of theater, but I'm fine without the glory, to be honest." She sipped her champagne. "It's their big day, after all."

"Mmm," he murmured noncommittally. "Well, it was nice chatting with you. I better get back to work. I hope you enjoy the rest of your evening."

"I plan to go home and fall into bed, so I'm pretty sure I'll enjoy it immensely." She lifted her glass. "Thank you."

"It was entirely my pleasure."

He tucked the tray under his arm, strolling back through the doorway. Jillian sipped the champagne while breaking down her equipment, stowing it in the various compartments of her camera bag. She'd just finished zipping everything up when the mother of the bride, beaming brighter than the blazing Christmas tree in the ballroom, came up to her, arms outstretched.

Jillian sat the half-empty champagne flute on the table beside her.

"Thank you," she said, grasping Jillian's hands, leaning in for an air kiss. "You were wonderful. It all felt so relaxed and happy. So right. I just can't wait to see the photos."

"I should have the proofs ready for your daughter to view after the holidays. And really, Mrs. Metcalfe, you shouldn't have." She indicated the tip envelope the other woman tucked into her hand. As she'd explained to the bride, she owned the photography studio, so tips weren't expected or necessary.

Appreciated, but not necessary.

"Nonsense," the woman said. "It's Christmas, isn't it? Or close enough, at any rate. Oh, there's Fiona and Jim getting ready to leave," she said, her attention drawn to the couple accepting their coats from the clerk. "I better catch them. Have a lovely holiday, dear."

Jillian smiled as the older woman toddled off, filled with the satisfaction of a party well-received and general good will toward men. She'd come with her daughter for their initial consultation, and Jillian was touched by her sheer delight in every detail of the wedding planning and the obvious bond the two of them shared.

Wistfulness hit her as it sometimes did, that she'd never know those moments with her own mother. Of course, she was lucky to have had her aunt as a wonderful stand-in, even when she hadn't been entirely thrilled with Jillian's decision to marry. In retrospect, her aunt had been right in her assessment. But now she was gone too, and Jillian felt…

Alone.

Aside from Katie, it seemed like all of the connections she established frayed almost as soon as they formed. Charlotte, Cooper… even her own blood relatives.

And now Jesse.

It was ridiculous, of course, since she'd known him such a short time – and hadn't really known him, come to that. She'd known only as much as he'd wanted to reveal. But something had been telling her more insistently each time she was around him that maybe, just maybe, this time it was for real.

Except that it wasn't. How could it be, when their relationship had been based on a blatant deception?

Disgusted with the self-pitying turn of her thoughts, Jillian tucked the envelope into her purse. Then she turned and ended up bumping into the man who came around the corner.

"Whoa. I'm sorry." Dark hair threaded with grey, bright blue eyes and a quick, easy smile. "Didn't see you there."

"It's no problem. Here, let me get that camera case out of your way."

"You're the photographer. Pretty wedding. I bet you got some great shots."

"With a couple as photogenic and, well, happy as Matt and Ashley, it would be difficult not to."

"Speaking of happy couples, my wife is going to kill me if she smells alcohol on my breath." He winced. "I'm the designated driver. One beer after one glass of champagne isn't going to impair me, but try telling her that. Anyway, I thought I saw some bowls of those little mints out here earlier..."

He started glancing around.

"Like this?" Jillian handed him the glass dish from the table.

"*Yes.* Thank you." He reached in, plucked one out. "You're a lifesaver. Want one?"

"Why not?" Jillian untwisted the wrapped mint, popped it into her mouth and then stuck the wrapper in her purse. She had to drive home herself, and though she didn't have to go far and was well within the legal limit after only half a glass, she didn't like to take chances when it came to getting pulled over. Especially not in this city. And especially not now.

"I'm taking these with me," he said in a confidential tone as he stuffed the few remaining mints in his pocket. "In case one doesn't do the trick."

"I saw nothing," she assured him.

"My kind of woman." He winked at her, flirtatious without being obnoxious about it. "You have a nice night."

"You, too. Good luck with your wife."

Jillian smiled a little as she hauled the case over her shoulder. The man's sunny demeanor seemed to have dispelled the worst of the emotional mists that were plaguing her. She got stopped twice more on her way to the back door

– the groom's mother, the wedding planner – delaying her departure. Luckily home was only a few blocks away. She was going to crawl into bed and then sleep until noon.

Hopefully, anyway.

Brian had reassured her today, but she couldn't help but worry. Bizarrely, Detective Gannon's death seemed to have something to do with both her basement and her Christmas decorations. Her thoughts flashed back to the morning when she'd discovered the tripped breaker, and wondered if there could be a connection.

The possibility of exactly *how* it connected was both perplexing and terrifying.

Had Gannon somehow bypassed their alarm and gone poking around in the basement? Why? And had he been the one behind poor little Killer's death?

Shoving aside the fear, anxiety and unanswered questions that once again wanted to intrude, Jillian exited the building. The night was bright and clear with a bite to the air that came as a welcome change from the close, stuffy atmosphere of the crowded reception.

She opened the hatch with the remote, stowed her equipment in the back.

She drove past Forsyth Park, the famous fountain currently festooned with garlands and bows. The street lamps reflected off the water, cast shadows on the Spanish moss hanging from the old oaks until it seemed to dance like a party of restless wraiths.

Despite her efforts to shove bad memories aside, the vision of Killer, his bushy tail shaking behind the mossy curtain, popped into her mind with such vividness that it almost seemed that he'd joined the party. Shaking his tail, shaking, shaking, while the wraiths writhed around him in grim celebration.

Disconcerted, Jillian blinked. It was only moss, swaying slightly in the chilled night air. A sight she'd seen hundreds of times.

So why did it seem... sinister?

Jillian swallowed, her mouth suddenly dry. Water. She should have had water instead of champagne on a nearly empty stomach. Coupled with fatigue of both the physical and emotional varieties, it was understandable that she felt a little off.

Nothing that a solid night's sleep wouldn't fix.

Jillian turned the corner onto her street, punched the button on the remote and watched as the electric garage door slid open. When Katie asked Jillian to move in with her after Jillian's marriage fell apart and Katie's grandparents died, leaving her the townhouse, they'd agreed to turn the detached garage into a studio for Jillian's photography business. It was more convenient – and certainly more economical – than renting a space downtown.

Jillian sat where she was for another moment, staring at the interior of her studio, now brightly lit by the overhead light. A brief flare of panic seemed to squeeze off her breath.

There was nothing to be afraid of, she told herself firmly. No cops waited to arrest her – or worse. No dead animals on her doorstep.

She'd gotten through far, far worse, so she would get through this, too.

With her heart racing and her mouth dry, Jillian scanned the access alley behind the townhouse. Was that someone, crouched behind that wall at the end?

No. No. It was just a trash can. Mrs. Franklin's trash can. Tomorrow was trash day.

She opened her door, but then quickly closed it. Her hand shook.

What the hell was wrong with her?

"Not going to let them get away with this," she murmured to herself as she pictured Mike's eyes through the hole in his mask, laughing, laughing. The laugh morphed into a sneer, and the face became Gannon's. Her current paranoia was their victory.

And she refused to let them have it. The fact that one was in prison and one was dead didn't matter at the moment. What concerned her were the emotional scars they'd left her with.

Opening her door again, Jillian climbed from the car, angry that her pulse continued to leap, her hands to shake. Furious with herself for this seeming backslide toward the terrified young woman she'd once been, she stalked around to the back of the car, began hauling her equipment into the studio. Despite the rage which seemed to bubble under her skin, she still handled everything with care. This wasn't just her career, it was her life blood. The camera was as much an extension of her as a paintbrush was to an artist.

When she had it all stowed away, the memory cards locked in the little fireproof safe in which she kept them – they were irreplaceable, after all – she punched the code into the pad to shut the garage door behind her.

Righteous with the sort of pure, unadulterated indignation that comes from having been woefully wronged one too many times, Jillian marched toward the back porch, slammed through the door into the kitchen.

The alarm, which they'd started using religiously, began its high-pitched shriek, scraping along the raw edge of her nerves. Jillian punched in the code, reset it, and then stabbed her still-shaking hand through her hair.

The light over the gleaming Wolf range brightened the otherwise dark kitchen, reminding Jillian that Katie was working the closing shift and wouldn't be home until much later. The kitchen closed, but the bar area stayed open until two a.m. on weekends.

Probably better, all in all, because Jillian hated for Katie to see her like this.

Jillian hated *being* like this.

She was tired, she thought as she slung her purse over the back of a barstool. So tired of it all. Hadn't she suffered enough? Couldn't fate or the Universe or whatever higher power cut her the tiniest break?

Feeling as weepy as she'd just been pissed, Jillian crossed the kitchen. Pulled a bottle of water from the fridge. Unscrewing the lid, she headed toward the doorway. The click of her low heels echoed like gunshots against the tile, the light in the hallway seemed a glaring beacon.

She stopped. Everything was too loud, too bright. Too… much.

Her own heartbeat sounded thunderous to her ears, the blood pumping through her veins nearly audible in a sort of rushing, gurgling pulse. The pits of her arms began to sweat even as her mouth dried up.

She took a sip of the water.

Was she having a panic attack? She'd had a few… before. The first when she'd woken up in the hospital after the assault, hooked up to tubes and probes and machines. The doctor had been forced to sedate her. She knew the physiological symptoms, the racing heart, the trembling, the shortness of breath. Tingling in hands and fingers. The sense of impending doom.

And while psychically she was experiencing some of those things, she didn't feel panicked. She'd felt angry, and then sad. And now she was terribly confused.

A panic… reaction, maybe. But not a full-fledged attack. And the emotions she'd been suppressing for a while were simply hitting her all at once.

A little steadier now that she'd thought it through, Jillian continued down the hall toward the stairs. The wallpaper – a flocked velvet featuring birds and trees in a shade of rose that Jillian still wasn't sure how Katie's grandmother had ever talked her grandfather into – seemed even more showy than normal. Garish, even. The color was so bright that she could swear that she heard the birds themselves shrieking in protest.

Jillian stopped again, held her hands –including the water bottle – over her ears, and tried to block out the noise.

Something not quite right, she realized. Something in fact very… wrong. You couldn't *hear* colors. Inanimate birds did not make sounds.

When her hip struck something solid, she realized that she must have staggered forward without knowing. Eyes popping open, she stared at the little table by the front door. At the unclaimed mail she'd left there yesterday for Katie.

Her thoughts veered of their own accord toward Jesse, toward the day he'd kissed her brainless right here against this wall.

You might not be able to hear colors, but she could swear she heard her own brain cells exploding – *pop, pop, pop* – every time she looked at his eyes. They were like blue pools of damnation. Leading her to hell, but right at the moment she didn't care.

Jillian shook her head. Where the hell had *that* come from? Blue Pools of Damnation sounded like a really terrible garage band.

And she *did* care. Logically, she understood his position, but emotionally was another matter. If she were being completely honest with herself, the fact that he hadn't shown up today while the police were here serving the warrant that *he* clearly arranged for felt like yet another slap in the face. She wanted to hate him for it. She really did. But she mostly just felt miserable.

Jillian turned toward the stairs a mite too quickly, because she lost her balance and dropped her water bottle in the process of steadying herself. "Well, crap." She looked down at it, spreading over the hardwood. "That's a mess."

She needed to clean it up. A mop. There was a mop in the utility closet.

She started to turn away to find the closet, the mop, but found her gaze drawn to the nesting dolls instead. They were all there. One, two, three, four, five, six, seven. Seven painted wooden figurines. Red, such a bright, vivid red except…

One of the dolls was blue.

"No," Jillian said, closing her eyes. Jesse's eyes were blue. The dolls were red.

She opened her eyes again.

The little doll was still blue.

"It can't be." She picked it up, looked at it closely. Dropped it to the floor with a choked scream.

It lay in the puddle of water, melting… melting. Oh God, everything was melting.

Jillian whirled around, slipping in the water and landing on her butt. She squeezed her eyes closed, trying to fight the sensation that she was melting as well, when the sound of the squeaking stair tread made her look up.

A man stood on the stairs, his face lost in the shadows. "Davis?" He descended another step, and Jillian's heart squeezed into her throat. "Alexei?"

But it couldn't be.

Gasping, Jillian scrambled to her feet, pressed her back against the door. "You're dead," she said to the apparition. "Dead."

When he – it – moved closer, Jillian fumbled for the doorknob. The alarm started wailing behind her as she opened the front door and fled, but it wasn't until she saw the headlights coming at her that she realized she'd run into the street.

CHAPTER SIXTEEN

LIKE the waters of the Red Sea, people moved out of Jesse's way as he strode through the halls of the police station, known to locals as The Barracks. It was good that no one stopped or questioned him as he might have had to kill them, and he didn't want anything to dull the razor sharp edge of his anger.

He located the interrogation area, took a deep breath before knocking on the door to the observation room. It wouldn't do to go in like a Tyrannosaurus Rex, creating carnage from everything that moved. He had to be a smarter hunter.

Detective Portman opened the door.

"Agent Wellington," she said, stepping back so that he could enter. "I…" Her voice trailed off when she saw his expression, and then she cleared her throat before shutting the door. "I see you've been apprised of the new development."

He counted to three before he could trust himself to answer. Five. Okay, let's try ten. "Apprised. Yes, I've been apprised." He glanced pointedly at his watch. "Hours after the fact."

"There were circumstances –"

"Circumstances," he cut her off "which precluded informing the lead investigator in the case that there'd been a development of some magnitude. Please. Do tell."

Her lips thinned, the café au lait tone of her skin taking on a few drops more cream. "Perhaps I should let you speak with Detective Goode."

She stepped back, and Jesse got his first look at the observation window – which he purposefully avoided – and the four men standing in front of it. One of them was Goode, the other detective assigned to Gannon's case. One of them was a narc whom he vaguely recognized. The third man was Detective Axelrod.

And the other was his brother, Jordan.

"What the hell is an ADA doing here at this point?" he demanded.

The men broke off their discussion and turned toward him. Jordan's dimples flashed in the first moment of recognition but then disappeared when he got a good look at Jesse's face.

"My brother's involved in this case?" he asked Goode.

"Tangentially," was the detective's answer.

"Tangentially?" Jesse demanded, looking all around him. "Unless someone with higher rank is around to indicate otherwise, I'm the *lead* in this case."

"No, you're the lead in the Losevsky murder. Gannon is one of *ours.*"

Jesse stared for a moment, and then scrubbed a hand over his face. "Gannon was also one of *mine.* Or have you forgotten the joint task force?" He glanced at Axelrod, who took a sudden interest in his shoes. "Or how about the fact that I gave you the grounds you needed for the warrant for

Ms. Montgomery's house? And yet you don't think I need to be informed that she's been arrested?"

"For public intoxication, not in connection with Losevsky's murder. Hence the presence of our narcotics officer," Goode nodded to the other man. "He got first crack at questioning her due to the nature of the charge, and we had to wait for the drug she took to wear off some."

"And where was she while this drug was wearing off?"

"We had her contained."

Jesse nodded, as if rage weren't percolating in his blood. "Contained. And I assume she received proper medical attention and treatment considering she was *hit by a goddamn car?*"

The room was quiet in the aftermath of his outburst, until Detective Portman cleared her throat. "You can see for yourself that she's fine."

Jesse didn't dare. He didn't dare look through the window yet.

"Look," Goode added in a conciliatory tone. "We would have called you when it seemed relevant to bring you in."

"When it seemed relevant." Jesse could feel his hands bunching into fists, so he purposefully flexed them. "I had to hear about this from Agent Parker, who heard about it from his sister, who heard about it from the neighbors when she arrived home in the early hours of the morning. I contacted my boss who – guess what? – hadn't heard anything either. He's conferring with *your* boss about that particular oversight right now. You're fortunate that my boss forbade Agent Parker from coming down here, as the ass chewing you'll be receiving from your lieutenant is nothing compared to what he would be dishing out."

He turned his attention to Detective Axelrod. "We've worked together for weeks now. But it didn't cross your mind that, hey, maybe Agent Wellington has a vested interest in this latest development?"

Axelrod looked up. "It's your vested interest that worries me."

"Excuse me?"

"You and Parker. You've been easy on the Montgomery woman from the get-go. Treating her like she's made of fucking glass." His bottom lip quivered before he firmed it and viciously said: "And now Nick is *dead.*"

"And you think Ms. Montgomery had something to do with that."

"I think that bitch was high as a kite last night, and you yourself saw her at The Shady Lady – which, interestingly enough, is the location Losevsky had written on her card. It's obvious she's into the drug scene, which means she knows something and lied about it to protect her sweet little ass. Just like Nick said. And Nick found something, something that would bust her, and now he's dead. Hung from his own chandelier with her Christmas lights, and some of those drugs stuffed in his pocket to make him look dirty. If you weren't too busy coddling her, you'd realize that him wearing your shirt amounted to whoever it is that she's been protecting having some fun at your expense. Flipping the bird at your investigation. *She killed him,* sure as if she'd done it with her own hands." The detective took a menacing step forward. "And I'm going to see that she pays."

"George," Detective Goode said with unflappable clam. "Tone it down or I'm going to have to ask you to leave."

"Tone it down?" Axelrod said. "It's not your partner lying on a slab." He glared at Jesse. "Although it *could* be, if this asshole continues to play patty-cake with suspects instead of doing his damn job."

"Your anger is understandable," Jesse said in a tone that belied his incandescent fury. "Considering your recent loss. But you're making some vast assumptions based on your personal feelings rather than any actual evidence to indicate Detective Gannon did not voluntarily hang himself. And if the autopsy *does* reveal foul play and you have screwed up this case's chances in court with your ham-fisted handling of a possible witness's rights, I will see to it that your *damn job* will entail a rent-a-cop uniform and the local mall."

"Um, if you'll excuse us for a moment," Jordan broke in, smiling charmingly as he pushed past the others. "I'd like to have a conversation with my brother. Outside. *Outside,"* he repeated in a pointed tone when he drew closer to Jesse. He emphasized it by grabbing Jesse's arm, all but dragging him into the hallway. Then he kept going, into the stairwell, where they were less likely to be overheard.

He turned, hands on hips, and stared at Jesse with eyes the exact same color as Jesse's own. "Now," Jordan said. "What the hell is going on?"

"That's what I'd like to know."

"Okay. Let me synopsize what I know. Ms. Montgomery was arrested last night after entering the roadway where she was struck by a passing car. She sustained only minor injuries, including scraped palms from falling to the pavement, as the car had been traveling at a slow rate of speed while looking for a parking spot. According to witnesses on the scene, she raved about melting dolls and ghosts on the stairway, indicating hallucinations of some sort. She reacted very… strongly when approached by the officers who responded to the scene. She's facing charges of assaulting an officer and resisting arrest as well as the public intoxication and entering the roadway while intoxicated. Also, jaywalking."

Jesse stared at him. "Jaywalking."

"That's what's on the report. My office, of course, is willing to plead her down should she be willing to roll over on her dealer. I think they're hoping to tack on accessory to murder as well, though at this point there's not enough evidence to sustain such a charge, although her fingerprints on the hanger found at the detective's residence does raise questions."

Jesse rubbed his forehead. "The lights came from her house. Of course her fingerprints were on them. But I've already established reasonable suspicion that Gannon may have entered the basement where the lights were stored. It's not a stretch to suggest he removed the lights himself. Do you know if her prints were found anywhere else in his apartment? And it's ridiculous that I have to ask you because I haven't been informed of that much."

"No prints anywhere else," Jordan said. "I can't believe I missed your name on that warrant."

"You didn't. I called Portman. Goode is right in that Gannon's death is their case, but wrong in trying to act like it's not connected to our original investigation. That was Axelrod's doing, I'm sure of it," Jesse muttered. "Asshole."

He pivoted and kicked the wall.

Jordan's dark brows scrunched together. "What else am I missing?"

"Other than the fact that a stupid turf war might tank the entire case?"

"What was he talking about? When he said that you and Parker have been treating this woman like glass?"

Jesse considered kicking the wall again. Or maybe ripping the stairwell door from its hinges. But he wouldn't lie to his brother. "Ms. Montgomery lives with Parker's sister. They've been friends for years."

"Oh. Well, that sucks. I guess he wasn't aware that she had a drug problem?"

"She doesn't have a drug problem. She has a cop problem."

Jordan simply stared at him and Jesse sighed. "She has a history with the Savannah PD." He gave his younger brother a rundown of Jillian's situation, of the complexities of the case.

"Wow. Okay. So I can see the defense coming back with a charge of malicious prosecution, given the prior history. Although Ms. Montgomery did enter the street and disrupt traffic. She did resist arrest. She did strike an officer. And she did – according to witness statements – appear to be intoxicated. The simple urinalysis was negative for all but a small amount of alcohol, but they're waiting on the results of the more exhaustive RIA tests, which should detect the presence of other drugs."

"It was LSD." He'd bet money on it.

"I thought you said she didn't have a drug problem."

"She said she doesn't."

Jordan snorted. "And people don't lie?"

Jesse ran a hand across the back of his neck to relieve some of the tension. "Brian has never seen her high or stoned. Neither has Katie. There were no drugs or paraphernalia found in the house or studio."

"So she decided to experiment. Detective Goode said she'd been at a party."

"She'd been at a *wedding,* where she was working as the photographer. And how stupid would she have to be to experiment with narcotics when she knew she was already under suspicion for having possible connections to a criminal organization known for peddling that particular drug? When police had been at her house that very morning, serving a warrant? Trust me, this is *not* a stupid woman."

"You seem a little defensive. Whoa," Jordan said when Jesse whipped around. He held up his hands, palms out.

"Don't kill me for making an observation. An *accurate* observation, if I might add."

Jesse paused, took stock of his behavior. Yeah, he was acting defensive. Probably because he knew that Jillian had been in police custody the entire freaking night, and he suspected, quite strongly, that they hadn't been particularly courteous hosts. The thought of her, already frightened and – for reasons that he couldn't yet explain – tripping on a hallucinogen, locked up, helpless, at the mercy of people who had reason to dislike her...

He punched the wall this time.

Jordan watched him shake out his hand, and then met his eyes with a level look. "She means something to you, doesn't she?"

Jesse froze. Admitting it out loud to an assistant district attorney was a good way to get his ass booted from the case. But this was his brother.

He dipped his chin in a quick nod.

Jordan scrubbed a hand through his wavy dark hair. "Shit. That's why you avoided the window. You didn't want your face to give you away."

"Something like that."

"Well, if you'd looked, you'd at least have seen that she's in good hands."

Jesse raised his head, and Jordan smiled his sympathy.

"She retained Ainsley as her lawyer."

JILLIAN tried to stop herself from rocking in her chair, but the action seemed reflexive. Her body's rote attempt at self-comfort that even her will couldn't override. Or maybe it was a lingering side-effect of... whatever it was that had caused her to hallucinate last night.

Something she'd eaten? Perhaps the hors d'oeuvres had been bad?

Either way, the end result was that the chair in which she sat in the interrogation room squeaked every time she swayed back and forth. The sound was like nails on a chalkboard, but at least it wasn't amplified. Her senses seemed to have mostly returned to normal. While that was an improvement, the dissociative nature of her mental state last night had at least allowed her to believe that the events were a hyper-realistic dream.

Sadly, she now knew better.

Her eyes burned from lack of sleep, and from the tears she hadn't been able to stop herself from shedding. Her nose felt stuffy and her head hurt, and the palms of her hands stung something fierce beneath the gauze the EMTs had wrapped them in. Her left knee was several shades of black and blue, as it, even more than her palms, had taken the brunt of her fall. It had swollen to twice its normal size, too, making walking on it difficult.

She had a red, tender spot on her side from being hit with a taser.

The other injuries were more painful, but this is the one that disturbed her the most. She didn't really remember hitting the cop in the nose with the palm of her hand, but apparently she had. She guessed her old self-defense training had come back to her when one of them grabbed her.

Her heart skipped a beat thinking of them with their hands on her, holding her down, and one of them shooting her with his taser to incapacitate her further. Granted, the situations were nothing alike – this time, the police had been doing their jobs. She could also acknowledge that she'd been hysterical – for multiple reasons, only one of which was having just been struck by a car.

Emotional and physical traumas coupled with the hallucinations were already enough to bring her to the brink. When the cops began manhandling her, trying to control her, PTSD had taken over and pushed her off the ledge.

"Would you like me to ask someone to bring you a blanket?"

Startled by the question, Jillian glanced over at her attorney. Ainsley Tidwell. A raven-haired, dark-eyed beauty who radiated control, she watched Jillian with patent concern. It was only then that Jillian realized her teeth were chattering, too.

"It's n-nerves," she admitted in a low tone, not wanting the cops to overhear.

"I made them turn the microphone off," Ainsley told her. "We can speak freely."

Jillian's disbelief emerged as a snort. "You'll have to forgive me if I d-don't trust them."

Ainsley smiled her cool smile. "I'd be disappointed in you if you did."

Jillian had never been so relieved to see another person as when Ainsley had shown up early this morning, looking like an avenging dark angel in a pinstriped suit. She hadn't been with it enough in the overnight hours to insist upon calling her attorney, but Ainsley informed her that Katie contacted her.

Thank God for Katie. Jillian was going to have to buy her a small island or something in order to express adequate thanks.

She'd initially been undecided about retaining this attorney, especially after finding out that she worked with –

basically for – Jesse's brother, but beggars couldn't be choosers. However, after watching Ainsley remain calm and unflappable in the face of the cajoling, threats and various histrionics from the detectives, Jillian didn't really care who she worked for. She was just glad to have the woman on her side.

Disgusted by the chattering of her teeth, Jillian clenched her jaw shut. "What happens now?"

"My guess is that they'll be back in here to question you again before allowing you to return to your cell. Same story as last time: you don't answer anything I tell you not to. Afterward, I'll start the process of getting you out of here."

"Quickly," Jillian said in a tone bordering on desperation. Then she glanced down at the jumpsuit she wore. "Orange is not my color."

Ainsley smiled, and then grew serious. "I'll do my best. They're working pretty hard to connect you to Detective Gannon's death, and some of the circumstantial evidence is working against us. I don't need to tell you how seriously law enforcement officers take the demise of one of their own. Particularly under questionable circumstances."

"No. You don't." Jillian's teeth began to chatter again. "I wonder what's taking them so long?"

"It's part of their technique," Ainsley said. "They wear you down, physically and mentally, hoping you'll eventually break and tell them what they want to hear."

"They can wait until hell freezes over," Jillian said. "I don't have a dealer. I can't explain what happened last night, but it did *not* involve me taking drugs."

The door opened and Jillian looked up, expecting to see one of the detectives who'd questioned her earlier.

Jesse walked through the door.

Blood rushed to Jillian's head and then seemed to drain away just as quickly, leaving her dizzy. It took several moments for her to realize that her attorney was speaking.

"... This is a surprise."

Jesse looked grimmer than she'd ever seen him. "Ms. Tidwell. I need a word with your client."

"I gathered as much." She raised an arm, gesturing languidly toward the chair on the opposite side of the table.

His lips thinned. "Alone."

She laughed, a musical sound of incredulity. "You're joking."

When he simply continued to stand there, jaw clenched, Ainsley glanced between them. She arched a brow. "You two know each other?"

"We met through Katie's brother," Jillian explained after a moment. Jesse still hadn't looked her in the eye. "I mentioned he was an FBI agent investigating that man's murder. The one at the laundromat. That's how this whole thing started."

"Yes, okay," Ainsley said. "I suppose I should have seen this coming." She turned to smile sweetly at Jesse. "A prior personal acquaintance doesn't supersede my duty to protect my client's interests. If you have any questions, you can ask them in my presence. Especially as I assume this is being recorded?"

His jaw clenched even harder before he finally nodded. "Yes."

Jesse lowered himself into the chair. Jillian noticed that he moved stiffly, his posture one of someone who was holding onto his control with both hands.

He finally looked at Jillian. "Are you okay?"

Jesse's voice was so low, so gruff as to be almost unrecognizable. Despite the fact that she still felt betrayed by his actions, she thought the concern in his expression was genuine.

But that wasn't enough to eradicate the bitterness that colored her tone. "Just dandy."

She thought his teeth would turn to powder if he ground them any harder. "What happened last night?"

"You mean you haven't read the police report in all its gory detail? Public intoxication, resisting arrest, assaulting an officer. It's a veritable bonanza of charges."

"Jillian," Ainsley cautioned, recognizing the reckless tone even as Jesse said: "I know what you've been charged with. I want to know what *happened.*"

They stared at each other across the table for several painful, heavy heartbeats, the air between them seeming to develop a tactile quality. Finally, she glanced at Ainsley, who was watching them both with patent interest.

"Tell him exactly what you told me," Ainsley suggested.

Jillian sighed, but then turned her attention back to Jesse. "From what point?"

An additional question hung unspoken in the air between them. *Should I mention our little tete-a-tete yesterday morning?*

It was partly a threat on her part, because she recalled that he'd said his boss would hand him his ass if he knew he'd been by to talk to her like he had – not in what one could call a professional manner.

But Jesse *had* left her house and then gone out to arrange for a warrant based on something he'd seen while he was there. So maybe he'd already come clean with his boss about being there, even if he hadn't divulged the personal aspect of their conversation. Or maybe he'd already laid bare every sordid detail.

Although if he had, Jillian didn't think he would be here, questioning her. That created a conflict of interest, didn't it? Much like Brian's? Brian had told them yesterday morning that if any further evidence turned up, his boss would almost certainly pull him from the case as he couldn't be expected to be impartial. Jillian gathered that at this point, Brian had been pulled.

As much as she was indeed hurt and upset by Jesse's actions, she still felt that having him on her side was better than getting petty revenge for what she saw as him using her.

If he was, in fact, on her side.

Jillian studied his face, tried to set her resentment aside. He appeared to be truly concerned about her situation, but could she trust him?

Jesse met her gaze straight on. "From whatever point you think is relevant," he told her.

He was giving her permission to reveal what he'd done, she realized. What he'd confessed to her that morning, about crossing the line. To lay it all out here, in the police station, with who knew how many cops as witnesses. Not to mention her lawyer. It might even help her legal case. It would almost certainly hurt Jesse.

Jillian opened her mouth. Closed it. And remembered the look on his face when he'd told her he would have done anything to keep her from walking out of the Y without him.

Finally, she cleared her throat. "After the cops and Brian left the house, I got ready for the wedding." She glanced up, saw something flicker in his eyes. Maybe gratitude.

Maybe something... deeper.

Shoving that aside for now, Jillian walked him through the events of the evening, up through leaving the reception. "I started feeling... odd on the way home."

"Odd in what way?"

"Hot. Shaky. Thirsty. And paranoid, I guess is the best way to describe it. A little like I was having a panic attack."

"Have you experienced panic attacks before?"

She nodded. "After Mike's attack. It got pretty bad. That's one reason I left Savannah, went back home after the trial. I thought getting away would help."

"Did it?"

"Not as much as I would have liked. I started seeing a psychologist."

"Did you take any type of prescribed medication to alleviate the attacks?"

"This information will be in your medical records," Ainsley said, possibly reminding her that whatever she said could – and would be verified.

"I realize that. No," she answered Jesse. "I was offered Xanax as well as a prescription sleep aid, but I didn't want to rely on chemicals. I took the PM version of over the counter pain relievers if it got too bad – the same one I took the night the house may have been broken into – but mostly I found other ways to deal with it."

"Like what?"

"Like running. Hiking on the trails near my home. That's how I found my way back to photography – I saw too many beautiful things in the mountains not to want to capture them on film."

"And you didn't use anything else, any other substance? Marijuana? It's known to have a calming effect."

"Not if you're terrified of having an altercation with the police, it's not."

For the first time since he'd entered the room, he smiled a little. "Touché. No medical history of epilepsy, schizophrenia, severe fever?"

She blinked. "No."

"There are a number of health conditions that can cause hallucinations, erratic behavior such as you allegedly displayed last night," Ainsley explained to Jillian, all the while eyeing Jesse. "I believe that's why he's asking."

Jesse nodded. "Your original urinalysis came back negative except for small traces of alcohol, well below the legal limit," he said. "We won't know until we have the results of the other tests back if there was anything else in your system. I'm eliminating other possibilities."

"Oh." She digested that. "You're not assuming I was simply high or stoned or whatever the appropriate term is here?"

"Ass. U. Me. Assumption generally doesn't work out well for either party." He paused. *"Did* you voluntarily ingest any illegal drug or mind-altering substance last night?"

"While photographing the wedding event of the season? Do I look like I'm insane? No," she said, stating it loudly and clearly. "I did *not* voluntarily ingest any illegal or mind-altering substances last night. However," she said and had both Ainsley and Jesse straightening. "I did eat some mushroom caps. Hors d'oeuvres," she explained. "I don't know much about it, but can't some varieties of mushrooms cause hallucinations?"

"They can," Jesse agreed. "Although I doubt they would be serving them at the wedding event of the season." He smiled, just a little. "However, we'll check with the venue, see if any other guests experienced similar symptoms. Tell me again about the champagne."

"What about it?"

"The timing, the circumstances."

"Ah, I drank it maybe fifteen minutes before I left. I was packing up and one of the servers stopped by, said he'd noticed how busy I'd been and that I must be thirsty or something like that."

"What did he look like?"

"Why?"

"Just humor me."

"Blond," she finally said. "Attractive. Late thirties, maybe. I didn't get his name."

"Did he take the glass away when you were finished?"

"I don't think so. No," she said after considering. "The bride's mother came up and thanked me and I sat the glass aside."

"Where?"

"On the little table near the coat room. Yes, because that's when the other man came up and asked if I'd seen the mints because he'd been drinking and didn't want his wife to know."

"Description?"

"Of the man or of the mints?"

"Both," he said, surprising her.

"Ah, maybe late forties, early fifties for the man. Short dark hair, graying at the temples. Very blue eyes. A dimple," she said pointing to her chin "right here. As to the mints, they were basically your typical peppermints, but they were wrapped in red plastic."

"You said he offered you one. Did you throw the wrapper away?"

"I... don't know." She rubbed her forehead. "Maybe I stuck it in my purse? I honestly can't remember."

"Did you have anything else to eat or drink in the half hour or so before you left the wedding?"

"No," she shook her head. "No. I'm sure of it. Why?"

"I think I can answer that question," Ainsley said, studying Jesse with interest before switching her gaze to Jillian. "It sounds to me like Agent Wellington is considering the possibility that you were drugged."

CHAPTER SEVENTEEN

JESSE strode out the front door of the police station, welcoming the cold air that slapped his face with all the enthusiasm of a jilted mistress. Given the fact that his blood was all but boiling beneath his skin, he considered it a shame that he lived in a climate that didn't lend itself to snow and sub-arctic temperatures.

He headed toward his Jeep.

"Jesse! Jesse, wait up."

He recognized the voice behind him. Of course he did, considering he'd dated its owner steadily for the better part of a year. Which meant that he knew that walking faster, pretending he hadn't heard her or any other avoidance technique would get him absolutely nowhere.

When Ainsley wanted to say something, she was relentless in her pursuit of the opportunity to say it. She would hunt Jesse down and make him listen until his ears bled if she had to. God knew she'd done it before.

He halted, and simply waited for her to catch up.

The wind had flushed her cheeks with a rosy hue that only accentuated her dark loveliness. She looked cool, capable and a little intimidating – and he knew it to be truth in advertising. As far as defense attorneys went, Jillian couldn't have done much better, with the exception of Jack himself.

However, Jesse couldn't help but wish she'd retained someone else. Not because he and Ainsley had parted on bad terms – they hadn't. They remained friendly still.

But Ainsley knew him pretty damn well, and was far too perceptive for her own good.

"Hey," she said, a trifle breathless against the bite of the wind. She wrapped her scarf around her neck. "How can you not be cold without a coat? Never mind." She shook back her dark hair. "You're like a human inferno, especially when you're pissed. And I have to say I haven't seen you this pissed off since..." she frowned. "Actually, I don't think I've ever seen you this pissed. Dissension in the ranks?"

He just stared at her.

"Yes, yes. I know you're not going to give me, the other team, any potential ammunition." She tilted her head. "Except that I get the feeling that this time, oddly enough, you and I might not be on opposite sides."

He started walking. "If you have something to say, say it. I have things I have to do."

"Yes, like try to prove my client may have been drugged involuntarily. I appreciate that, by the way."

"I'm not doing it for you."

"No, you're doing it for her."

Jesse stopped. Glared down at her. "I'm doing it because it's my *job* to investigate what happened. Not to form a hypothesis based on a personal agenda, but to, you know, look for actual physical evidence based in *fact.*"

"Something I've always admired about you," Ainsley said as she hustled to catch up after he started walking again. "Your integrity. And if your integrity happens to turn up evidence that my client may have been drugged without her knowledge or consent –"

"Assuming she's telling the truth about what happened."

"Alright, assuming she is telling the truth, and you find evidence which supports her claim, I trust that you will let me know and/or try to convince the cops to drop the charges. Because clearly, if her intoxication wasn't her choice, she can't be held liable for any actions resulting from said intoxication."

"Watch your step," Jesse said, pointing out a tree root which had lifted a piece of the sidewalk.

"See? You're a gentleman. As well as a man of ethics. Which is why I trust you will take not only my client's cooperation but also her victim status into consideration."

"Is there some reason you're buttering me up?"

"I'm only looking out for the best interests of Ms. Montgomery."

"By treating me like a fresh dinner roll."

Ainsley smiled. "It must be very, very difficult for you."

"Being mistaken for a carbohydrate?"

"Being attracted to a woman who is a principal figure in an investigation."

He stopped so suddenly that she bumped into him. "You know," he said slowly. "I'm getting pretty damn tired of people suggesting that I have so little control over my dick that it interferes with me doing my damn job."

Ainsley pursed her lips. "I didn't say anything about your dick. And, speaking from personal experience only, I don't recall you having any control issues with that particular appendage."

"I'm not going to talk to you about my dick. I'm not going to talk to you about Jillian. And I'm for damn sure not going to talk to you about an ongoing investigation."

"Jesse, wait. Will you just *wait,* damn you?" she said as she grabbed his arm to bring him around. She studied his face, her dark eyes growing serious. "This is more than just a simple attraction, isn't it? No, don't answer. I know you can't." She blew out a breath that sent one long strand of dark hair flying upward.

And then she squeezed his arm. "I'm sorry. I chased after you mostly because I wanted to give you a hard time, because I could tell that you were pissed off at the situation. And that was at least in part, I surmised, from the tension I sensed between the two of you. But don't worry," she told him. "I doubt it would have been obvious to anyone else who was observing. The tension, I mean. Your anger was pretty damn visible. It's only that I know you so well, particularly when it comes to gaging when you're sexually attracted to someone. But I didn't realize... wow," she said. "You've really fallen for her, haven't you?"

"I have to get to work."

"Right." She dropped his arm. Smiled again, like the shark he knew her to be. And then her expression softened. "I hope you will take this in the spirit it's intended when I say good luck."

Jesse sighed. Ainsley might be a shark, but every food chain needed its apex predators – and this time he couldn't fault her choice of client.

"At least she's in good hands."

"Why, Jesse Wellington. I do believe that was a compliment. Maybe I should buy a lottery ticket, since it seems to be my lucky day."

"Bite me."

"Been there, done that, but under the circumstances, wearing the T-shirt seems a bit tacky." She smiled again. "I'll talk to you later, Jesse." And then she turned and walked away.

Jesse watched after her a moment before walking the short distance to his Jeep. Jesus. Talk about being the eye at the center of a storm. His brother was the ADA. His ex-girlfriend was the defense counsel. And his…

What? he considered as he pulled into traffic, heading toward East Henry. What exactly was Jillian to him? Nothing, really. An acquaintance. An acquaintance with whom he'd shared some conversation. And an earth-shattering kiss.

And that was bullshit. He'd been more honest with her yesterday morning than he was being with himself right now. She might not technically be anything to him, but he was flat out lying if he didn't admit that she had the potential to mean… a lot. A whole hell of a lot.

Everything.

His hands tightened on the wheel while he waited at a red light, and the reality of that set in. He must have sensed it the first time he laid eyes on her. That damn click. And then he'd been stupid enough to spend more time with her than was wise, given the situation. Stupid enough to put his hands on her. To taste her.

And now he knew that one taste was never going to be enough.

If he couldn't find any evidence that she'd been drugged, she faced some serious charges. Charges that could possibly see her doing a little time. The thought of it made him sick. Seeing her in that orange jumpsuit – looking pale and exhausted and frightened – was an image that unfortunately would remain burned into his brain.

The purely analytical part of that brain wondered why he was so convinced she hadn't taken any drug voluntarily. Was he, in fact, allowing his dick – or his emotions – to cloud his judgment?

Maybe, he admitted. Maybe a little. Which meant that he was going to have to keep his distance from her until this case was resolved, one way or the other.

But setting his personal feelings aside and looking at it logically, it didn't make sense for Jillian to have done what she was accused of doing. Especially with no prior history of use. No evidence of drugs or paraphernalia in her possession. Goode had tried to make an issue of the envelope of cash found in her purse, but Jesse confirmed it with the mother of the bride that she'd given it to Jillian as a tip. He'd hated doing it, as there were potential professional ramifications involved in questioning her clients, but it was better than allowing the cash to be used against her as more evidence that she was involved with illegal narcotics. That she carried around envelopes of cash with which to make her buys.

When he reached East Henry he parked around behind Jillian's townhouse, knocked on the back door, where Brian let him in.

The other man looked haggard.

"How is she?"

"Well, she looks better than you," Jesse answered as he walked past him, into the kitchen. The spotless, almost militantly organized space he recalled from before was a total mess. "Holy shit."

Brian's lips thinned. "I sent Katie over to Davis's house so she could get some sleep before trying to put this place back together. I've been working on the other rooms, but she doesn't want me to touch the kitchen or Jillian's studio."

Jesse glanced up sharply. "They trashed her studio, too?"

"Nothing's broken that I can see, but Jillian is going to have to look it over. It was tossed pretty good."

Jesse shook his head in disgust. "This wasn't necessary."

"No, it wasn't. This was some assholes with attitude taking advantage of the opportunity to exact a little revenge on the woman who'd done one of their own wrong. Or two of their own, if you believe Jillian had anything to do with Gannon. Which some of them do. And I wasn't around to discourage them from going well beyond the parameters of looking for drugs into malicious destruction, so they had some fun. Luckily they didn't break anything – at least not that I've noticed so far. The door was open, so they didn't have to bust it down. And since they didn't have a warrant covering the electronics, they left the computers alone. I was afraid they would have taken them. I guess they knew that if they went too far, they'd have not only me to deal with but a lawsuit on their hands."

Jesse ran his hand through his hair. "So much for professionalism."

"There are some excellent cops in the SCMPD, but unfortunately Jillian has gotten on the wrong side of a number of those who aren't so excellent. I'm relieved to hear that she's okay. I was worried as hell about her."

So was Jesse. He still was. "She looks a little worse for wear, but if she'd been seriously mistreated, Ainsley would have been raising hell."

"Ainsley?" Brian raised his brows. "As in your ex?"

"Jillian retained her. She consulted with her the other day, and Katie called her early this morning."

Brian huffed out a laugh. "Well, that had to have been interesting. I'm sorry I missed it. So what is it we're looking for?"

"In the absence of evidence to the contrary – which we won't have until we get back the results of the RIA tests – I'm operating as if Jillian did in fact have some sort of hallucinogen in her system. The descriptions from the paramedics, the cops on the scene and the doctor who checked her over were all consistent with someone who was either tripping or experiencing a psychotic episode of some sort. I called the manager of the venue for the wedding and checked with the local emergency rooms, and no one else reported any similar symptoms, which rules out the bad mushrooms Jillian floated as a possibility."

"Bad mushrooms?'

"The appetizer she ate. She suggested perhaps they were of the magic variety."

"That's one way to make a wedding more interesting. But since that wasn't the case, I guess you have an idea for how else she could have ingested a psychedelic without knowing."

"She said a waiter offered her a glass of champagne, and she consumed half of it before leaving. That much checked out with the urinalysis. She apparently also ate a wrapped mint, offered to her by a male guest. I sent Bristol over to the Gingerbread House with Detective Goode to get a name for the waiter and see if there's a chance the glass was still sitting where she'd left it and hadn't been run through the dishwasher yet. I'm not holding my breath, though."

"Goode? What happened to Axelrod?"

"Let's just say that his lieutenant thought it might be a good idea for him to take some time off to pull himself together. So I've got Goode and Portman for now. Speaking of which," Jesse said when the front doorbell rang "that's probably Portman right now. Mateyo suggested that we mix up the teams to help promote better inter-agency relations. Yeah," Jesse said when he read Brian's expression of disgust. "That was pretty much my reaction as well."

"I guess we can't just pretend she's a Jehovah's Witness and wait for her to give up and leave."

"Better not."

With a sigh, Brian headed toward the front door, with Jesse at his heels. It wasn't that Brian – or Jesse – had anything against the detective personally. It was just that they had... divided loyalties, you could say, when it came to this case. Although Jesse was trying his hardest to keep his loyalty to his oath and to the truth uppermost in his mind.

Brian opened the door, greeted Detective Portman. She stepped into the foyer, and then raised her brows when she saw the state of the parlor.

"Your pals had some fun looking for drugs here last night."

With tremendous dignity, Portman straightened her spine. "Just because we work for the same police department doesn't make them my pals, Agent Parker. And it certainly doesn't mean I approve of them trashing your sister's house in the process."

Brian rolled his shoulders. "Sorry. I guess I'm just a little frustrated."

"I don't blame you. I heard about Ms. Montgomery's previous... altercations with certain members of the force. I can't speak for the actions of others, but I am sorry that there still seem to be some who are more interested in petty revenge than in the fact that the woman in question was the victim of a heinous act perpetrated by those who should have had more honor."

He stared at her, and then nodded. "I appreciate that."

"Do you know what happened to Jillian's purse," Jesse asked, deciding that it was time to change the subject. "She said she slung it over a barstool last night."

"Ah, I don't recall seeing it. But then Katie may have moved it somewhere else after the cops searched it. Maybe Jillian's room."

"Lead the way."

They followed Brian up the stairs, and Jesse gave the wallpaper a glance. "Even without the aid of a hallucinogen, this stuff is pretty loud."

"My grandmother," Brian said, shaking his head "had questionable taste. I was glad they left me the beach place, which they didn't put a lot of money into decorating, meaning it escaped most of her whims. I never could have lived with this shit," he nodded at the walls "but Katie's more tolerant."

There were three bedrooms on the second floor, a generous master suite complete with fireplace and sitting room, and two other bedrooms that shared a bath. Katie used the smallest bedroom for her office, leaving Jillian the larger bedroom at the back.

Jesse had been in dozens of homes over the course of his career, either investigating or making arrests, but he'd never had the itch between his shoulder blades that he experienced now.

He felt… weird. Guilty. Sort of like a peeping tom.

Which was ridiculous, because not only was he doing his job, he was doing this at least partly in order to help Jillian. If his theory was correct, and she *had* been drugged, finding evidence of it would go a long way toward getting her out from under suspicion. A suspicion that on the basis of the evidence at hand seemed warranted. But sometimes even when puzzle pieces appeared to fit together, the picture they formed just wasn't quite right.

And the picture of Jillian as a drug abuser involved – at least peripherally – with a Russian organized crime ring wasn't one that struck him as true.

And he assured himself that that was logic speaking, and not any part of his anatomy.

Jesse stopped at the door to the room, glanced around. It was... tasteful, he guessed would be the best way to describe it. Neutral walls which showed off some of her photographs, simply and beautifully framed. Soft bedding with splashes of color in the pillows.

All of which were currently thrown on the floor, along with most of the contents of her drawers and closet.

The sight of a lacy bra artfully arranged on top of the otherwise barren dresser made his jaw clench. He would bet money that someone put it there intentionally, so that Jillian would be well aware that some of the cops she'd long feared and avoided had had their hands on her most intimate articles of clothing. So that she'd feel violated once again.

Portman made a noise behind him, and Jesse turned to see that she'd noticed it, too.

"Again, it wasn't my doing, but I feel the need to apologize on behalf of the department. I can promise you, most of us wouldn't do this sort of thing."

"There are a few people who've been waiting for the opportunity to take Jillian down a peg or two," Brian said, his face suffused with color. Then he glanced at Portman. "Gannon was one of them."

She frowned. "You think that the fact that he hung himself – or was hung – using her Christmas lights has something to do with what happened with Mike McGrath?"

"I don't know," Brian said. "But that, the dead squirrel in the basket – somebody sure does want Jillian to pay for something. Or they want her under suspicion."

She murmured something noncommittal, and Jesse unclenched his jaw. "Ms. Montgomery said she carried a small black handbag last night, with a silver chain strap. Let's see if we can find that in this mess, hopefully with the mint wrapper intact."

"You really think she was drugged by someone at the reception?" Portman said. "That she was set up?"

"I don't know. But I do know that something about this whole thing stinks."

They each took a different area of the room, started picking clothes and bedding and books and whatnot off the floor, laying it on the bed or draping it on the big stuffed chair in the corner. Jesse took the bra off the dresser, refusing to think of it on Jillian's body. He wasn't going to contribute to any further violation of her privacy. Not wanting her to realize that the cops had pawed through her undergarments with the intention of upsetting her, he placed any item of lingerie he came across in one of the dresser drawers.

He lifted a T-shirt, found a box which held loose photos, a number of which were scattered on the floor.

There was a picture of Katie in her chef's get-up standing outside her restaurant on what must have been opening day. Another of Katie, Brian, Jillian and a couple people he didn't recognize forming a human pyramid on the beach. One of an older woman, her head covered in a scarf, smiling proudly beside Jillian in her high school cap and gown.

"Her aunt," Brian said from over Jesse's shoulder. "That was her first bout with cancer. She lost the second one a few years ago."

"Rough," Jesse said.

"Yeah, she was the only real family Jillian had, other than a couple of cousins who she doesn't see much of."

Jesse glanced at the photos again. It looked to him like Katie and Brian had become her family.

"Ah, that's her mom and dad," Brian continued, gesturing to a photo of a couple holding a small girl between them, which from the cloud of reddish-gold hair could only be Jillian. Under it was another photo of an incredibly lovely woman in a... whatever you called those fancy dance costumes. A tutu, he thought. She held her leg at an impossible angle behind her while standing on the toes of the opposite foot. White feathers decorated the red-gold hair she wore pulled into a tight bun.

"Her mother, I presume."

"Yeah. I guess she told you she was a professional ballet dancer back in Russia."

She had, and Jesse knew it from reading her file anyway. Jesse studied the young woman – probably no more than twenty – who bore a striking resemblance to her daughter. There was another photo, an infant wrapped up in a blanket, and Jesse wondered if it was Jillian. He flipped it over, saw that the writing on the back was in Russian. But someone had translated it underneath.

Alexei. My heart. Underneath was a date. Jesse frowned, and then did some mental math. This photo was taken about six years before Jillian was born.

"Found it," Detective Portman called out from the opposite side of the room.

Jesse turned to see her lifting it in the air. He sat the box of photographs back down.

"You have some gloves on you?"

"I do." Brian pulled some out of his pocket, passed them over.

Jesse pulled on the gloves, took the purse from Detective Portman.

"You said you're looking for a candy wrapper?" Brian said.

"Mint," Jesse clarified. "Jillian said she ate one right before she left, maybe stuck the wrapper in her purse. They were in a dish and one of the wedding guests came looking for them, offered her one and then dumped the rest of them in his pocket. Said he didn't want his wife to know he'd been drinking."

"Plausible."

"Yeah. And it might be less plausible that someone laced a bunch of mints with a hallucinogen and convinced her to eat one, but unless the champagne glass pans out, I don't know how else she could have ingested it."

"If she didn't do it voluntarily," Portman pointed out.

"If," Jesse agreed. "But if you look at the time she left the reception – and we have verification for that – and the time the driver who hit her placed the call to nine-one-one, there's only about a thirty minute difference. Most hallucinogens take that long to kick in."

"So maybe she took it when she got into the car."

"Because after a long, stressful, tiring day, she decided to experiment with drugs that generally tend to keep you awake for at least seven or eight hours?"

Portman shrugged. "Maybe she thought it would relieve stress. Who knows? People do stupid, nonsensical stuff all the time."

That, they did. But Jesse still didn't buy it. Not this time.

He dumped the contents of the purse onto the bed. It was a small handbag, thankfully, the dressy kind that women sometimes carried to fancy events, and not the bottomless pit variety that he was always halfway convinced contained a small department store or perhaps an entire civilization of which scientists were previously unaware.

Wallet – containing credit cards, driver's license, a few dollars, but no wrapper. Lipstick. Pens. A few stray coins and a receipt for gas. A small package of tissues. The cops had taken her cell phone and the envelope of cash as possible evidence.

If they didn't give her cell phone back when they released her, Jesse would remind Brian to make sure she had a backup phone to use until hers was returned. Given the situation, she couldn't be without the security a cell phone could provide.

"Check the little inside pocket," Brian said from over Jesse's shoulder.

Jesse did. It contained a tampon.

And now he felt even more like a creep.

"Maybe it fell out," Brian said. "When the other cops went through it. Or maybe her car."

"I can go look in the car," Detective Portman offered.

Brian fished a ring of keys from his pocket. "Here you go. It's the silver SUV out back."

"Thanks. I'll be back."

Portman left and Jesse began stuffing things back in the purse.

"It was kind of a longshot anyway", Brian murmured. "But thanks for trying."

Jesse glanced up. "I'm not looking for evidence as a favor to you."

"I didn't think you were."

Frowning, Jesse continued returning things to the purse. "I have to remain impartial. If the evidence goes the other way and it points to her being a user, then she'll have to face the music. I hope you understand that."

"Are you trying to convince me or yourself?"

Jesse stopped, glared at Brian, and then shook his head. "I'm just saying.'" When he went to put the package of tissues back into the purse, he noticed that part of the cellophane was red instead of clear. He pulled the package out, looked closer.

And then pulled the small, red wrapper from where it had become lodged inside.

"Bingo."

He pulled a small evidence bag from his pocket, dropped the wrapper inside. And stared at it, knowing that he was basically full of shit. He was pretty much desperate for his theory to be correct. For Jillian not to be a user. It wasn't an ethical position for him to take, as an investigator.

But as a man, he didn't much care.

The realization scared him.

"I love Jillian like a sister," Brian said, drawing Jesse's attention. "But Katie *is* my sister. And if Jillian is doing drugs and she got them from Losevsky, well, that sucks, but it's not the end of the world. You know? Given that this would be a first offense she'd probably get off fairly lightly. But if it's deeper than that, if McGrath – despite him saying he has no knowledge of any of this – is behind some sort of revenge plot, that puts Jillian, and by extension Katie, in more danger. And if, God forbid, this isn't some kind of payback and Jillian is somehow…" he circled a finger around "connected to Losevsky's organization, that's just almost too damn scary to contemplate."

"So you'd rather Jillian just be on drugs."

"Yeah," Brian admitted. "God help me, I would."

"That still doesn't explain the squirrel."

"A warning not to admit where she bought the drugs."

"Which brings us right back to her being under the scrutiny of Losevsky's organization."

"You're right. Shit. Maybe it would be better if this is McGrath getting his rocks off. And Gannon, I don't know. Maybe he knew we were going to connect him after you found that toothpick outside."

"Maybe," Jesse said. But he had the feeling that all of the scenarios they'd kicked around were entirely too simple. That there was something else they were missing.

He glanced over at the box of photos. "Do you know if Jillian has any relatives still in Russia? Cousins or anything?"

"If she does, she's never talked about them. I was under the impression that her mom sort of cut all ties when she ran off with her dad."

Jesse considered that for a moment, and then decided it probably wasn't important. "I'll drop this by the lab, ask them to put a rush on it. I guess we should tell Portman that she can stop searching the car."

They headed back down the stairs and Jesse glanced over at the spot where he'd pinned Jillian against the wall and distracted, bumped into the table, spilling the fruit basket and several of the wooden dolls onto the floor.

The same table she claimed to have bumped into last night while hallucinating.

Jesse frowned.

"What?" Brian said when he realized that Jesse had stopped.

"Weren't there seven of these doll things?"

"I don't know," Brian admitted. "I picked up the ones I could find and put them back on the table."

"There were seven," Jesse said. "So either one is still missing, or one of the cops took one."

"Does it matter?"

"Maybe not," Jesse admitted. But something, some feeling he couldn't exactly identify, made him want to locate the other doll.

The doorway to the parlor stood on the other side of the table, and Jesse glanced around that corner, scanned the floor. He remembered Jillian saying that she'd dropped it. In the throes of her hallucination, she'd imagined that it had turned a different color, and when she picked it up, the doll's face melted. Or appeared to melt. So she'd dropped it on the floor.

Jesse bent down, saw a small roundish shape on the far side beneath the chair. He reached under, drew it out.

The face was, of course, intact. That little Mona Lisa smile.

A *blue* Mona Lisa smile.

Jesse glanced at the other dolls on the table. The very red dolls.

"Son of a bitch."

His furious tone brought Brian closer, and Jesse glanced over his shoulder. "She wasn't hallucinating everything. The bastard's been in the house."

CHAPTER EIGHTEEN

JILLIAN'S hand trembled when she lifted it to press the doorbell. It was an unfortunate outward manifestation of the fact that internally, she was a mess.

Being the target of apparent psychological warfare tended to have that effect.

But she couldn't – wouldn't – go into hiding. She wouldn't allow herself to be driven from her house. She wouldn't let Mike or… anyone else turn her back into the woman who'd run away, run home, who'd married the wrong man because he was familiar and safe and she was desperate for the safe and the familiar.

Jillian refused to be that person. This was the second time in her life that someone had brought a fight to her, and she wouldn't leave the ring again.

When no one came to the door, Jillian considered that perhaps Mr. Pratt was napping. Or maybe he wasn't home. Although she'd seen a nurse go inside a short while ago, so she assumed that he was here. Perhaps he was with the nurse, who'd come to assist him in caring for his brother. The elder Mr. Pratt had been bedridden following his stroke, incapable of speech or caring for his personal needs. The younger Mr. Pratt might be a pain in the butt, but she couldn't fault him in the way he took care of his brother. He could have stuck him in a care facility, but wanted to adhere to his wishes to finish out his life in his own home. Nurses came by regularly.

Jillian was just about to give up when she heard the thump of a cane hitting the wood floor on the other side of the door. She pasted a smile on her face.

The door creaked open, and Mr. Pratt peered at her through thick glasses, his thinning white hair sticking up in tufts. He looked not unlike Ebenezer Scrooge having been disturbed from a long winter's nap.

He frowned when he recognized her.

"Mr. Pratt. I hope I'm not bothering you."

"Bah," was his response, only furthering the resemblance. Then he glanced down at the festive tin she held in her hands.

"I made *pryaniki*. Cookies," she explained, when he glanced up sharply. "My mother's recipe. I make them every year at Christmas. Your brother expressed a particular fondness for them last year, so I wanted to be sure to bring some by for both of you."

"Surprised you've had time to bake cookies, what with all of the commotion at your place over the past couple weeks."

Jillian could almost feel herself shrinking, like a turtle pulling back into its shell. She cleared her throat. "Yes, I'm sorry about all of that. I hope it hasn't disturbed you or your brother too much."

"Cops all over the place, flashing lights and sirens. You putting up a fuss in the middle of the street. What do you think?"

She thought that he was a crotchety old jerk, but she couldn't deny that he had a point. "Again, I apologize for the disturbance."

He peered over her shoulder. "You got some kind of van parked outside today."

"We're getting a new security system." Because someone had gotten into the house. Twice.

That they knew of.

He frowned and then stood aside. "You might as well come in."

Jillian's heart sank a little. She'd hoped to make the handoff at the door. "Thank you."

He grunted.

He smelled a little odd, she noted as she walked past. Like... talcum powder, maybe? Her aunt had been a nurse, and frequently smelled similar, as at that time it was used to make latex gloves easier to don. Elderly people, she knew, often used talc or cornstarch as a grooming item.

The smell brought a wave of familiarity that was both comforting and depressing.

He led her into the parlor. The townhouse was set up in a very similar manner to Katie's, though being an end unit it featured more windows on the wall across from the fireplace.

Despite that – and the low fire burning in the grate – it seemed dimmer, more oppressive.

Possibly because there were no holiday decorations, no season's greetings from friends and family displayed on the mantel. Quite a bit different from last year, when she'd delivered the cookies to Mr. Pratt's brother. The older man had had a small tabletop tree and an old-fashioned radio tuned to a jazz station playing Christmas carols. Jillian was charmed.

She was suddenly very glad that she'd brought the cookies. Scrooge the younger Mr. Pratt might be, but it still saddened her to think of anyone spending this time of year in such a bleak fashion.

He gestured her toward a seat. "Would you care for a drink? Some hot tea, perhaps? It's a bit chilly for these old bones today."

"I'm afraid I can't stay that long. But I do thank you for the offer." She slowly lowered herself onto the sofa.

"Is something wrong with your leg?" he asked, frowning.

"Ah, it's still a little stiff," she admitted. "From... my collision with the car."

He nodded, and then dropped into the wingchair beside the fireplace with considerably more agility than she'd displayed. Resting his cane against the arm, he glanced at the tin as he balanced it on his lap. "They're not laced with anything, are they?"

Jillian blinked. "Pardon me?"

"A joke," he said, surprising her again.

Jillian smiled, uncomfortably. She wondered if that was somehow a reference to her arrest? She knew the neighbors had to have discussed the circumstances as they'd interpreted them – which probably amounted to her being a junkie, and likely crazy to boot.

Or maybe just an acknowledgement of the fact that they hadn't always seen eye to eye.

"Not unless you consider sugar a drug or a poison."

He watched her for a moment, and then pried the lid from the tin. "Your mother's recipe, you said?"

"Yes. She was from Russia. This is an old family recipe. A traditional spice cookie. They're very good with tea."

He leaned over, drew the scent into his nostrils with a single, prolonged inhale. "They smell wonderful."

"Thank you."

He re-secured the lid. "It's important, don't you think, for family traditions to be passed down? Mother to daughter. Father to son."

"I guess that would depend upon the tradition," she said. "But in this case, I'm glad that I have this particular legacy by which to remember her."

"Honoring the dead is important." He paused. "Especially those who are taken from us far before their time."

She tilted her head. "You know about my parents?"

He shrugged. "Mrs. Franklin likes to hear herself talk."

That she did. Jillian had forgotten that she'd mentioned the way her parents were killed. It was last summer, when a young woman had drowned in the waters off Tybee. Mrs. Franklin had pontificated for days on the dangers of swimming in the ocean, and why she never got near a body of water any deeper than her bathtub.

Of course, statistically you were much likelier to be killed in your bathtub than you were in the ocean, but Jillian hadn't brought that up.

"Do you fear the water?" Mr. Pratt asked, seeming to read her mind.

She glanced at him, startled. "No. That surprises some people, but I was only five when it happened. I seem to have blocked it out, or maybe just didn't fully understand what was happening at the time."

He seemed to consider that as he stared at the fire. "Perhaps that is the benefit of experiencing a tragedy at such a young age. We are not aware of the extent of our loss. When we are older," he looked back at her. "It is very difficult to let go."

The moment stretched out, with only the soft crackle of the fire and the ticking of the mantle clock to break the silence.

"I'm so sorry about your brother," she said, thinking that might be what he was talking about. "Is his health continuing to decline?"

"It certainly does not improve."

Jillian didn't bother to ask to see him. Mr. Pratt had already told her months ago that he didn't like outside germs to be brought into his brother's environment. The nurses he put up with because there was no other choice.

"Well, if you will convey my holiday wishes to him, I would appreciate it."

"I'll let him know that you stopped by." He sat the cookies aside so that he could rise. "Thank you for the gift," he told her. "You are a lovely girl."

Surprised by the compliment, Jillian swallowed. "Thank you."

"I'll see you to the door."

When they reached the entry, Jillian noticed some dusty footprints on his wood floor. "Oh. I'm sorry. I'm afraid I must have tracked that in. The new alarm system," she explained. "They had to cut through the plaster in a few places. There's quite a bit of dust around."

He stared down at it. "It's of no concern."

She smiled, a slightly more genuine expression than when she'd arrived. "I hope you have a wonderful holiday."

He raised his head, and his bright blue eyes held some dark emotion – sadness or bitterness, she couldn't tell. But it was gone as quickly as it had appeared. "You do the same."

Jillian heard the door close behind her as she limped down the steps. Her knee bothered her, but she'd refused to take any sort of pain medication. Not after her experience the other night. She didn't want chemicals of any sort altering her system. She'd just have to tough it out.

She was halfway down when she noticed that Brian was standing on the sidewalk just down the street talking to someone.

Jesse.

Her heart did an uncomfortable lurch.

With the radar he seemed to have where she was concerned, he looked past Brian's shoulder, spotted her on the stairs. His mouth set into a grim line.

Well, she wasn't exactly thrilled to see him either. She'd been released on bond yesterday, but hadn't laid eyes on him since he'd questioned her in the interrogation room. The lingering humiliation of that caused her cheeks to flush. Sure, he'd seemed to believe her story – had in fact gone out of his way to look for evidence that she hadn't voluntarily ingested some illegal substance that night – and, according to Brian, was the one who'd discovered that the house had been broken into, the smallest *matryoshka* switched with a blue one. At least she hadn't hallucinated that.

But she had hallucinated other things. Things that were more disturbing.

She started down the steps again, hoping to make it back up hers and inside before Jesse could speak to her. If he spoke to her. Two different agents – or one agent and one detective, anyway – had questioned her about the nesting dolls and whether she knew anyone that would want to mess with them – and her. The detective – his name was Goode – hadn't liked it when she'd mentioned Mike or one of his cronies, but she didn't much care if she offended him. At the moment, she was pretty damn offended that someone had killed her squirrel and apparently drugged her. The results of the more extensive blood tests had revealed LSD. Not good for her legal case, but at least Jillian knew that she didn't have a brain tumor or some other condition that caused her to hallucinate.

That was something.

By the time she hit the bottom step, a strong hand grasped her under the elbow.

She looked up into Jesse's eyes. Those damned, devastating eyes. "I'm fine."

"You're limping."

"I've been limping for three days. I've managed so far."

"Don't be stupid," he said in a low tone.

Jillian's back went straight as a telephone pole. "I would extend the same advice, although in your case it doesn't seem to be a behavioral choice."

He narrowed his eyes, but then tilted his head toward Mr. Pratt's house. "You really want to do this in front of an audience? He's watching out the window."

Of course he was. Mrs. Franklin probably was, too. "Fine," she said and accepted his support going down the steps and then back up. When they reached her front door, he let go.

Jillian drew in a deep breath, but not from exertion. She'd been essentially holding hers so that she didn't have to smell him, all soapy clean and male.

"I was afraid you were going to pass out," he murmured, and she jerked her head up to meet his gaze. A smile lurked around the corners of his mouth, but quickly faded. "Are you okay?"

It was the same question he'd asked her in the interrogation room, in almost the same tone. And while she was tempted to give him the same smart aleck reply, she found that she lacked the energy to hold onto her anger.

"Mostly," she said, opting for honesty instead of a platitude. "It's hard to sleep. Not that being awake is much easier, but…"

She could tell that he understood what she meant. Problems always seemed to double in size when you lay awake in bed at night.

"Brian said you won't take anything. Not even the prescribed medication."

She shook her head. "I want to feel like I'm in control of at least one thing right now."

He glanced away, and then back. "I'm sorry."

She thought that he was talking about more than her difficulty sleeping. About the fact that he'd lied about his occupation, and then added insult to injury by formally questioning her.

About the whole damn situation.

"Me, too." Not that she thought she was at fault here, but she was still sorry. Sorry that they hadn't met under better circumstances, perhaps.

Brian cleared his throat, and Jillian realized that he'd joined them on the porch. "You should go inside," he said.

Jesse nodded, and then looked back down at Jillian. "There are some things we need to discuss."

Jillian considered leading him into the parlor, as it conveyed a sort of formality that was probably appropriate under the circumstances – and helped keep the professional distance that he was so determined to maintain. Not that she could blame him.

However, the den was more comfortable, and quite frankly she was more concerned with her own comfort than his professional distance at the moment. Spending several nights in a jail cell would do that, she guessed.

She waved her hand around, indicating that he could sit wherever he liked, and then lowered herself onto the deep leather sofa. She lifted her leg, stretching it out beside her.

When she glanced up, Jesse was watching her with a frown. "What did the doctor say about your knee?"

"That it will probably be stiff and sore for a while. He was right."

"Do you have a brace?"

"Why do you think I'm wearing these sexy loose pajama pants?"

"It might be a good idea to try heat to relieve the stiffness."

"Is that medical advice or a pick up line? Sorry," she said when he gave her a look. "Jail altered me. I'm no longer able to control my inner smartass."

He stared at her for several more moments before glancing around in a clear bid to change the subject. "Looks like you got the place straightened back up."

She lost a bit of her sass. "Brian and Katie and Davis had everything back in place by the time I got… out. I wouldn't have known they'd trashed the place if things in my studio hadn't been arranged in a way that let me know someone else had handled them. Plus, the bastards broke open my safe to search it for drugs. Thank God they didn't destroy or take the memory sticks from the wedding. I would have been ruined professionally." She glanced up. "By the way, I had an email from the mother of the bride."

"I had no choice but to ask her to confirm that she'd given you the cash as a tip."

Jillian sighed. "I know. And luckily she's a lovely woman who's not prone to leaping to conclusions, so unless I fail to deliver her daughter's photos, I doubt she'll post horrible reviews about me on Yelp." She glanced at Jesse. "I want you to know that I appreciate your tact. And the fact that you also didn't leap to conclusions."

"Like I said, that's something I try to avoid until I have evidence that bears out my conclusion. In this case, the evidence bears out the fact that LSD was present in the mint you consumed. There were traces on the wrapper."

Jillian sat up. "So that's proof that I was drugged."

"Not precisely," Jesse said. "It's proof that there was LSD in a mint which you, by your own admission, consumed voluntarily."

"But I didn't know –"

Jesse held up a hand to forestall her outraged protest. "I know. That's your story. And luckily for you, we were able to talk to the waiter who offered you the champagne. When he said he had his eye on you that night, he apparently meant it. He saw the man who came over to talk to you, saw most of that exchange."

Jillian digested that. "So the nice man with the wife whom he didn't want to know he'd been drinking… drugged me? Why? How? That bowl of mints was sitting on the table. Anyone could have picked one up and eaten it."

"According to the staff at the Gingerbread House, those mints were not part of the wedding package. They didn't place them there."

"So he drugged the mints, placed the bowl there and then offered me one in the hope that I would eat one? What if I'd refused?"

Jesse shrugged. "Maybe he waits for another opportunity."

"So you think this was target specific? That he wanted to drug me in particular? For what reason? Is he a sex offender or… who is he? How awful for Matt and Ashley, that one of their guests would do something so terrible. Did you arrest him?"

Jesse was quiet for several moments. "Are you finished yet?"

"Finished with what?"

"Asking questions that paint a nice, neat scenario in which the fact that you were likely drugged bears no relevance to the rest of this case."

Jillian opened her mouth to protest again, and then realized that was exactly what she was doing. She slumped back against the sofa.

"Was he even a wedding guest?"

"Not that anyone recalls inviting, based on his description. Seems he slipped in, did his thing, slipped out, with no one the wiser."

"Surely you can identify him somehow, though. Security cameras? Or fingerprints on the wrapper?"

"The only fingerprints on the wrapper were yours. And we're working on it."

Jillian glanced at the cold hearth, and suddenly longed for a fire. She pulled the throw on the back of the sofa over her shoulders. "I don't understand," she finally said. "A friend of Mike's…"

Her voice trailed off and she looked up at Jesse. He leaned forward in his chair. "Jillian. I've spoken with Mike McGrath. I really don't think he's behind this."

"You mean you went to…"

"The state penitentiary. Yeah. And while there's certainly no love lost on his part for you, I don't think he has the resources, the clout or even the brains to plot something this elaborate. Getting one of his buddies to pull you over, drop a dime bag in your car? Maybe. Getting someone to bust out the windows on your car? Maybe that, too."

"You think that was part of… whatever this is?"

"Possibly. The timing is certainly interesting. But my point is that this type of psychological warfare – the missing

T-shirt, the squirrel in the basket, the drugged mint, messing around with your dolls so that you *know* someone was in this house – that takes planning and knowledge and a flair for the theatrical. And possibly a deep-seated grudge."

She swallowed. "Against me."

"Well, you do seem to be the epi-center."

"I don't understand."

"Neither do I. Not yet. But I will. And Jillian." He waited for her to meet his gaze. "I am going to ask you questions. Maybe tough questions. And I want honest answers. Is that understood?"

"You think I've been lying?"

"Not really. But I also don't know that you've been as forthcoming as you could be."

Jillian threw up her hands. "I don't know what you want from me. I told you, and those detectives, and Agent Bristol, and Brian, everything that I know. Which, when it comes to drugs or men being murdered or why Detective Gannon had my Christmas lights at his house *isn't very much.* I don't know anything else, okay? I don't have any answers. And I think that if you're going to question me, I should call my lawyer."

"We can do that," Jesse agreed. "We can set this up formally, either at the Barracks or my office. If that's what you want."

Jillian's shoulders slumped. The last thing she wanted was to go through that again. But she didn't think it was smart to say anything else without talking to Ainsley.

She looked at Jesse. His expression was calm, stoic. But his eyes...

They reflected all of the turbulence that Jillian felt herself.

"I want to trust you."

A muscle ticked in his jaw. "I want you to trust me, too. I want you to trust that I will do my damnedest to find out why this is happening and who's behind it. To get justice for those who've been harmed. But if there's something you want to tell me that you're afraid I will use against you... call Ms. Tidwell. I don't want to do anything to hurt you, Jillian. I'm going to be straight and admit that the thought causes me a lot of anguish. But I will also do my job. To the best of my abilities."

Jillian believed him. And, if she were being completely honest with herself, admitted that she respected him even more for that integrity. If he'd told her that he would be willing to look the other way, just for her, it would have tarnished something. She'd had too many dealings with people in positions of trust who abused those positions.

It made her fall for Jesse a little bit more.

"What did you want to ask me?"

He looked at her, something warm and possibly triumphant in his eyes. And then he surprised her.

"Who's Alexei?"

CHAPTER NINETEEN

ALEXEI Markov, Jesse thought as he read through the file on his laptop, was a man whose life had gone from shit to golden and back to shit again. Raised in an orphanage until age five – when he'd reportedly begun to show an almost uncanny aptitude for the dance arts – he'd then been sent to live and train in what Jesse thought of as ballet boot camp. He'd risen through the ranks, earned a spot as a principal dancer in a major ballet company, toured Europe, receiving accolades wherever he went.

And then apparently he'd lost his head.

Burnout. Jesse had seen it happen to another superior athlete he'd known, a college friend whose parents had signed him up for swim lessons before he could walk, chauffeured him to five a.m. practices and meets that consumed his weekends, pushing him to be faster and stronger and better, all with an eye toward Olympic gold. Colleges scouted him, scholarships poured in, but his first season on the university swim team was dismal. He missed practice. He showed up hungover to meets. He basically no longer cared. His whole young life had been focused on a singular goal, without any real consideration as to whose goal it happened to be. He'd been pushed and prodded because he'd shown an aptitude. But aptitude didn't always equal passion. And passion was perhaps the more important ingredient in long-term success.

Alexei Markov, it seemed, suffered the same plight as the guy Jesse'd known in college. He'd grown sick of feeling like his life was not his own. He missed performances. Copped an attitude. Acquired tattoos that appalled his employers and had to be covered with heavy stage makeup. Had brushes with the law for drinking and fighting, and – being considered something of a heartthrob – left a trail of broken female hearts behind.

Hence the title of the Associated Press article included in the file: *The Bad Boy of Ballet.*

It was one of the few articles in English, and mostly glamorized his rise and fall. Other press clippings had been translated from Russian, and by the photos and gossip indicated that the bad boy of ballet had fallen in with even worse company, becoming bosom buddies with a man named Nikolai Igorevich, whose father Vitaly was reportedly a key figure in Russian organized crime.

Bingo. The puzzle was beginning to take shape. Looking at the dates, descriptions of criminal activity and the notations from Interpol claiming that Igorevich had dropped off their radar around two years ago, it was simply too much coincidence to believe that he – or a faction of his organization – wasn't now operating in Savannah.

Jesse examined a photo of the younger Igorevich and Markov together at some charity event for the arts that the father held annually, part of his cover as a legitimate businessman and patron of the arts. One of the items they'd auctioned off was a pair of Markov's ballet shoes.

With that thought in mind, Jesse navigated to the information he had on Vitaly Igorevich. Aside from ballet, the man was also a patron of the theater, taking a particular interest because he had fancied himself an actor in his younger years. Assuming he'd discovered that crime was a hell of a lot more lucrative, he'd changed careers but never quite gotten over the bug.

The theatrical element, as Jesse'd come to think of the crime scenes he'd investigated, began to make a bit more sense.

Jesse frowned, returning to the photo of the other two men and zooming in on the image. Something about Markov seemed familiar. And he didn't think it was because he'd seen the man's photo somewhere before, despite the fact that Markov was something of a minor celebrity. Jesse didn't exactly follow ballet.

Pushing that aside as something to consider later, Jesse continued through the file. Markov's behavior continued to deteriorate until he quit the ballet, although there was some dispute as to who quit whom. Rumors circulated that he'd been fired, that he was in rehab, in a psych ward, in jail, though there was no record of any of those things. He did, however, go to ground somewhere out of the public eye.

Less than a month later, he was killed in a fiery car crash – reportedly the result of a combination of high rates of speed and intoxication. The dancing world mourned.

Perhaps more relevant to Jesse's case, two days before Markov's car crash, Nikolai Igorevich had been shot to death in a law enforcement sting.

A noise outside had Jesse looking up. A light mist fell, creating a cocoon effect, but he knew the usual sounds of the dock. The water lapping against the hull, the start of a motor, the shriek of seagulls, the occasional muffled footsteps as other boaters came and went. But Jesse was docked in the last slot, so people rarely walked down this far.

He sat the laptop aside, pulled off his glasses and listened.

Footsteps on the dock. Stopping beside his boat.

Easing his feet to the floor, Jesse walked barefoot out of the cabin, past the head, toward the door. He'd left a nightlight shining in the galley, but rejected the urge to turn it off as he passed. It might alert whoever was out there that he'd heard them.

The face of the man who'd bumped into him on River Street flashed into his head, followed by another image of what had been left of Losevsky. Not to mention Gannon's dead, bulging eyes.

Jesse didn't kid himself about the nature of the organization he was investigating – particularly after reading about some of the crimes attributed to Igorevich. Crimes very similar in their horrific nature to what had been done to Miron Losevsky. He also acknowledged the reality that if they felt he was getting too close, they wouldn't hesitate to take action. Kill him, take his boat out to sea, dump his body overboard. Neat and clean.

Or maybe they'd want to leave a splashier message – no pun intended – since dramatic displays seemed to be their style.

The boat swayed a little, indicating that someone had boarded. Holding his service weapon at the ready, Jesse put his back to the wall beside the door.

The pounding surprised him. Assassins didn't tend to knock.

Curious more than alarmed now, it nonetheless took Jesse another moment to get his physiological fight response under control.

"Jesse?"

Jesse froze when he recognized the voice. Then cursed under his breath. Making sure the safety was on, Jesse stuck his sidearm in the back of his waistband and covered it with his shirt.

He unlocked the cabin door.

Jillian stood there, shivering in the cold night air, moonlight bouncing off her fair skin and hair – slightly damp from the walk down the dock – so that she looked like a mermaid or a siren having just emerged from the deep.

The description was apt, he considered. Because he was pretty sure she was about to lure him into doing something stupid.

"What the hell do you think you're doing?"

She stiffened. "I need to talk to you."

He should send her on her way. Or better yet, call Brian and have him pick her up – maybe lock her in her room while he was at it. Or put her in a damn safe house.

Instead, Jesse pulled her inside and closed the door. He didn't bother to hide his frustration. "Where's Brian?"

"He was watching TV when I left. Why?"

"Why?" Jesse rubbed his hand down his face in lieu of throttling her. *"Why?* Maybe because he's supposed to be watching you?"

Jillian's expression turned mutinous. "And he's been *watching me* for three days. But I'm not a child, or a dog. Nor am I stupid, so don't even suggest that I'm not aware that I seem to be a… a target of some sort. I don't understand it, but I acknowledge it. However, I might be able to understand it if you would tell me what the hell is going on!"

"I can't –"

"Discuss an ongoing investigation. You've told me. Brian's told me. And back to the fact that I'm not stupid, I understand how these things work."

"Yet here you are."

"You didn't answer my calls."

"Because I had a feeling they weren't made with the intention of asking me how my day was or my opinion on whether powdered or granulated sugar makes the best cookie."

Her hands clenched at her side. "It isn't fair to keep me in the dark. It's my life that's in upheaval. I gave you my mother's journal. I've turned over my electronic communications. I've given a formal statement. I've cooperated with everything you asked of me."

"And the Bureau, the Justice Department and myself all appreciate it."

"Don't be a smartass."

"I would be a dumbass, but you've got that position all wrapped up."

"Dammit, Jesse." Tears filled the corners of her eyes, making them shimmer like mossy pools until she stubbornly blinked them back. "Don't treat me like I'm stupid."

"Then don't do stupid things. Jesus, Jillian. You know you shouldn't be here. For multiple reasons, not the least of which is that you put yourself in danger!"

"I'm not asking you to protect me. Yes, I knew there would be risk involved in coming here, but deemed it acceptable. And I'm not asking you to show me the answers to the big test or reveal state secrets or whatever else you're thinking. I just want to know what you found out about my brother!"

Her brother. Alexei Markov.

The son whom her mother had borne out of wedlock when she'd been a mere sixteen. The son she'd given up because she was a rising ballet star and the child's father one of her instructors. Her married instructor, and a very influential man in his realm.

It was no wonder young Alexei had shown an aptitude for dance.

Jesse steeled himself against the tears. Or tried to, at any rate. He'd watched numerous suspects, witnesses, victims break down over the years. He'd seen people weep in raw pain and grief, watched others turn the tears on and off like a sympathy-inducing faucet. He couldn't say he was completely immune, but a crying woman didn't strike fear into his heart the way it did with some men.

But this woman's unshed tears made something inside him damn uncomfortable. He wanted to soothe her. He wanted to slay dragons for her.

He wanted her, period. And when you got right down to it, he was the one in danger.

"Don't cry," he said, rather stupidly.

"I'm not crying, you jerk."

"You look like you're about to."

"I'm *not* crying," she repeated, straining the words through her teeth. "Though I am considering punching you."

A slight smile lifted the corners of his mouth, and Jesse couldn't resist the urge to reach out and stroke her cheek with the backs of his fingers. "Haven't you had your fill of assaulting law enforcement officers lately?"

"That's not funny."

"No it's not." He sighed, and let his hand drop. He really shouldn't discuss this with her. He really shouldn't be here with her. But it probably wouldn't hurt to let her know.

And then call Brian to get her the hell away.

"I haven't found out much more than what we already knew from your mother's journal, the emails and from what you told me about your conversations with Alexei himself. What I have discovered… let's just say that it confirms some of my suspicions about your brother's questionable connections."

Jillian searched his face and apparently decided that he was telling the truth. Looking defeated, she eased herself onto the padded bench behind the table that comprised his dining area. She sat silently for a moment, and then folded her hands on the table.

"I didn't know," she told Jesse. "I truly didn't know that he was involved in anything illegal."

"Unless he admitted it, how would you?"

"I feel like I should have guessed."

"Because you're psychic now? Or did he give you any reason to suspect he had ties to organized crime?"

"No." She shook her head. "But the last time we Skyped, he seemed really agitated. Nervous. I attributed it to the problems he was having with his career, maybe a problem with alcohol. I read the articles in the Russian press that reported that he was spiraling out of control, but he assured me it was exaggerated. He said that he had some things to take care of to get back on track, basically, and that he might not be in touch for a short while, but he didn't want me to worry. And then he was gone. I didn't think… I didn't think it was relevant. To your investigation. How could it be, when he was dead?"

Jesse hesitated, and then sat down on the bench. He was careful to keep a couple of feet between them.

"The other night you said you waited two weeks before trying to contact him after that session."

"That's right. He'd said he might be MIA, plus it was right around Christmas. I was busy, and figured he might be, too. But after a couple weeks passed, I sent several emails, all of which went unanswered. I tried both his agency and the ballet company, but they had no information. At least none that they were willing to share. A week later, I got a Google alert – I'd set it up to follow his name in the press – with the report that he'd crashed his car."

Jesse considered. "You said you'd been communicating regularly with him for six months?"

"Around that. And at first it was pretty difficult given that he only spoke a smattering of English and my Russian was pretty basic. I'd started learning it after my aunt died and I found my mother's journal in the safe deposit box… I wanted to translate it myself. It seemed too private to hire someone else. As I told you the other day, it was a shock to learn that I had a half-brother. I didn't really believe I would find him, but I had to try. And then when I thought I had, I couldn't be sure it was him, despite the fact that his background matched what my mother described." She glanced up. "She'd been so proud of him, of his dancing. He was only twelve, I think, when she died, but already considered a prodigy. I still can't believe she never told my father."

"Sometimes people bury a secret so deeply inside themselves that the thought of revealing it becomes equivalent to ripping out their guts."

Jillian smiled a little. "Not the most eloquent of visuals, but I know what you mean." Then her expression turned pensive. "I didn't tell Cooper. My ex-husband," she explained. "I didn't tell him that I had a brother. Our marriage was already shaky – had been pretty much from the exchange of vows – and my aunt's death seemed to drive another wedge between us. Things weren't good, so I didn't want to share it with him. I didn't even tell Katie. I used my aunt's computer to search for Alexei and her email to communicate with him. Cooper thought I was having an online affair."

"Understandable."

She nodded, studied her clasped hands. "I'm ashamed to admit that I let him continue to think it. It was a handier excuse for the divorce rather than admitting that I'd rushed into marriage after a really bad experience because I wanted to feel… safe. So in a way, I guess Alexei became my secret, too."

"That explains why we couldn't find any record of you communicating with anyone in Russia – you weren't using your computer or your own email."

Jillian glanced up sharply. "You searched my email?"

"And your phone records and your passport and your credit card activity. I can see by your face that you feel violated, and I'm sorry for that. But I'm not sorry for doing my job or for following leads which pointed – probably rightfully so – to you. You may not have realized your relationship with your half-brother was relevant, but at this point I think it's safe to assume that it is."

Jillian drew a deep breath. "If you'd found those emails between Alexei and I before I told you about them, you would have thought that I'd been hiding something from you."

"Without your explanation and the evidence you provided, both with the journal and the emails? Absolutely. And though it would have pained me and would have devastated Brian, I'd have hauled you in for questioning. And I probably wouldn't have been as nice as I was the last time you sat across the interview table from me."

Jillian stared at him for several moments and then shook her head. "I should be offended by the lack of trust in that statement. I should feel hurt that you would kiss me the way you did and yet still be willing to lock me up. I don't understand why it makes me feel better."

"I said it would have pained me."

Her smile was wry. "Speaking as someone who spent a weekend behind bars, I can guarantee it would have pained you a lot less than it would have pained me."

They stared at each other for several moments, with only the lap of the water against the boat to break the silence.

"Thank you," she finally said. "For telling me what you could."

"I'm going to have to kick Brian's ass for letting you drive all the way out here by yourself."

Her eyes shifted to the side. "He didn't exactly let me. I waited until he fell asleep on the sofa."

"What about the alarm?"

"I silenced the door chime. But I left a note."

"A note." Jesse stabbed his hands into his hair, resisted the urge to pull it out. "A lot of good a note would have done if one of your brother's former friends decided to run you off the road or invite you in for a friendly little question and answer session."

"But why would they be interested in me? No, wait. Hear me out. Alexei's dead. He's been dead for almost two years. So why now?"

"Maybe he told you something that they'd rather not be known."

"Like what?" She threw up her hands. "Say they discovered he'd been communicating with me. You have the emails. I told you what we talked about on Skype. It was basic getting-to-know-you stuff. It's not like he passed along nuclear codes or something."

"That would be an entirely different investigation. But Jillian, just because *you* know he didn't tell you something compromising, it doesn't mean other people share that knowledge. They may want to eliminate you solely on the possibility."

"Okay." She drew a shaky breath. "I've been thinking about this – and given the fact that I've basically been incarcerated in my own home, I've had plenty of time to think. I didn't want to believe that Alexei was involved with something criminal, but being realistic, I had to acknowledge that it might explain some of what's happened. But if, as you've suggested, the things that have happened *do* have something to do with my brother and the people he was involved with, then why haven't they just shot me? Or run me over with a car when I was out running? Or any of the myriad ways they could have eliminated me that wouldn't have drawn attention. They've had plenty of time and almost endless opportunities. Why drag things out like this? Why mess with my head? *That* doesn't make sense. It's not like I've done anything to inspire malice."

Jesse had been asking himself the same question. And aside from the fact that whomever they were dealing with seemed to enjoy putting on a show of sorts, he didn't have an answer. Not a logical one, at any rate.

"I don't know yet," he admitted. "And until I do, you're going to have to promise me that you won't pull another stunt like tonight. I know you're not dumb, but I don't think you appreciate the type of people we're dealing with. I also understand your impatience and frustration. I even understand that feeling like a hostage in your own home takes you back to a mental and emotional place that you'd rather not revisit. But this," he gestured toward the pepper spray on her wrist "nor your basic knowledge of self-defense are a match for someone who would sneak into a place that they know is being monitored by law enforcement and take the time to flay a man's flesh from his bones.

"Yeah, it's an ugly picture," he said when she winced. "But it's one I want you to keep front and center of your mind. Whoever is behind this is a psychopath, Jillian. An extremely violent psychopath who we have reason to believe has already been in your house. The fact that it was your dolls – the nesting dolls you inherited from your mother – that were messed with is not a coincidence. It's a message. Until we understand that message, you need to consider yourself in mortal danger. Being stuck at home with a babysitter might suck, but it's better than being dead."

Face pale and sober, Jillian once again studied her hands. When they trembled, she pulled them back onto her lap.

"I wanted to talk to you tonight because I wanted answers, but also because I feel better. Being with you," she explained. "Not because I don't think Brian is competent. I know he is. But he also coddles me like a baby sister. It's just the way he is, and I know that he means well. But it drives me crazy to be treated as if I'm a child to be patted on the head and sent to bed while the grown-ups figure out what to do. Infantilizing me doesn't make me feel safer. It makes me feel like a victim again, and like you said, I don't want to revisit that place. I *can't* revisit that place and retain my sanity. You don't tell me as much as I'd like you to, but at least you're straight with me when you do share information. Knowing what I'm up against is… empowering, I guess. I feel more prepared. And as much as it irks me to be left out of the loop, I also like knowing that you're ethical. Given my past experiences, ethical carries a lot of weight."

She waited a beat, and then looked directly at him with both vulnerability and determination shining in her eyes. "That click you mentioned? It happened for me, too."

"Jillian." Alarm bells started ringing in his head.

"I know," she interrupted before he could say anything else. "I know that you won't – can't – act on it."

"Not for a lack of wanting to."

She nodded. "I just felt like I should say something in case… I don't mean to sound fatalistic, but in case things don't turn out quite the way we hope. Like you said, this person – or persons – has already been in my home. He's drugged me. He killed that poor animal. And he's probably murdered other people. It's terrifying," she admitted. "But I don't want to hide under the bed. And I don't want to waste time pretending that I don't feel the things I feel."

"Jillian." This time his voice held angry frustration. "Nothing is going to happen to you. Do you hear me?"

"You don't know that."

"The hell I don't." He reached out, cupped her face. "No one is going to touch you. No one."

Except, apparently, for him.

It was a bad idea. A terrible idea. But Jesse leaned forward anyway, placed his lips very lightly against hers.

She responded with an eagerness for which he wasn't prepared. Foolish of him. She'd been through a tremendous amount of emotional upheaval lately. Emotional upheaval often manifested – given the right provocation – in the physical expression of sex. And she'd just told him, in so many words, that she wanted him.

He should back off now, barricade her in the head and call Brian to come pick her up. Or maybe he should barricade himself in the head.

He should do a lot of things. Just not the thing he was doing.

But Jillian made a small, wanting sound, and the feel of her hands pressing into his back, trying to pull him closer, combined with the smell of her, the taste of her, started to snuff out the last flicker of resistance.

He sank into the kiss, sank into her.

He was a man who didn't think overmuch about sex. Not to say it didn't occupy a fair portion of his waking thoughts – and sometimes his non-waking ones – but he didn't tend to analyze it. If he was attracted to someone and she was legal, available, sane and consenting, he saw no trouble with occasionally scratching an itch. But aside from a few long-term relationships, he didn't worry about the potential implications of scratching.

He worried a little now. Even as his blood pulsed and his body thrummed with pleasure. And it wasn't just because he knew – professionally speaking – that he'd crossed a line.

Somewhere in the back of his head, he knew that professional ethics wasn't the line that should concern him.

"I'm sorry," she said, jerking away. "I didn't mean to… lunge at you like that. I really should go."

"Yeah," he agreed. "You should."

And he should be the one to make sure she went. Yet they both remained where they were, their chests rising and falling with the rapidness of their breathing. As clichéd as it was, the attraction was magnetic. He felt unable to pull himself away.

Jillian was the first to break eye contact. "I'll call you when I get back so that you know I arrived safely." She started to rise.

"Jillian," Jesse said, pulling her back down. He raked a hand through his hair as if that would jump start his common sense, but feared that was hopeless. "Stay."

"I'll be fine," she assured him. "Really. There's no need to call Brian or…"

She trailed off when she finally recognized the look in his eyes. "We shouldn't."

"You're absolutely right. Stay anyway."

"Jesse…" her breath eased out on a tender sigh. "I don't want to put you in a bad position."

"It says something about my state of mind right now that my first thought was that any position we tried would be fine by me. But honestly?" He shook his head. "I've eliminated you as a suspect. Yeah, you're part of this investigation and as such I should keep my hands to myself – at least until the case is closed – but I'm going to risk blowing your image of me as Captain Ethics to admit that at this point I don't much care. If I thought there was a chance I'd have to arrest you, I'd push you outside and bolt the door. Probably," he amended. "It's difficult to say for certain when you're wearing those damn boots."

She smiled, but it faltered.

"Hey." He cupped her cheek. "I know the timing isn't the best, but this... feels right. I don't know how to explain it beyond that."

"The click."

"The click," he agreed. He'd been more or less hooked from the moment he laid eyes on her.

"I don't want to get you in trouble," she protested. "Or be something you regret."

"I'm pretty adept at getting in trouble all by myself. But luckily I'm also pretty damn adept at what I do, so they put up with me. And Jillian... I could never regret this. Never regret you."

Jesse leaned in slowly, giving her time to back away if she really didn't want this. When she didn't, he took her mouth with a patience he didn't usually possess. He wanted her to know that this wasn't just a fast, meaningless coupling between two people who were hot for each other. Difficult as it was for him to believe, it felt like so much more.

He tasted her mouth, nipped her generous bottom lip, lightly sucked her tongue. Once she was back with the program, he worked his way down the side of her neck, opening his mouth over the tender area where it connected with her shoulder. She tilted her head, pulling the thick curtain of her hair aside to grant him easier access. When he used his teeth, her nails dug into his flesh.

The slight sting inflamed him.

He wanted her. He wanted to claim her, to possess her in a way that he'd never quite experienced before and that he was pretty sure wasn't politically correct. But he just didn't give a damn.

The soft sweater she wore – slightly damp from the mist – clung to curves that made Jesse praise whatever higher power designed the female anatomy. Running his hands along her ribcage, he slowly lifted the fabric, pulling his mouth away from hers long enough to yank the sweater over her head.

He tossed it aside, unconcerned as to where it landed, and stared unabashedly at her very pretty breasts.

Curious, he hooked his finger in the elastic waistband of her stretchy pants, and lowered them an inch.

"I've been told," he murmured "that when women wear matching undergarments, it means they plan to have sex."

Jillian's cheeks colored a little. "Sometimes."

"This time?"

"I didn't plan to, no. I expected you to be more angry than amorous. But in the interest of returning the favor of straightforwardness, I may have worn them on a… contingency basis."

He nodded. "A more cynical man might think that you'd planned to seduce me into telling you what you wanted to know."

"A more cynical man would be an asshole. And wrong."

Jesse accepted the ire in her tone. "I can be an asshole, Jillian. Fair warning."

She shook her head. "I honest to God don't understand why I like that about you."

"Because I don't bullshit. Or coddle you unnecessarily."

"Maybe. Maybe that's exactly it." Jillian hesitated and then reached up, undid the center clasp of her bra herself.

She ran her hand up her torso, flushing slightly as she cupped her own breast. The noise Jesse made in response sounded more like an animal than a man.

It caused him to hesitate. Given her history, he didn't know if she had any difficulties with physical intimacy. He didn't want to trigger some sort of post-traumatic stress. "I want you to tell me if I do anything that makes you uncomfortable."

"I appreciate your sensitivity," she told him "but when I said I don't want to be coddled, it goes for this, too. Treat me like a woman, Jesse, not a hothouse flower. The same woman you pushed against the wall and kissed breathless before. I promise I won't break."

Watching her, Jesse pulled the gun from the back of his waistband and placed it on the table. Then he leaned forward, pushing her against the bench so that he could take her into his mouth. Her back arched, one hand threading into his hair to bring him closer. He explored her breasts with his lips and tongue, her fingers tightening slightly when he did something that she particularly liked. The slight discomfort coupled with the pleasure of finally being able to touch her caused his erection to pulse almost painfully against his jeans.

"God, that feels so good," she murmured.

"Hang on. It's about to feel a whole lot better." He sat up, ran his hand down her leg, over her high-heeled boot. "Some day, when we have more time and more room, I want you to wear these for me." He glanced up. "And nothing else."

Her lips turned up in a sexy smile with the slightest trace of shyness around the edges. It was an irresistible combination.

He unzipped one boot and then the other, cursing the narrow confines of the galley when he bumped his elbow on the table, but he finally managed to get her tight, stretchy pants down her legs. She was left wearing a pair of silky red underwear that put him in mind of a Christmas treat just waiting to be unwrapped.

"Ho, ho, ho," he murmured.

"Is that a candy cane in your pocket or are you just happy to see me?"

"Sweetheart," Jesse corrected "that's the North Pole."

When she laughed, Jesse grinned. You had to love a woman who appreciated a truly awful pun.

Hooking his thumbs under the elastic, Jesse slowly began to pull. When she was totally bared, all fair skin and fiery gold hair, with the long, toned legs of a runner, Jesse thought that in that moment he was probably the most fortunate man on earth.

Then he frowned, touching the fading bruise on her knee.

He glanced up. "It makes me sick, thinking of what could have happened."

She reached up, laid her fingers against his lips. "Don't. I don't want to think about that. Not tonight."

Understanding, Jesse nodded. This time was for them. The close quarters of the cabin, the almost infinitesimal rocking of the boat combined to create an insular world, one from which he'd try to keep reality from intruding. At least for a little while.

Jesse pressed his lips to her knee before stretching her leg back out, admiring the shapely length of them.

"Jesse," she whispered after a few moments of him staring.

"Mmmm?"

"I'm naked."

"I've noticed."

She looked at him with exasperation. "Yet you remain fully dressed."

"I'm enjoying that contrast right now. Kind of a little master/slave fantasy. Or maybe a kinky Santa with his apprentice elf."

She laughed. "You're such a man."

"And thank God for it."

Jillian's laugh turned to a gasp when he braced one foot against the floor and lowered himself, kissing her between her legs. The gasp became a groan of pleasure that ended on his name and didn't hurt his ego one bit. But this wasn't about him. He wanted to please her not because it was some sort of proof of his sexual prowess. He simply wanted to make her feel good.

Really, *really* good.

To that end he slid first one finger and then another inside her, stroking her as he used his lips and tongue to push her closer and closer to the edge. One of her knees bumped the table, so Jesse draped both of her legs over his shoulders, holding her thighs in place. She squirmed, her breath coming in short pants.

"Oh God, Jesse. I can't."

She could. She would. Jesse pinned her left leg to the bench with his shoulder so that he could slide his fingers into her again. He curved the middle one, causing her to buck against him. Then he strategically used the stubble on his chin.

The orgasm seemed almost violent in its intensity, her inner muscles pulsing against his fingers as a hoarse cry ripped from her throat. He wouldn't at all be surprised to find a few strands of his hair clutched between her fingers.

Jesse continued through the aftershocks, until the hands that had been pulling him closer began to push him away. Untangling himself from her legs, he admired her skin, all flushed and dewy over limbs that had gone boneless. He smiled when she finally lifted her eyelids to half-mast.

"Hi."

She made a small sound.

"Everything okay?"

"I think I'm dead."

The smile turned into a grin.

"I hope you don't mind if people send flowers here," she told him. "I don't have the energy for a proper burial."

"That's a shame. And here I was just getting started."

She feebly lifted a hand. "Go ahead. I won't hold the necrophilia against you."

"As generous as that offer is, I prefer my partners to be responsive." He leaned down, pressed a kiss to her stomach and made her shiver. "Looks like there might be some life left in you after all."

Jillian struggled to sit up, and Jesse helped haul her upright. Her hair was tousled, her eyes slightly dazed, and Jesse felt pretty damn good, considering. When she looked at his mouth with hesitation before leaning in and tasting him, tasting herself, Jesse decided that he could probably feel a whole lot better.

"As exciting as the whole oral sex on the ridiculously narrow bench thing has been, maybe we could move to the berth for part two of the night's proceedings. Assuming you're still up for it, that is."

"A berth is a bed, right?"

"Right."

"I'm up for it. I think I re-bruised my knee on the table."

"Let me see." Ignoring the urgency of his body for another moment, Jesse examined her legs. He frowned when he saw a darkish mark on her inner thigh. "I think I might have bruised your leg with my shoulder, actually."

"Totally worth it," she assured him.

Jesse's lips twitched. "If you're not careful, you're going to inflate my ego."

"I'll deal with that regret at a time when my body isn't shaking little pom-poms and cheering your name."

Laughing, Jesse stood, offered her his hand. When she took it he pulled her flush against him. Looking into her eyes, he ran his hands down her slender back, cupped her magnificent ass. And then lifted her so that her legs wrapped around his waist.

"Don't fall," Jillian said when the boat swayed slightly beneath them.

"I have excellent sea legs," he assured her and proved it by walking unerringly to the stateroom. When his shins touched the berth he dumped her backward onto it, following her down. The control he'd exhibited up to this point began to slip at the feel of her pinned beneath him, her long legs hugging his. He kissed her with the urgency he'd been holding at bay.

She responded as hungrily as she had before he'd brought her to satisfaction, the small noises of desire she made driving him crazy. Jillian pulled at his shirt, and Jesse leaned back long enough to rip it off over his head, toss it aside. She began fumbling with the button fly of his jeans, causing him to groan.

He grabbed her hands. "Let me," he said. "If you touch me too much I'm afraid this will all be over before it begins."

Jesse rolled to his side, opened his fly and shoved the jeans down his legs. Since he'd pulled them on after his shower, he wasn't wearing boxers. His erection sprang free.

He grabbed a condom from the little drawer built into the berth, covering himself with an eye toward speed rather than finesse. He felt like a randy teen. Gathering Jillian beneath him again, he plunged.

Her sharp cry brought his head up. "Did I hurt you?"

"No." She shook her head. "Don't stop. Please don't stop."

He didn't. Probably couldn't at this point, so it was a relief that she didn't ask it of him. Lights flickered behind his eyes as the heat and the slickness and the rhythm caused pressure to begin gathering at the base of his spine far before he was ready. Jesse tried thinking of something that would slow it down, but Jillian slid her nails down his back, teased her fingers along the crack of his ass and drove him crazy. Mindless with the desire to claim, to possess, Jesse hooked his hands under her legs and shoved them back so that he could take her harder.

Sweat rolled off his forehead, dripped down his face as their bodies slid slickly together. He looked down to see Jillian biting her lip, her head tilted back against the pillow, the pale line of her neck exposed. It looked like she was close.

He leaned down, said something very raunchy in her ear as he ground his pelvis against hers.

She shattered.

Turned on beyond anything he'd ever experienced, Jesse continued until the pressure at the base of his spine became too great. Holding Jillian's hips in place, he thrust one last time.

His release temporarily blinded him. Jesse felt like he'd come apart at the seams.

When he finally managed to make his eyes work again, he realized that they were in danger of falling off the end of the bed. Somehow, they'd managed to turn sideways.

Jesse rolled, bringing Jillian with him so that she lay limply against his sweaty chest. He thought perhaps they were glued together.

He raised a hand, laid it against the back of her head.

"I only thought I was dead before," she told him after several moments. "This time I really am."

"We'll have a double burial at sea."

"My God," she said, sounding stunned. "That was... I don't know what that was."

"Really great sex."

"I don't think I can move my limbs."

"Probably a good thing we waited," he agreed. "If we'd done this that day in your entryway, they would have found our corpses standing there, mummified against the wall."

She snorted. "I probably shouldn't find that image so amusing, considering."

"I have a fairly macabre sense of humor sometimes," he admitted. "It tends to come with the job."

At the mention of his job, Jillian went silent.

"Hey." He tilted his head so that he could see her face. "No regrets, remember?"

"I was just thinking about how strange life is. Of all the men I possibly could have gotten involved with, I never would have believed it would be a cop."

"Agent, technically."

"Federal cop." She leaned up onto her elbow. "So you're like a regular cop on steroids."

He smiled at her teasing tone. "If you're gonna go, go big."

"I'm not going to touch that innuendo with a ten foot pole."

"You already did. Without the pole."

Shaking her head, she leaned down to kiss him. "That... thing you said? I liked that."

"I sensed that you did. You've got a dirty mind, Jillian Montgomery, and an angel's face. If you were to tell me that you love to fish, I might have to declare you the perfect woman."

She smiled, leaning in to kiss him again, but Jesse stopped her when he heard another noise outside.

"What's wr –"

Jesse pressed his finger firmly against her lips. Meeting her eyes, he shook his head. "Wait here," he whispered.

She nodded, her eyes widening in distress. "Please be careful."

Jesse rolled off the bed, snatching his jeans from the floor and pulling them on even as he hustled toward the table to retrieve his gun. He cursed himself for leaving it there to begin with, but that was something to worry about later. Palming it, he once again eased toward the door.

Jesse listened for a repeat of the noise he'd heard previously, but all he heard was the soft lap of water. Then it happened again. It sounded like a moan, barely audible.

With one final glance toward the stateroom to make sure Jillian had stayed put, Jesse eased open the door and crouching, moved onto the deck. Taking cover as best he could, Jesse maneuvered into a position where he was relatively protected.

No one shot at him when he lifted his head in order to be able to see the dock.

It was empty. Jesse frowned, wondering if maybe he'd mistaken the groaning of the dock itself, or one of the boats, for a human sound. But he didn't think so.

Rising up a little more, Jesse scanned the area. The sky was grey and close, but at least it was no longer raining. The drying sweat on his skin caused him to shiver, and Jesse wished briefly that he'd taken the time to don his shirt. A car pulled into a nearby parking space, the gleam of headlights illuminating part of the dock. Shielding his eyes so that the glare didn't ruin his night vision – not the best anyway, considering he wasn't wearing his glasses – Jesse used the unexpected gift of light to examine the dock more closely. There appeared to be a dark substance forming a thin trail on the planks.

Jesse rose to his feet, peering more closely.

What he saw ripped a string of vicious curses from his throat.

CHAPTER TWENTY

JILLIAN stared at her stained hands, not really seeing them. All she could see was that man, that poor man, blood gushing out of the horrible wound in his neck.

Her fault. It all seemed to be her fault. Or connected to her, anyway. To her brother.

But none of it made any sense.

Jillian listened to the hushed air of the hospital's chapel, fruitlessly hoping to hear an answer. First that man Losevsky was killed, and Jillian's business card found among his effects. Then Detective Gannon died – and though she still didn't have all the details regarding what happened, she knew that it somehow tied to her and Katie's Christmas decorations, of all things. And now this other man had been attacked and was barely clinging to life. Jillian didn't know who had attacked him or why, but she'd gotten the distinct impression that Jesse suspected it was also connected.

And those were just the incidents she knew of. Being out of the loop as she was, she realized there could be more.

But while it seemed logical to lay those crimes at the feet of the organization with which her brother had associated, it still defied understanding as to what that had to do with her.

But it did. It obviously did have something to do with her. The dolls, the drugs, the poor squirrel – there was no way to overlook the fact that someone was messing with her. Someone wanted to draw her in to their sick little games.

But she still couldn't figure out *why*.

"Jillian."

Jillian looked up to see Katie standing beside the pew.

"I called your name three times," her friend said.

"I guess I didn't hear you."

Frowning, Katie sat her purse on the padded bench and then lowered herself beside Jillian. "Are you okay?"

"I have no idea."

"Your hands," Katie breathed on a horrified exhale, causing Jillian to curl her fingers inward.

"The blood isn't mine."

"Well that's a relief. Jillian, what happened?"

Jillian turned her head. Katie had been… distant was perhaps the best descriptor to use, over the past few days. Jillian couldn't say she blamed her. Her life had been turned upside down, almost as much as Jillian's. It was her grandparents' home – her home, really – that had been invaded and searched and virtually ransacked by the police. Katie who insisted on the new alarm system. Katie who sat up with Jillian to make sure she didn't have a concussion. Katie who called Ainsley when she found out Jillian was in jail, involuntarily tripping and too frightened and confused at the time to demand her attorney.

"I'm so sorry," Jillian said.

"For what?"

"For being such a pain in your ass. For getting the house trashed. For endangering you. For screwing up Christmas. Pick one."

Obviously exasperated, Katie shook her head. "None of those things are your fault. And it's not quite Christmas yet, so you can't say you screwed it up."

"Close enough."

"Look," Katie said "I know I've been a little quiet the past couple of days. But it's not because I'm angry at you or plotting how to kick you out. It's beyond silly, but if you want to know the truth, I was a little hurt. That you told Jesse about your brother. But you'd never mentioned one word to me."

"I told Jesse because he asked me directly. And because it seems to be a major development in his investigation."

"I told you it was silly."

"I'm sorry for not sharing with you. I don't really have an excuse, except to say that I was in kind of an odd emotional place at the time. My aunt died, and my marriage – which you'd been opposed to, with good reason – was failing. You were looking around for properties to rent for your restaurant, and it seemed like everything was sort of falling into place for you and my world was falling apart. I retreated, I think. My relationship with Alexei was easy because there were no expectations, no history. No pressure. So I sort of kept it to myself."

Katie considered that, and then tucked a stray curl behind her ear and studied her own well-manicured fingers. "I don't have to tell you that you've been like the sister I never had. And I guess I've gotten used to being basically the most important person in your life since your aunt died and you got divorced. It's totally selfish of me, but I can see that there's something perhaps equally important developing between you and Jesse, and it's made me feel a little possessive." She shrugged. "So I guess we're both ridiculous."

"I thought you wanted me to be involved with Jesse."

"I *do!* That's why it's so ridiculous. Although I have to admit, I wasn't expecting you to become quite so… involved tonight." She arched her eyebrows.

"Is it that obvious?"

"You have beard burn on your neck."

Jillian lifted a hand to cover it, and then remembered the blood. She'd been able to clean off most of it, but some still remained around her nails. She let her hand fall back into her lap.

"What happened?" Katie repeated softly.

"I was frustrated with being kept in the dark," Jillian said "considering it was my brother. So I waited until Brian fell asleep and then snuck out."

"Yeah, I got that part," Katie said wryly. "The mistake you made was re-engaging the alarm as you left, because it gave the warning noise when I came in. Needless to say it woke Brian, who freaked out when he saw your note."

Jillian grimaced. "I don't think he's very happy with me. And I can't exactly blame him."

"He was pretty steamed when he left to follow you out to Tybee."

"They think it was his car turning into the parking lot which frightened away the attacker. Brian circled around once, looking for my car, and after he found it he parked. His headlights were what illuminated the... blood."

"A man was stabbed," Katie said. "I know that much."

"His throat was cut."

Katie winced.

"But the person who attacked him was startled, probably by Brian's headlights. So his hand slipped. I think one of the carotid arteries was probably cut, but not the other. There was still so much blood."

"You did CPR?" Katie nodded toward Jillian's hands.

"You know my aunt insisted that I learn essential first aid. Jesse and I took turns applying pressure to stop him from bleeding out. I don't know how successful we were. He's still in surgery."

"You tried," Katie said. "That's all anyone can ask."

"I feel like it's my fault."

"What?" Katie exclaimed. "How could this be your fault?"

"He was my brother. I know I didn't actively cause any of this, but my decision to try to find Alexei, to get to know him, somehow led to what's happening. The man," Jillian said "the man who was attacked tonight. He was –is – a friend of Jesse's. He's an artist – I've seen his gallery on River Street. I don't know why he was coming to see Jesse, or why someone wanted to kill him, but it hurt Jesse." Jillian remembered the impotent fury on Jesse's face. "And so now I feel even worse, because this seems to be personally affecting all of the people whom I… care about. I feel like I should go away somewhere or something. See if whoever is doing this will follow me and leave you guys alone."

"That is the dumbest shit I've ever heard."

Jillian and Katie both looked up to see Jesse silhouetted in the doorway.

Jillian clenched her jaw. "It may sound dumb, but it's how I feel. Your friend might *die.*"

"My friend might die," Jesse agreed, stepping further into the room and letting the door close behind him. "But that's not on you. We don't have enough evidence yet to know why he was attacked. If it's for the reasons I suspect – namely the drugs – it could be on me, because I sought LeRoy out and questioned him. Or you could say it's on LeRoy for living a lifestyle that put him in contact with the underbelly of Savannah. But actually? The only person this is really on is the one who wielded the knife. And if I hear you say anything about acting like human chum again, I will dump your ass in a safe house so fast your head won't even have time to spin."

Beside her, Katie drew in a sharp breath. "Um, I think I'll just… wait outside for a minute. I'm sure there's a vending machine that sells coffee somewhere. Come find me when you're ready to leave, Jillian."

Jillian barely noticed her friend picking up her purse and sliding down the pew. She was too busy glaring at Jesse.

"If you keep treating me like a child," she told him in a low tone "we're going to have problems."

"If I was treating you like a child, I'd haul you over my knee and spank you. Don't tempt me."

"What happened to acknowledging that I'm a mature woman capable of making my own decisions?"

"When your decisions involve deliberately putting yourself in danger, I'm forced to question that capability. Dammit, Jillian. I know I haven't given you a lot of reasons to inspire confidence, but I'm *not* going to let this asshole hurt you. Not again."

"What do you mean you haven't inspired confidence?"

Jesse stared at her for several moments, and then looked away. "He – and I use that term generically, because we don't know if it's the work of one person or one person commanding a group of people – got into your house. He killed your pet, for lack of a better term. He messed with your heirlooms. He drugged you. All while I was supposedly watching you. I suspect he had something to do with the death of a cop I didn't like and he almost succeeded in killing a man I do, essentially right under my nose." He hesitated, and then met her gaze. "I don't blame you for doubting me."

"Jesse," Jillian pushed to her feet and moved toward him. "I don't doubt you. That's not at all what I meant."

She realized that much like her, Jesse was taking responsibility for things that in reality were not his fault. "You're not the only investigator assigned to this case," she reminded him.

"I'm the lead."

"And you're the one who figured out that this had something to do with Alexei. And that I'm not a secret drug-runner for the Russian mob, which is what the Savannah cops were determined to believe about me. If not for you rooting out that mint wrapper and having it tested, interviewing the bride's mother to find out that no guest matching that man's description had been invited to the wedding, finding another guest who'd seen him leaving, proving I didn't make him up, Ainsley wouldn't have had the ammunition to push for those charges against me to be dropped."

"You had the journal and the emails as leverage, and it helped that you cooperated without making us get a warrant."

"Not to mention the fact that Ainsley is a tough negotiator."

Jesse snorted. And then rubbed his hand over his face. "I'm sorry. For being high-handed."

"The fact that you can recognize that you were is encouraging. That you would apologize for it, even more so."

His gaze drifted to her mouth. "I have incentive to stay on your good side. And to that end," he suddenly looked uncomfortable "I should probably mention that Ainsley and I used to, uh, date."

"You…" Jillian swallowed her surprise. "Really."

"About a year ago, for several months."

"Well, this is awkward."

"Tell me. But given what happened tonight, I don't want you to hear it from anyone else, which you would have, probably sooner rather than later. We got off to a rocky start on the honesty front, so I don't want to keep things from you if I can avoid it."

Jillian tried to figure out if she was comfortable with having Jesse's ex as her attorney. And then recalled how utterly professional Ainsley had been thus far, not to mention damn effective. She didn't seem to be the type to let her personal life interfere with her job. And it wasn't like they were going to be forced to compare notes.

Plus, she liked her. Maybe she liked her a little bit *less* than she had, but she liked her.

"Well, you at least exhibit good taste. Not only is she gorgeous, but she's intelligent and successful."

"I'm going to refrain from comment, because anything I say here is bound to be the wrong thing."

"Let's just consider the matter dropped."

He looked at her funny.

"What?"

"You don't want to rehash my previous love life? I thought women loved that stuff."

"Do you want to hear about my ex-husband?"

"Point taken." He held out his hand to her.

Jillian moved the couple steps it took to bring herself flush against him. Rising onto her toes, she pressed her mouth to his.

He wrapped her in his arms, kissed her back with an enthusiasm that bordered on ferocity. And then reluctantly pulled away.

Watching her eyes, he ran a hand over her hair before stepping back. "I just talked to the surgeon. Right now, they're putting LeRoy's chances at about fifty/fifty."

"That's better than I expected, to be honest. He lost so much blood."

"Thank you," Jesse said. "For helping."

"I certainly wasn't going to stand there and wring my hands while the man bled to death. Have you found out anything? About... who might have done this?"

"Not anything I can say. I know you hate being kept in the dark."

"It's not your fault. You're doing your job." She crossed her arms. "Are you going to be in trouble? For me... being there tonight? Detective Goode gave me the fish eye when I said that I'd come over to see if there were any new developments regarding my brother. He kept looking at the closed door to the stateroom as if he had x-ray vision and was trying to find evidence that we'd been intimate."

"You let me worry about that."

"But it's what I feared would happen. Yet I came over anyway."

"Would you stop trying to take the rap for everything? I'm the one who asked you to stay."

"But –"

"Don't make me spank you after all. Actually, on second thought…"

He waggled his eyebrows and Jillian smiled a little at his attempt to lighten the mood. Then she succumbed to a huge yawn.

"You should get some sleep," he told her.

"Am I free to go now? Or do the detectives have any more questions?"

"If there's follow-up it can wait until tomorrow. Let's go find Katie. Brian will follow the two of you back."

Jillian sighed. "Brian's going to kill me."

"He's under strict instructions not to. And look at it this way: if you hadn't snuck out and come to see me, he wouldn't have followed you, and his arrival wouldn't have startled the attacker and LeRoy probably wouldn't have had even a fifty/fifty chance. So you did a good deed."

She gave him a look. "You're just saying that because we had sex. Which I probably shouldn't be mentioning in the chapel."

"Sure you should, considering it was really excellent sex. If that's not a gift from some higher power, I don't know what is."

Jesse's cell phone started to ring.

"I have to take this," he said after checking the screen.

"Go ahead. I'll be out in just a minute. I have to get my purse."

Jesse was already involved in the conversation as he walked to the door. He opened it to a commotion – it looked like a couple nurses were trying to corral a disoriented and disorderly patient – so Jesse gave a head tilt to indicate that he'd be down the hall. Jillian nodded, and then walked back toward the pew to get her handbag. As she bent over, she heard the door once again open behind her.

"That was quick," she said, standing up, and then she glanced over her shoulder.

Shock rendered her incapable of screaming.

CHAPTER TWENTY-ONE

THE cafeteria was closed for the night and just down the hall from the chapel, which made it a good place to have an impromptu meeting.

"LeRoy is out of surgery," Jesse said to Detectives Portman and Goode. "Agent Bristol is in the process of reviewing the marina's surveillance footage." The cameras were limited mostly to the area around the office, though, so Jesse didn't hold out much hope.

"Does the doc have any idea how long it might be before we can interview him?"

"Assuming he regains consciousness at all," Jesse said with a bitter edge of regret "she expects him to be critical for at least the next twenty-four hours."

"Great," Portman said, while her partner eyed Jesse.

"You said you knew this LeRoy was an addict?"

"No, I said that a number of years ago I bumped into LeRoy at a party held by a mutual acquaintance. He extoled to me the mind-opening virtues of hallucinogens. Acting on the possibility that he still dabbled, I visited his gallery. He insisted he knew nothing. I told him that if he changed his mind, he could find me at the marina."

"So you don't know for certain that he was visiting you because he had information vital to the investigation. He could have just been stopping by to see an old… friend."

Jesse ignored Goode's thinly veiled innuendo. "Could have," he agreed instead. "In fact, he could have been simply out for an evening stroll in the delightful December rain. But the fact that he's lying in a hospital bed fighting for his life after having his throat slit as he approached my boat sort of indicates to me that the first possibility is more logical."

"There was no evidence that the perp hid on any of the nearby boats," Portman interjected, trying to steer the conversation back on track. "And we talked to the other residents at the marina. No one saw or heard anything."

"I didn't expect they would have. There aren't that many of us who live there, especially at this time of year, and the ones who do aren't that close by. I barely heard anything, and I was right there." Jesse considered that. "The perp had to have slid into the water. I would have heard his footsteps on the dock if he'd run away."

"How come you didn't hear his footsteps approaching?" Goode asked. "Or your friend LeRoy's, for that matter."

Because he'd been busy having mind-blowing sex at the time. A fact which made him feel guilty, but he still wasn't going to share that with the detectives. He wasn't about to give anyone a reason to lodge a formal complaint and risk being removed from the case. Especially not now. Jesse did try to abide by a staunch code of ethics, but he'd also been known to bend the rules as long as it didn't compromise an investigation. Jillian was no longer an official suspect, so to his mind their private relationship was none of anyone's business.

"I was talking to Ms. Montgomery at the time."

"Talking."

"That's right. She wanted to discuss the information pertaining to her brother."

"Given the circumstances, I'm surprised her attorney lets her talk to you without her presence. But wait." He snapped his fingers. "She's an old girlfriend of yours, isn't she."

"Are you trying to imply that my former relationship with the defense counsel has had a negative impact on this investigation?"

"Not really. Just find it interesting, is all. You being so closely acquainted with so many of the people involved in this case."

Jesse felt his hackles rise, but he refused to take the bait. Not when the hook was so clearly dangling there alongside it.

"It's a small world," he said to Goode, and then suggested that he and Portman talk to LeRoy's live-in lover, who was currently in the waiting room outside the ICU. "He was overwrought when I spoke with him earlier. Maybe you can get a more coherent statement from him."

After the detectives left, Jesse took a moment to control his anger. Goode, with whom he hadn't worked very long, had obviously been talking to Axelrod. Since the man was grieving his partner, Jesse tried not to hold that against him. Still, it was a pain in the ass to have to put up with the territorial hostility. That hostility would probably be on full display tomorrow at Gannon's memorial service. Especially since the lab results from one of the detective's pairs of sneakers had come back positive for the concrete dust matching the sample from Jillian's basement. Meaning Gannon had indeed been snooping around inside. Axelrod wasn't keen on having his partner cast in a questionable light when he wasn't around to explain his actions.

Jesse wished the man was around to explain his actions, also, though for entirely different reasons.

Jesse considered the fact that Gannon's bloodwork indicated he had enough cold medicine in his system to make him groggy if not outright knock him out. Had he ingested the medicine to somehow ease the pain he might feel when he hung himself? Jesse doubted it. There was still no real answer as to *why* the man would have committed suicide, unless he was indeed somehow connected to Losevsky's organization. But there was no evidence to support that, aside from the LSD tabs in his pocket.

The whole thing seemed staged.

Just as Losevsky's attack was staged, for maximum dramatic impact. Irena's death was quick and brutal, but then she'd been in jail at the time, so the choice of methods was limited. It was the same method, in fact, as the attack on LeRoy. Which suggested that someone had wanted him quickly dispatched. Probably because he had incriminating information, as had Irena. That LeRoy was almost killed on his way to see Jesse suggested that either he'd been under surveillance as a potential problem, or that whoever attacked him was already at the marina.

Maybe because they'd followed Jillian there.

Uncomfortable with that thought, Jesse considered Jillian's point that whoever was behind all of this had had plenty of opportunities to dispatch her. Just like they'd dispatched Irena and almost LeRoy.

So why had they made such a production out of Losevsky's death? A warning to other people who worked for the organization, following some unknown infraction? And they still didn't know why he'd had Jillian's card.

And what about Gannon? Jesse still found it hard to believe that the man killed himself, let alone that he'd donned Jesse's shirt and chosen Jillian's Christmas lights as his rope.

All of it seemed designed to draw attention to Jillian.

So she was right. It didn't make sense. If they thought she knew something – like Irena and LeRoy – it seemed far more logical to simply kill her. Unless there was some other reason to… put her in the spotlight.

Jesse realized that he'd been ruminating longer than he'd intended, and walked out of the cafeteria to find Jillian, who was probably asleep in the hall by now.

Instead, he found Katie.

"Hey," she said. "I was just coming to find you guys. Is Jillian ready to go?"

Jesse looked over her shoulder. "You haven't seen her? Did you check the chapel?"

"I peeked my head in but it was empty. I thought she was with you."

Feeling the first fingers of alarm beginning to dance up his spine, Jesse pushed past her and shoved open the door to the chapel. Like Katie said, it was empty.

"Maybe she went to the bathroom or…"

Katie's voice trailed off as Jesse bent down, picked up an item from the floor beneath the pew.

Jillian's cellphone.

The fingers which had been ticking his spine reached up to grab his throat.

CHAPTER TWENTY-TWO

"*THROUGH* here."

Jillian held onto the hand of the man who'd so surprised her, following him through a door and down a covered walkway that led to the hospital's parking garage. They didn't enter the garage, though, instead taking a footpath that led toward some sort of maintenance yard, where air conditioning units whirred as they maintained the hospital's interior climate.

"Here," he said. "The machines should provide enough noise to..." he waved a hand in the air "obscure, I think is right word. They will obscure our conversation."

Still stunned, Jillian could only blink. "I thought you were dead."

Alexei Markov – beloved international ballet star and the brother she'd never met in person – nodded. "You were meant to. As was the rest of the world. It was the only way."

Jillian studied his face. He'd done something to it, something surgical. His chin was perhaps a tad more pointed, his nose less pronounced. His hair was a mousy shade of brown, whereas once it had been golden. But the eyes were the same. The same shade of green as her own.

Their mother's eyes.

"The only way to what?" she finally said. "And why do we have to obscure our conversation? Who do you think is –"

He cut her off with a shake of his head. "Not yet. Let me see your bag."

"My what?"

"Your purse," he said in Russian.

It took Jillian a moment to translate, and then she frowned. "Why? You already tossed away my phone."

Alexei sighed. "I am sorry," he repeated. "I know that you are probably questioning my…" he waved his hand again "intentions. As well as your safety. But I promise you, on our shared blood, that I mean you no harm. I wish only to protect you."

Jillian weighed the advisability of trusting this man she didn't in reality know, a man who'd proven to not only have connections to a dangerous criminal organization, but who'd obviously faked his own death. It was probably the height of stupidity to have left with him.

But he would have fled if she'd attempted to alert Jesse or anyone else, of that she had no doubt. He'd told her as much when he'd surprised her in the chapel. So she'd gone with him, not only for curiosity's sake, but because she felt that if she wanted to get to the root of the trouble she'd been experiencing, this was her best – maybe her only – chance.

Her intuition – which she'd learned to trust – told her that Alexei had no intention of physically harming her. Not right now, at any rate.

She handed over her purse.

Alexei acknowledged her show of trust with a small nod, and then he rooted through the contents. To her shock, he pulled out a pocket knife and slashed the lining.

She started to vocally protest when he extracted a small object, something that looked like a button-type battery.

Scowling at it, he then clutched it in his fist. "Wait here," he said, and then handed her back her purse.

He strode back toward the door with the sort of feline grace that marked him as an athlete, sure in his own body. When he disappeared from her sight, Jillian crossed her arms against the very early morning chill, glancing around. She half expected an assassin to leap out from behind a piece of machinery, or Jesse to come charging around the corner. He would be frantic when he realized she was gone. Frantic and furious. Jillian had wanted to leave a text on her phone in the drafts so that he didn't think she'd been abducted, but Alexei insisted there wasn't time. He would explain, but only if she came with him in that moment. It was too risky for him to stay.

Of course, that's what any abductor worth his salt would say. The adult equivalent of *hey little girl, I've got candy.*

But she didn't think her brother was psychotic. At least, she really, really hoped he wasn't.

Only seconds later, Alexei reappeared.

"Was that some sort of tracking device?" she asked him.

"Yes. I suspected your movements were being closely monitored. They would want to know if you... deviated from your routine. I placed the device on a cart in the hallway. It is better if they do not know you have left the hospital grounds."

"I haven't left the hospital grounds."

He looked at her. "Not yet."

Jillian got the impression that he was about to ask her to do just that. "I can't leave without telling my roommate or the FBI agent who brought me here."

"Do you really think your lover will let you stroll off with a man who is supposed to be dead? A man who has brought you to the attention of a very dangerous criminal?"

He raised his brows. "A man who he likely believes to be a dangerous criminal himself?"

Jillian wasn't going to take the time to ask him how he knew that Jesse was her lover. "I think that if you have something to say, you should tell Jesse, too, especially if it pertains to dangerous criminals. He can probably grant you immunity or –"

Alexei snorted. "There is no immunity from death. And if the law enforcement community here gets their hands on me, I can promise you that I will truly be dead this time. Surely you, of all people, understand this."

"You think the cops are corrupt."

"I know this, at least of a few of them. A few of them – like your lover – I think are honest. But that does not mean I am willing to entrust them with my safety. Or yours."

"Your English has improved remarkably," Jillian noted.

"I have had two years to work on it. To my regret, the accent is... stubborn. Please," he said in a low voice. "Trust me. If you were to be hurt any more than you have been, I could never forgive myself."

Jillian studied his pleading expression, and then sighed. "Where are we going?"

"Someplace that I know is safe for us to talk. Afterward, I will let you contact your FBI agent. I promise."

"Tell me one thing… did I hallucinate you the other night, or were you really in my house?"

"I was there. I hoped to talk to you that night, but obviously I chose a poor time."

"How did you get in?"

"I climbed tree and came in through an upstairs window that was not wired into your alarm. Your roommate's lover left it unlocked after he opened it to hide the fact that he'd been smoking."

"How do you know that? And do you know who drugged me? Who messed with my – our – mother's dolls?"

Alexei's mouth formed a bitter line. "That is the least of what he's done. And I will explain everything. Just not now. And not here."

Jillian considered that she was probably making a huge mistake. And that Katie, Brian and Jesse would fight over who got to kill her when they found out she'd left with Alexei of her own free will.

But she wanted answers. *Needed* answers. It was the only way to make this nightmare end.

"Okay. But if I feel the least bit threatened at any time, I'm screaming bloody murder and ditching you, brother or not."

His smile revealed long dimples in his cheeks. *"Energichnyy."*

"I'm not familiar with that word."

"It means that you have spirit."

"I also have pepper spray, so don't make me use it."

He slung his arm over her shoulders. "I will try my best."

CHAPTER TWENTY-THREE

"THAT'S the last one," Katie said, emerging from the swinging door. "She isn't in any of the bathrooms on the main floor."

"She's not at the car. Any of the cars," Brian added. "I checked yours, mine and Katie's."

"Okay," Jesse said. He'd been trying to stay cool. After all, there was a chance that Jillian's phone had simply fallen out of her purse when she retrieved the bag from the pew. But if she wasn't in the restroom and she wasn't waiting at the car – an off chance to begin with – and she wasn't at the vending machines near the cafeteria, there weren't a whole hell of a lot of other reasonable options as to where she could be.

"Shit." Jesse dragged a hand down his face. There had been several people in the hall when he'd emerged from the chapel. How could anyone have gotten in there and... removed Jillian without someone noticing? There was only one exit door, and the stained glass windows weren't operable. She had to have left under her own steam.

But that didn't mean that someone hadn't intercepted her once she'd done so.

"Find Goode and Portman," he told Brian. "They went off to interview LeRoy's boyfriend. Maybe they decided to follow up with Jillian while they were here. I'm going to alert security and have them look at their surveillance footage to see which direction she took after leaving the chapel. If those options are unsuccessful, we call in more manpower and start a full scale search."

"What can I do?" Katie asked from beside him, her voice thin and worried.

"If you can think of anyplace else she might have gone, check there," he said, rather than telling her to let them handle it. He knew how frustrating it was to sit and wait, feeling helpless. "And you can check with the nurses' station on this floor, see if any of them recall seeing her."

The Parker siblings dispersed on their separate missions, and Jesse strode down the hall and around the corner, toward the security office.

He rapped his fist on the door.

It opened to reveal a man with a graying brush cut and military bearing, his hand resting on the butt of his firearm. His nametag read *Coleman*. "Can I help you?"

"Special Agent Wellington," he said, offering his identification. "I'd like to see your surveillance footage from the corridor outside the chapel, about thirty minutes ago."

The man handed Jesse back his badge. "Why?"

Because I said so trembled on the tip of Jesse's tongue, but he figured that finesse would get him what he wanted more quickly than attitude. "Because we seem to have a missing female who was last seen in the chapel."

The man looked Jesse over, and then stepped back. "Come in. Burns," he called to another man sitting in front of a bank of monitors. "Pull up footage from camera nine, starting forty minutes ago. Best to begin a few minutes back," the man said as an aside to Jesse "so you don't miss anything."

"I appreciate it."

He walked further into the cramped room, which was filled with monitors and the smell of doughnuts.

"You want one?" Coleman asked, gesturing to the open box. "They're still pretty fresh."

"I appreciate it, but no." Jesse didn't think he could stomach food right now, which was an indicator of his level of anxiety.

"Got it," the man named Burns said, and Jesse moved closer to the monitor. "I'll fast forward it to save time, but if you see anything you need to look at more closely, just holler."

"Thank God for this digitized shit, huh?" Coleman said, biting into a glazed pastry. "Hell of a lot easier than when everything was on cassette."

Intent on watching the action on the screen, Jesse ignored the man's comment. That area of the hospital wasn't extremely busy at this time of night, considering the cafeteria was closed and visiting hours were long over, so there wasn't a whole lot of action to be seen.

"That's you going into the chapel, ain't it?" Coleman said from behind him.

"That's me." And there went Katie, leaving to allow him and Jillian some privacy. A few minutes later he saw the disoriented patient wander around the corner, trailing an IV pole, and then the two nurses chasing after him. It was right around that time that Jesse exited the chapel, talking to

Portman on his phone and heading toward the empty cafeteria for their discussion. He'd just rounded the corner when another figure entered the screen, moving swiftly toward the door Jesse had just closed behind him.

"Stop!" he said. "Back up just a bit, will you?"

When Burns had carried out his request, Jesse studied the still image. The man had kept his head down as he walked, but when one of the nurses accidentally backed into him, he glanced up. In that moment, his face was visible.

"You recognize him?" Coleman wanted to know.

"Yes." Jesse's heart climbed into his throat. It was the man who'd bumped into him on River Street. He was sure of it. "Keep going," he told Burns.

The footage started again, in real time rather than fast forward, and Jesse realized he was holding his breath. The door to the chapel opened again, and the same man emerged.

This time accompanied by Jillian.

"That the women you're looking for?"

Jesse nodded in response to Coleman's question. "Freeze that again, will you?" he said to Burns.

The man did, and Jesse leaned closer. Jillian's face held obvious shock. And the man's face…

"Can you print a copy of that image for me?"

"Sure," Burns said, and Jesse pulled out his phone, scrolled through the photos he had stored there. One of which was from the file he'd been sent from Russian authorities. Not exact, he thought... but too close to be ignored.

When Burns handed him the printout, Jesse shook off his own shock – and a growing sense of betrayal – and thanked both men, calling Brian as he walked out the door.

"You find her?" Brian wanted to know.

"Not exactly." Jesse's voice was tight. "But she left here with her brother."

CHAPTER TWENTY-FOUR

"YOU favor her. Our mother."

"Mostly in the coloring," Jillian said. "Unfortunately I didn't inherit her grace and superb athletic ability, like you did. I'm more of a runner than a dancer, and only an average runner at that."

"I know." Alexei smiled to take the sting out of the mild insult. "I have followed behind you on occasion."

Jillian sighed. "I can't believe I didn't notice you. I thought I was more aware of my surroundings than that."

"Don't... what is correct phrase? Beat yourself up. I have become very good at concealing my presence."

His sister looked around at their surroundings, a sparsely furnished basement apartment in a townhouse behind and down the street from hers. "I'll say. You were practically in my backyard all this time."

"I took lease on this place close to one year ago. After I got word that Vitaly Igorevich had established himself in Savannah."

"All this time," she said, her eyes sad. "And you never approached me, never let me know that you were alive."

Uncomfortable and slightly defensive, Alexei jerked his shoulders. "I could not. I was not certain that Vitaly knew who you were, though my suspicion was strong enough to bring me here, into..." he searched his mind for the right phrase.

"The lion's den?" Jillian suggested.

"Yes, this. I worked hard to get away from Vitaly, to convince him that I was dead. Putting myself in his territory again was uncomfortable."

She studied him. "But you were worried about me."

He nodded. "It did not seem a... coincidence," he said. "That out of all of the places in the world Vitaly could have fled, could have reestablished his business, that he would choose the same city in which my sister resides. So I knew. He suspected that I still lived. And that he could get me to reveal myself in one way, by bringing threat to my family."

"Family whom you'd never even met."

"But still family." He reached out to squeeze her hand. "My only family. And that would be important to him." His voice turned hard. "An eye for an eye."

"Alexei, please." Jillian brought her other hand forward so that his was clasped between both of hers. "Tell me what's going on."

Alexei wished he didn't have to tell her. Wished he could be the older brother she deserved. Wished he hadn't made the choices that he did. But he had, so there was no other recourse but to deal with them.

"I was bored," he explained. Which sounded like such a flimsy excuse for what happened. "Bored with ballet. Not dance," he tried to explain "but of feeling like a piece of property more than a man. I was tired of having my every move dictated, no time for myself, no decisions left to me to make. So I rebelled." He shrugged. "You know this part."

"You told me that you went a little wild. And I read the articles written about your *fall from grace,* as one reporter called it."

He nodded. "I partied. I drank. I got in fights and I made love with equal abandon. I skipped practices. I also experimented with drugs."

"Ah," Jillian said. "The LSD."

"Among others, but it was my favorite. Some people have bad experiences," his smile was rueful. "As you know. But for me it opened my mind, allowed me to see things from different perspective. It took me out of the prison that my life had become. Nikolai was my dealer, and he became my friend. A very dangerous friend, as it turned out."

When Jillian said nothing, merely waited with an expectant air, Alexei continued. "Vitaly's organization, it is like that vine that grows around here in summer…"

"Kudzu?"

"Yes, that is it. It starts out small, but it keeps growing, wrapping around you and eventually smothering everything it touches. When I realized that it held me," he clenched his fists to show the strength of the grip "it was too late. I tried to distance myself as much as possible, and was able to use my career as an excuse. But one night… something happened. Something that made me realize that I could not allow myself to continue to associate with people like this. Something that scarred my soul. And made me immeasurably angry."

"I hope it's not worse than what happened to that man, Losevsky."

"Miron," Alexei nodded. "He was one of Vitaly's... I guess the word would be *mules*. He transported and dealt drugs, yes? But he was careless in his relationship with one of the whores – sex slaves, really – and when she escaped, she was able to give his name. His error was dealt with in the manner you heard about in your local media."

Jillian's face turned pale. "Sex slaves?"

"I apologize. I thought perhaps your FBI agent would have told you."

She shook her head. "He tells me only what I beg out of him, or things he thinks I need to know. He doesn't want to risk compromising the investigation."

"He is man of integrity." Alexei nodded his approval. "I determined this after watching him and researching his background."

Jillian smiled, just a little. "I'm glad you think so. And that man of integrity is going to be furious if I don't contact him soon."

"Is that your polite way of telling me to hurry along my story?"

"Well, I'm southern *and* half Russian, so hurrying a story is basically sacrilegious. But in this case… yes."

He grinned, enjoying her, but it quickly faded. "That night, the night that changed things, I was at party at Nikolai's house. Alcohol, drugs, prostitutes – every vice you can think of was provided. But there was one girl there – very young girl, still a teen. She went into Nikolai's bedroom with him, and I could hear her crying. Concerned, I listened at the door. They argued. The girl claimed to be pregnant. He laughed at her, said he didn't care. The bastard could be anyone's. She said the child could only be his. This made sense, as Nikolai did not like to share his women. He preferred virgins. Anyway, they fought some more, and then the argument turned very ugly. The girl was screaming at him, and I started to open the door, to intervene. But there was a shot. Nikolai killed her. A single bullet that exploded her brain."

"How horrible it must have been for you."

"More horrible for her, I would say. But yes… I thought of our mother. Of what I'd learned, from the journal you shared, about how a powerful man had impregnated her and then callously discarded her. I recalled the heartbreak in her words when she recalled the pain of having to give… to give me up. I got very angry. Nikolai exited the room, saw me and stopped. And then he smiled. Said something like *problem solved,* and then urged me to return to the party. He would have his men clean up the mess. *The mess,* as if this young girl's life were equivalent to a dog piddling on the carpet. It was then that I knew that I had to do something."

"Oh Alexei." She squeezed the hand she still held. "I'm so sorry."

He shrugged. "It was my bed to lie in. It took me a while to figure out the best way. I wanted justice for that dead girl and the baby she carried. But I knew that some of the police were in… Vitaly's pants?"

Jillian laughed, and then slapped a hand over her mouth. "I'm sorry. I feel terrible for laughing right now. But I think the phrase you're looking for is *in his pocket."*

Alexei smiled. "Ah. And I guess the other sounds more like… I can understand why you found it amusing."

"A little unintentional comic relief," she said. "And I guess it's the same in most countries – some of the police are interested in serving and protecting the public, and some are there for their own power and material gain. I guess you found some that you felt you could trust."

"I did. And I helped them set a trap for Nikolai. But unfortunately, one of the cops who was not so trustworthy must have gotten word to him, because he was expecting them. There was a fight, lots of gunfire. Nikolai was killed."

"Making you enemy number one with his father."

"Precisely. One of the police officers that I trusted, he helped me to fake my death. An unclaimed body was placed in my car, the records from my teeth," he tapped them "were exchanged, because the body was burned beyond recognition when the car exploded. Part of the plan."

"But Vitaly didn't believe it?"

"He may have at first. But he was devastated, enraged at the loss of his son. He went after the police officers involved in the raid, those who had survived. The one I trusted was killed. Tortured. I am sure he must have told Vitaly everything before he died."

Jillian closed her eyes. "It's all starting to make a terrible kind of sense. Now he really does want you dead. And he's using this campaign against me to… what, lure you out?"

Alexei felt nauseated. Sick at her misconception. "No, he wants to kill *you*. He only wants to make certain that I am around to see it."

CHAPTER TWENTY-FIVE

SHAKEN, Jillian stood in her darkened kitchen, arms wrapped around her waist as if to keep herself from flying apart.

"The house is empty," Alexei said. They'd checked it from top to bottom before he was willing to leave her alone.

"You got in," she reminded him. "As did this Vitaly or whoever he sent to mess with the *matryoshka*. And whoever took Jesse's shirt."

"That was before you changed the alarm system," her brother reminded her. "And I have checked the windows upstairs, and none of them are unlocked." He frowned. "I suspect that detective may have had something to do with it."

"The detective? You mean Detective Gannon?"

"The one who is dead, yes."

"You saw him here?"

"The same night he and the other detective were here to question you, the dead one – Gannon – he came back later, alone. I saw him outside when I was returning from…"

When he trailed off, Jillian's brows drew together. "Returning from what?"

His gaze shifted to the side. "I had a… discussion with the two idiots who broke the windows in your car."

"You –" Jillian stopped and shook her head. "I don't think I want to know, because I have a feeling that *discussion* in reality means something entirely less benign, and I'm going to tell Jesse everything we've discussed. I'd prefer not to implicate you any more than I absolutely have to."

Happy to change the subject, Alexei went back to his original point. "Perhaps the detective did something to the alarm, or found a way around it. Maybe he was one of those in Vitaly's pocket."

"I don't even know how he died," Jillian said. "Jesse wouldn't say, and the newspaper report was evasive. But the cops came here and took away a bunch of our Christmas decorations, of all things. I'm assuming they had something to do with his death."

Alexei frowned. "Christmas decorations."

"The lights in particular."

Alexei made a noise of disgust. "Vitaly. It is message to me, I am sure of it. The party I was at, the one where Nikolai killed the girl. It was a holiday party," Alexei explained.

"Oh."

After hesitating for a brief moment, Alexei leaned forward to place a kiss on her forehead. "Call your FBI agent. Tell him everything. I will wait until he is on his way so that you are not alone."

"I wish you would wait and talk to him yourself."

She knew it was a futile hope even before he shook his head. "I cannot be taken into custody. You know this."

"He'll want to know where we went."

"And you will tell him. They will likely search the apartment, but they will find nothing. I have made plans to move to another location. I hope they will not waste time looking for me, when I have given them enough information to understand that it is Vitaly whom they should be seeking."

"I'm afraid I won't see you again," Jillian admitted.

He hesitated. "You will. Now call your agent."

Alexei waited while Jillian dialed Jesse's cell number from the house phone, smiled sympathetically when Jillian winced at his tone.

"He's on his way," Jillian said. "And he ordered you to stay put until he gets here."

Alexei smiled, revealing those charming dimples. "It is unfortunate for him that I do not take orders very well any longer." He caught Jillian in a brief but fierce embrace. "Take care of yourself, *mladshaya sestra*"

Jillian watched as he slid out the back door, graceful and elusive as a feral cat. When he'd gone, she quickly set the alarm. And then eyed the pistol Alexei had insisted on leaving with her. She'd taken a firearms course when she'd moved back to her hometown, but her ex-husband hadn't been a fan of guns so she hadn't acquired one. But at least she knew how to shoot it if someone broke in before the cavalry got here.

Which turned out to be a remarkably short time.

The pounding on the backdoor within minutes after Alexei's departure caused her to palm the pistol. It wasn't until Jesse demanded that she open the door that Jillian laid it aside.

With a shaking hand, she punched in the code to turn off the alarm she'd just set, and then opened the door to a furious and fuming FBI agent. Who had his own weapon drawn.

Jillian sucked in a breath.

"Where is he?"

"He's gone."

Jesse brushed past her, seeming not to believe what she'd said.

"Jesse…" Jillian shut the door and then followed after him as he began searching. "Alexei isn't here."

"You'll have to forgive me if I don't quite believe you." He disappeared down the basement stairs. After he'd returned, Jillian once again locked the deadbolt on that door before following him past the open powder room and toward the den. Deciding that the Christmas tree wasn't hiding any errant Russian ballet dancers in its branches, he moved on to the parlor. Finally, he rounded the corner to head upstairs.

Jillian stifled a sigh and followed him. "Look, I know you must be upset with me for leaving but –"

"Upset?" Jesse said, coming to a stop in the upstairs hall. "Why would I be upset that you waltzed out of the hospital with your supposedly dead brother – at least the man you claim to be your brother."

Jillian gaped. "He *is* my brother."

"Fine, let's say he is. He's also a man who was a known confident of one of the foulest criminals Russia has ever produced. A criminal who has apparently graced our southern shores, bringing his stench with him. A criminal who has brutally murdered or attempted to murder three, maybe four people within the past month – that I know of. And you left the hospital with the one man we know is connected to him. Voluntarily. Leaving your cell phone – the one means I might have of tracking you or communicating with you – behind. Of course that's not upsetting."

"Just let me explain."

"Oh, you'll explain alright." He opened the door to Katie's bedroom, checked under the bed, the en suite bath and the walk-in closet.

Jillian decided to simply wait in the hall while he repeated the process with the office and her bedroom. When he was satisfied that she was indeed telling the truth, he holstered his gun and pulled out his cell phone.

"He's not here," he said to someone, probably Brian, while Jillian muttered "Told you."

He sent her a glare and then engaged in a bunch of cop speak, no doubt organizing the search Alexei had hoped they wouldn't waste their time with. Jillian interrupted him to give him the information about Alexei's apartment, because she didn't want to appear to be withholding anything. Jesse stared at her while he passed along the address.

"What was he driving?"

"He wasn't."

"How did you get here from the hospital?"

"We walked for a block or two and then caught a cab. You can probably call the company to verify that." She gave him the name.

He issued some more orders over the phone, never taking his eyes off of her. Jillian started to feel unnerved. There was no warmth in his gaze, in his tone. He looked and sounded like a stranger.

Like a cop.

When he ended the call, he shoved his phone into his pocket. And then he backed her against the wall.

"Jesse, you're frightening me."

"Then we're even," he said in a low, dangerous voice, placing his palms on either side of her and caging her between his arms. "Do you have any idea how *fucking* terrified I was when I found your phone, but couldn't find you? Or how sick I felt when I saw the video of you leaving the hospital with Alexei?"

"I'm sorry. I understand that you're upset. There wasn't time –"

"There wasn't time," he interrupted with a nod, as if that were a perfectly reasonable explanation.

"Jesse –"

"No. Not yet. I don't want to hear it yet."

She could feel the tension vibrating in his arms as he leaned into them, leaned into her. His mouth, when it took hers, demanded rather than coaxed. She could all but taste his fury.

Jillian raised her hands to his chest, started to push him away, but her fingers curled in, clutching at his shirt instead. When his tongue parted her lips, it was a moan rather than a protest that escaped them.

The sound snapped whatever thin leash might have been holding him back, and Jesse yanked her pants down her legs, growling when they got hung up on her boots. He brought her left leg up, unzipped that boot and tossed it aside, not taking the time to deal with the other. Her pants were dangling from one leg while he undid his fly. Her underwear he simply ripped aside. Within moments, he was inside her.

Jillian cried out with the shock of his sudden possession. She grabbed onto his shoulders, feeling them shake from the adrenaline coursing through his body. Knowing that he was in the grip of an emotional storm, she held on tightly and didn't resist. Couldn't resist. All of the fear and frustration and anger and uncertainty of the past several weeks coalesced into pure, animalistic lust. They mated there in the hall outside her bedroom door, permeating the air with the smell of musk.

When the tension finally broke, it was with every bit as much intensity as a summer thunderstorm.

With his forehead resting on the wall a mere inch from Jillian's ear, she could hear, feel every labored breath Jesse exhaled. And then finally, the raspy words.

"Don't ever scare me like that again."

"I won't. Not by choice."

Slowly, he let go of her legs until she was standing, albeit shakily. He adjusted himself, and then bent down to help her put her leg back into her pants.

When she was clothed again, he stood and met her gaze. His was resolute. "Take a few minutes to get cleaned up, and then we'll talk. And you're going to tell me. Everything."

CHAPTER TWENTY-SIX

JESSE braced his forearm on the window frame, peering through the glass at the birds in the courtyard next door. A robin – at least he thought it was a robin – splashed in a fancy pedestal bath while a pair of smaller birds, maybe sparrows, shared the bounty from one of the many feeders. He imagined that in the warmer months, the pots scattered around held blooming things that would attract hummingbirds. Red. He seemed to recall reading that hummingbirds were attracted to red.

He wasn't quite sure why he was thinking about birds.

Probably because it was easier than thinking about the fact that an extremely dangerous psychopath had Jillian in his sights. Or supposedly had. But given the fact that the information Alexei passed to Jillian regarding his role in setting up a sting had checked out, Jesse thought that the events of the past month made sense. If Igorevich wanted Jillian dead, he could have killed her, a multitude of times and in a multitude of ways. As Jillian herself had pointed out.

But subtly threatening her, drawing law enforcement attention to her, was one way to in turn draw Alexei's attention. The Christmas… imagery, for lack of a better turn, was a message. As was the presence of the LSD at both

Losevsky and Gannon's deaths. Messages that only Alexei Markov would fully understand.

They had an APB out for Markov – as well as Igorevich, who, now that they knew who they were looking for, met the description of the man who'd given Jillian the laced mint at the wedding. Jillian had spent the day answering questions. Now that it was strongly suspected if not outright confirmed that the notorious Russian criminal was the man whom they were after, all of the alphabet agencies wanted in on the case. Jesse had hated like hell to subject her to it, but didn't have a choice. From this, he couldn't protect her. And at least she'd had Ainsley there to safeguard her rights.

Not to mention that with her cooperation, they had a chance of bringing Igorevich down. So right now most of the law enforcement officials in the area were inclined to view Jillian favorably.

"Oh. I didn't know you were ba…"

Jillian's voice trailed off when Jesse turned away from her bedroom window.

"Wow." She yanked the edges of the towel, which was the only thing covering her, closer together. "I'm sorry, it's really inappropriate under the circumstances, but you look… incredible."

Jesse glanced at the dark suit he wore, and then back at Jillian. "I could say the same thing about you."

"My hair is dripping wet, you could fit a week's worth of groceries in the bags beneath my eyes and I'm wearing a towel."

"Your point?"

She shook her head, smiling, but the smile quickly faded. "I would ask how the funeral was, but that has always struck me as an inane question. Funerals are never pleasant."

"There was quite a turnout, as you'd expect, with lots of pomp and circumstance."

Jillian bit her lip. "I read one article online that claimed he committed suicide. And another that suggested foul play."

"There's still some question," Jesse admitted "although the evidence is leaning toward the latter." Particularly since Gannon had a fairly significant amount of sleep-inducing cold medicine in his bloodstream. Which might explain why he didn't put up more of a fight if he didn't hang himself willingly.

The question remained as to why Gannon had been targeted, either murdered or forced into taking his own life. Was he on Igorevich's payroll? Or had he run afoul of the man's organization somehow?

"He had a little boy."

"Yeah." Jesse nodded at Jillian. "And that sucks."

She looked down at the floor, where water from her hair had dripped. "I want to do something. To help." She glanced back up. "If there's a scholarship fund or something that's been set up…"

"There is," Jesse said. "I'll get you the information." And he would be making a donation himself. He might not have liked Gannon, but the man hadn't deserved to die. And the kid sure as hell didn't deserve to grow up without his father. "You're shivering," Jesse noted, wanting to step forward, take her in his arms and warm her. But if he did that, he didn't quite trust himself to stop there. "I'll let you get dressed."

He started toward the door.

"Is the policewoman still downstairs?" Jillian asked as he drew even with her.

"I relieved her. Brian is keeping watch outside, though. He'll follow us to the safe house."

Her tired eyes drifted closed. "I hate this. Christmas is in two days. People should be with their families instead of babysitting me. Brian should be with his family. *You* should be with your family."

Jesse hesitated, and then reached forward to cup her face between his hands. "Maybe I am."

Her eyes popped back open. "You —"

"Jillian?"

Katie's voice came from downstairs, interrupting her. Jillian sighed her dismay.

"I need to talk to her. She's leaving to spend Christmas with her parents at their new place in Florida."

"I know. Brian told me. You were supposed to go, too."

"So was he," she sighed. "And anyway, I wouldn't want to put them in danger."

He stroked his thumbs over her cheekbones before releasing her. "Get dressed. I'll tell Katie you'll be right down."

He started out the door.

"Jesse?"

He glanced back over his shoulder.

"As far as Christmas gifts go, that was the best one you could have given me."

Jesse wasn't one to speak carelessly or to say things he didn't mean, but the words that came to him seemed to be the right ones. "Consider it the first of many."

JILLIAN hadn't taken the time to dry her hair, so she shoved the thick, damp mass of it into a bun and secured it with a few bobby pins as she descended the basement stairs. She wanted to go ahead and give Katie her Christmas present – a series of framed black and white photos Jillian had taken of the restaurant – so she'd had to quickly retrieve them from where she'd hidden them in her studio.

With all that had happened in the past few weeks, she hadn't even had time to wrap them. She was going to see if there was a pretty bag in the storage room to shove them in before she handed them over. Her inner Christmas freak demanded that she make the effort, no matter how crazy her life had become.

And her life had certainly become crazy. She'd been harassed, drugged, jailed, met the brother she'd thought was dead and… fallen in love.

No matter how improbable it seemed to her logically, her heart knew that she'd recognized Jesse right from that first moment. From that first click. If circumstances had been different, she imagined that their relationship would have progressed a lot more slowly, with more caution on both of their parts. But life or death situations tended to cause people to throw emotional caution to the wind.

Regardless, she had little doubt that they would have reached this place eventually. When she was with him, it just felt right. Like… home.

Padding barefoot across the cold concrete floor, Jillian wished she'd thought to slip on her shoes before coming down here, but she didn't want to hold Katie up too long. It was twilight now, and her friend had to drive several hours to reach her destination.

Shivering slightly despite the sweater she'd thrown on over jeans, Jillian opened the door to the storage room and flipped on the light. Although they'd straightened things up after the cops had raided their decorations, seeing the space where the missing tubs should be made Jillian's stomach twist. She still didn't know how exactly the lights connected to Detective Gannon's death, but her mind filled with all sorts of bizarre and terrible possibilities. She understood why he couldn't, but she wished that Jesse had told her exactly what happened. Sometimes it was so much worse to have things left to the imagination.

Jillian opened up one of the remaining tubs, searched through wrapping paper and bows and ribbons, but didn't see any bags. Shoot. Maybe she could just stick a bow on the photos?

Not perfect, but better than nothing.

Selecting a large red one from the tub, Jillian then replaced the lid.

Her hand flew up to stifle a startled scream as she turned around. "Mr. Pratt," she said in confusion. "What are you doing here?"

He smiled, his expression sympathetic. "I'm sorry dear. But I'm afraid it is time."

"Time for…" the question trailed off when Jillian realized that his accent was different. Not southern. In fact it sounded…

"No," she said, backing up until she was pressed against the wall. The wall which now featured a hole where a section of shelving had swung out, unnoticed by her as she'd rummaged through the Christmas wrapping. She gaped at it, and then turned her head back toward him in disbelief.

"You're not really Mr. Pratt's brother."

"Allow me to introduce myself," he said in Russian. *"I am Vitaly Igorevich."* He executed a brief bow before casually aiming a silenced gun at her head. "And I would advise you not to scream."

CHAPTER TWENTY-SEVEN

SHE considered screaming anyway.

Jillian didn't even have her pepper spray. She hadn't thought to put her bracelet on after her shower, since she was in her own house. And guarded by federal agents.

Still in shock over the revelation, she nonetheless was able to reason that being shot in her own basement was preferable to being dragged off God knew where to suffer some possibly more horrible fate. Almost certainly more horrible.

Not to mention she refused to be used as a pawn to lure her brother.

But Mr. Pra… *Vitaly Igorevich,* she mentally corrected, put a stop to that plan before she could open her mouth.

"I have your brother," he said, pulling out a cell phone with the hand not holding the gun. He swiped the screen with his thumb, bringing up a photo of Alexei, tied to a chair in a windowless room. A room that closely resembled this one, minus the tubs of decorations. He was visibly beaten and bloodied, his chin resting on his chest.

Jillian's hand once again flew to her mouth.

"I will kill him slowly, with as much pain as I can extract, if you do not come along quietly. More, I will kill your friend and your lover while they wait for you upstairs. How easy to surprise them. Who would suspect an old man?"

"You're a monster," she said.

He shrugged, and then gestured with the gun toward the door that she'd never known was hidden in the wall. She wondered if Katie knew. Almost certainly not. And once it was closed again, they'd have no idea where she'd gone. They'd think she'd somehow left or been taken from the building, when in reality she was just next door. They might talk to the man they believed to be Mr. Pratt – the crotchety but harmless elderly neighbor – to ask if he'd seen anything, but they'd have no reason to suspect him.

Jillian certainly hadn't.

She peered at him now, noting that the accent wasn't the only thing that was different. He stood straight, making him taller than he'd always appeared, and nothing about him seemed infirm. She knew that he wasn't nearly as old as he'd pretended to be.

She tried desperately to think of a way to stall, to somehow alert Jesse, but the thought of him coming down the stairs, unaware that he was walking into danger, was more than she could bear. Igorevich would kill him. She had no doubt.

"Let's go."

With a brief flare of panic, Jillian gave one last thought to making a run for it, but knew that it would mean consigning three people she cared about immensely to death. She feared it was already a certainty for Alexei – and herself – but at least Katie and Jesse would be spared.

She hoped.

Trembling all over, she pulled away from the wall. Surreptitiously, she dropped the ribbon on the floor behind her. Like a giant breadcrumb.

Igorevich glanced down at it, and then smiled a little smile that caused ice to form in her veins. "Pick it up."

Jillian bent down slowly.

"Don't try anything," he added when she considered doing just that. One well-placed snap kick could dislocate his kneecap. He might get off a shot, but he wouldn't be strolling up the stairs afterward.

But she would likely be dead, and Jesse – or Katie – would be imperiled if they came down to investigate why she was taking so long.

Jillian stood. He motioned again with the gun. And though she tried to move, Jillian found that her legs had turned to jelly.

Impatient with her now, Igorevich reached around with his free hand and grabbed her by the hair, pressing the gun into her temple as he yanked her toward the door. He pushed her through, and then closed the door behind him, sliding a lock into place. They were in a room not much different than the one they'd just left, only this one was much smaller. Jillian noticed a black case of some sort standing in the corner, alongside a music stand and a couple of large chest-style freezers.

When he noticed Jillian staring, Igorevich nodded toward the case. "I'm not sure if you knew that your neighbor played the trumpet. A jazz quartet in his younger years. The room beside this one is soundproofed, as he didn't wish to disturb anyone when he practiced. Considerate of him, was it not?"

Jillian swallowed. He spoke of Robert Pratt in the past tense. "You killed him."

"Of course," he said nonchalantly, and then patted the top of one of the freezers. "I'm afraid he wasn't able to enjoy the *pryaniki* after all."

When Jillian only stared at the freezer in horror, Igorevich went on to explain. "I needed to be close to you without arousing any suspicion. After researching your neighbors, I discovered that Mr. Pratt lived alone and had no close relatives to miss him if he failed to make contact. Except for his adoring brother, of course."

He executed another short bow, as if she should applaud his performance.

And it was a performance, she realized. He'd been remarkably convincing as a harmless if annoying old man. From his flawless English – complete with southern drawl – to his bird-watching and cranky demeanor.

"The door," Igorevich continued in that oddly proud manner "was my own addition. It took a great deal of time and engineering in order to accomplish it without your knowledge, but the fact that you and Miss Parker are so often away from the house was helpful."

"You're the one who messed with the alarm. Who took Jesse's shirt."

"Why would I have need, when I had direct access?" He shook his head. "No, that was the idiot cop, although I do confess to tripping the breaker and turning on all of the light switches after he'd gone, just to create a bit of confusion." He shrugged. "A man has to have some fun. I do not know why the cop was – what's the word – *snooping* that night, although I suspect he wished to find evidence that the federal agents were protecting you. His timing was unfortunate. I don't mean to be indelicate, but I'm afraid he saw one of my brother's nurses leaving at a very late hour and in a rather…

unprofessional state of attire. I feared it would eventually arouse his suspicion."

"Your brother's..." Jillian stopped, realizing what he was implying. He'd had nurses – or women dressed as nurses, at any rate – stopping by on a regular basis as if to tend to his brother. Knowing what she knew now, Jillian highly doubted that those women were here in any kind of care-giving capacity. They were probably prostitutes – or, as Jesse had mentioned – some sort of sex slaves.

The ball of nausea in her stomach became coated with a layer of anger.

"But enough about me," Igorevich said with false cheer, gesturing toward the door on the opposite wall. "Let's go see your brother."

KATIE glanced at the kitchen clock. "I hate to rush her, but I really should be going. Maybe I'll just run downstairs and hurry her along."

Jesse glanced up from the fresh cup of coffee he'd been blowing on, frowning at the basement door. "I'll go," he said, setting aside the coffee. "That way if there's something she doesn't want you to see, she won't be upset."

"Thanks." She offered him a smile. "And just so you know, the only reason I feel even remotely okay about leaving her is that I know you would defend her with your life."

"So would Brian. Or any of us, really. It's our job."

She only smiled again. "Not in the same way you would."

Jesse hesitated with his hand on the basement door. "I hope you don't mind my being here, because after we catch this guy, I plan on that happening a lot."

Her smile turned into a grin. "I was counting on it."

With his own lips curving, Jesse started down the stairs. "Jillian?" he called when he neared the bottom. "Are you about finished? Katie wants to leave."

When no answer was forthcoming, Jesse frowned. "Jillian?"

Light shone around the crack of the storage room door, but other than the hum of the heating unit, no other sound could be heard.

Acting on an instinct that he didn't question, Jesse removed his sidearm from the shoulder holster he'd worn beneath his suit. He moved quickly but quietly toward the storage room.

Jesse pushed open the door, gun at the ready. The room was empty. He checked behind the stacks of plastic tubs, just to be sure, but there was no sign of Jillian.

Jesse repeated the same process with the other rooms. The laundry room, the mechanical room, the other storage area and the half bath – none of them yielded either Jillian or any clues as to where she might have gone.

Jesse pulled out his phone and strode toward the basement's front entrance. "Hey," he said when Brian answered. "Did Jillian come outside? Are you sure?" he asked when the response was negative. "Check her studio."

Jesse peered out through the iron bars which both decorated and guarded the front windows. The sidewalk was empty. Checking the door, he noted that the deadbolt was engaged. Just to make sure, he slid it back and opened the door.

Jillian wasn't in the little alcove beneath the front stairs.

Shutting the door and relocking it, Jesse responded to Brian. "Are you positive she's not there?" he asked again, checking the basement rooms one more time. "No, she isn't upstairs. I was in the kitchen and she would have had to pass me on her way up from the basement. She had to have gone outside."

But how? Jesse considered. The deadbolt was engaged, and she hadn't brought her key down with her to relock it after she went out. Not to mention that Brian was outside. Unless he'd been napping, she couldn't have snuck past him.

Snuck past him...

The phrase conjured up the sense of betrayal he'd felt when he'd watched the video of her walking out of that hospital with Alexei Markov of her own free will.

But he shook it off. She wouldn't just walk off, Jesse assured himself. He'd verified, as much as possible, that she'd been telling the truth about everything Alexei told her. And beyond that, he felt it in his gut. She'd been straight with him.

She was in love with him. He wasn't – couldn't be – wrong about that.

With that settled in his mind, he started thinking about an even worse possibility than her leaving again.

Namely, that she'd somehow been taken.

Jesse's gut clenched, and he had to concentrate to hear Brian over the odd ringing in his ears. Jillian wasn't in her studio. The other man was sure of it.

"We're going to search every inch of this property. She can't just have walked through the wall."

Jesse ended the call, and stared at the open door to the storage room for one brief second before yelling Jillian's name.

The sound of his own voice bouncing off the concrete was the only response.

CHAPTER TWENTY-EIGHT

SOMEONE was crying. Through the haze of pain, Alexei was almost certain that he heard the sound of weeping. Female weeping. It embarrassed him to admit he'd always been a bit of a sucker for a woman's tears.

Shh, he started to say, but his mouth wouldn't work. His jaw... he tried to shift it slightly, causing agony to radiate so sharply through his entire head that he very nearly blacked out again.

Something very cold, very wet, hit him in the face. He didn't dare attempt to shake it off, but he did blink his eyes. Or he tried to at any rate. The right one was swollen shut, and the left appeared blurry. He couldn't seem to lift his chin from where it rested on his chest.

Someone cursed in his native language. Then a hand twisted into his hair, yanking back his head. *"Open your eyes."* The imperative was spoken in his ear. *"Or I will cut them out."*

Cutting them out did not seem to be such a terrible idea, given the amount of pain they were causing him. But Alexei sensed that it was best to at least attempt to respond to the command.

His left eye inched open.

"That's it," said the voice from above him, and Alexei blinked the blurry features of Vitaly Igorevich's face into focus. Three angry red scratches ran down one side of it, but otherwise it was his real face, his real hair. Not the disguise he'd worn to trick Jillian and – to Alexei's great regret – himself. When he'd left his sister's house last night – at least he thought it was only one night ago, although it seemed much longer – he'd been surprised to bump into the old man outside.

Even more surprised when the old man had jabbed a needle into his shoulder, injecting a fast-acting temporary paralytic of some sort.

When Alexei came to, he was tied to this chair. And his body remained essentially unresponsive to his commands, so that he hadn't been able to defend himself from the blows Vitaly delivered.

Much as he used to when Alexei had foolishly considered him a friend – before he knew the extent of his and his son's evil – Vitaly smiled and patted him on the cheek.

Alexei cried out.

"Does that hurt?" Vitaly said. "Good." Then he turned Alexei's head to the side.

"No." The word emerged as no more than a harsh whisper, and one that was garbled at that.

Jillian was handcuffed to some sort of heavy shelving on the wall beside him. Her hair – so like the pictures he'd seen of their mother – was damp and loose around her face, which was pale and blotchy from crying. A dark splotch marred one cheek.

Apparently Vitaly had struck her.

Righteous anger swelled, but behind it came a sense of helplessness and disappointment. He'd worked so hard to protect her, and instead he'd played straight into Vitaly's hands. And now he was in no condition to save her.

I'm sorry, he tried to communicate with his one working eye, since his mouth didn't seem to want to cooperate. Jillian's lip trembled, and in her eyes he saw the mirror of his helplessness.

Until Vitaly chuckled, and then her gaze went incandescent with anger.

"I'm been discussing, with our lovely Jillian, the various ways I've considered prolonging your emotional torment. Should I slowly flay the flesh from her lovely bones, as I did with that fool Losevsky? Or since you seem to have a soft spot for whores, perhaps I should turn her over to one of my establishments and provide you with videos of her being fucked to death?"

He ran a hand over his chin, as if considering. "Both have their individual appeal, although the latter would certainly last longer and create less of a mess." He glanced around. "And though the soundproofing has held up admirably so far, I'm not sure I trust it that far. I could gag her, of course, but hearing her scream and knowing there is nothing you can do to help would be so much more traumatic for you, don't you think?"

A sound of raw fury roiled up from Alexei's gut, emerging from his throat broken and raspy.

"Do not worry," Vitaly said in Russian. *"I won't leave you out of the fun."* He gestured toward a gas can in the corner. *"Since you wanted everyone to believe that you'd died by fire, I decided to grant you your wish. Eventually,"* he added.

He started to say something else but then his attention was caught by a flashing red light near the ceiling.

"That was faster than I expected," he said with a frown, and then turned to look at Jillian. "That indicates the front doorbell," he explained, pointing to the light. "Which we cannot hear due to the soundproofing. I suspect it will be one of your FBI guard dogs, who must be missing you by now."

Vitaly started toward the door, and then paused. "I almost forgot."

He walked back to retrieve the wig he'd used to make himself appear to be an older man with balding white hair. Then he touched the three scratches on his cheek, which Jillian had apparently given him at some point. "I'll have to say I had an altercation with a cat that was attacking one of my birds."

He stooped his shoulders, taking on the mien of Adam Pratt, crotchety old man.

"You young people don't do anything foolish while I'm gone."

"ALEXEI. Alexei!" Jillian said for probably the twentieth time.

But after mumbling something unintelligible to her, her brother appeared to have passed out again. Not that it surprised her. She didn't know how he was even alive, given that almost every visible inch of him was black, blue or bleeding.

Tears sprang into Jillian's eyes, but she blinked them clear. She didn't have time to cry or to panic. Since Alexei didn't seem capable of helping at the moment, she'd have to manage on her own.

When she'd fought with Igorevich after he'd refused to let her go near Alexei, he'd once again grabbed her by the hair. Her bobby pins had come out, sending her hair cascading down her back. But more importantly, one of the bobby pins was now lying on the floor in between her and Alexei. If she could just get hold of it, she might be able to use it to pick the handcuff lock.

Escaping from handcuffs was one of the self-defense tactics she'd learned after she was attacked. It had been quite some time since she'd tried it, but it was worth a shot.

At this point, it was her *only* shot.

She wouldn't allow herself to think about the things that Igorevich had said. If she did, she would curl into a blubbering ball, which wouldn't do a damn bit of good.

Jillian stretched her arms as far away from the shelving unit as she could, and then reached out with her bare foot to try to slide the bobby pin closer. It was just beyond the reach of her big toe.

"Dammit."

She let out a frustrated breath. There seemed to be a clock ticking away in her ear, because she knew that Igorevich could return at any moment. And once he did, it was all over. Of that she had no doubt.

Steeling herself against the certain discomfort, Jillian yanked at the cuffs until they bit into her skin, the metal pressing hard against the bones in her wrists. She winced, biting her lip on the philosophy that one pain distracted from another. Having gained a fraction of an inch in her reach, she once again stretched out her leg.

"Turn... your knee..."

Startled, Jillian almost fell. After regaining her balance, she looked at her brother. The one eye that wasn't swollen shut appeared focused on her.

"You will be able... to stretch... your leg...farther."

His voice was weak and raspy, but she thought she understood his point. If she turned her knee in toward her body, she could slide her foot a little further out. And as a dancer, he would know all about stretching.

Jillian took Alexei's advice, shifting her position. She could just touch the bobby pin with her toe.

She laughed her relief, sending a smile toward Alexei. He winked his good eye.

Okay, and now to slide the pin toward her rather than inadvertently kicking it away. Jillian forced herself to pause and take a deep breath, and then carefully lifted her foot and placed her toe down on the thin piece of metal. Bending her knee, she slid it backwards across the concrete.

When it was close enough to her that she could stand up straight, Jillian loosened the tension on the handcuffs, which had torn little chunks of flesh from her wrists. Blood trickled down her arms, but she couldn't think about that now. She had to focus on picking up the bobby pin with her foot and then getting off the rubberized piece and bending one side of the pin at a ninety-degree angle. That much she remembered.

Concentrating fiercely on not losing her balance, Jillian grasped the pin between her toes and lifted it. She may not quite have Alexei's athletic grace, but she was fairly flexible. She bent her knee, bringing her foot up toward her cuffed hands.

The door opened, causing her to drop it.

No!

Desperate, panicked, Jillian stared at the pin. It took her a moment to realize that someone was rapidly approaching her. She looked up, expecting to see Igorevich's gloating face, but a little cry of surprised joy emerged when she realized it was Jesse.

He gently touched the bruise on her face with his free hand and then kissed her hard on the mouth.

"We're going to make this quick," he said to her in a low voice as he released her. "Brian is distracting him at the door. Backup is on its way." He glanced at Alexei. "And an ambulance."

"I have a bobby pin," Jillian said, indicating her cuffs.

"I have a universal key."

"You win." She held her hands still while he unlocked the cuffs. His jaw went tight when he looked at the blood. "It's fine. I'm fine." She shook out her hands, reveling in the freedom. "How did you –"

"I'll tell you when we're out of here."

He then turned toward Alexei. "I don't guess you can walk."

Her brother gave a weak approximation of a smile. "Perhaps… I could… pirouette."

Jesse handed Jillian a knife. "Cut the ropes. I'll have to carry him out."

Wincing in sympathy over his poor, battered body, Jillian tried to be gentle as she sawed through the ropes that bound his arms and legs to the wooden chair. Alexei gritted his teeth, but didn't issue a single complaint, despite the fact that she knew he had to be in tremendous pain.

When the last rope was through, Jesse handed Jillian his gun. "Hold this while I pick him up."

Jillian took his sidearm, almost crying as she watched Jesse bend in preparation to lift her brother over his shoulder.

Then the flashing red light caught her eye.

"Wait, that's –"

The shot struck Jesse somewhere near the neck. Jillian turned toward the doorway, screaming her shock and rage even as she fired.

CHAPTER TWENTY-NINE

"*SINCE* you couldn't come to Christmas, we're bringing Christmas to you."

Jesse watched his mother set up a fully lit and decorated tree in the corner of his hospital room.

"Christmas was last week, Mom." He knew, because the date was written on the chalkboard on the wall that held his current nurse's name and other pertinent information. And he could read it because someone had finally brought him his glasses.

Addison Wellington turned her pretty blond head, giving him The Look. "And I couldn't exactly have decorated your cubicle in the critical care unit, now could I?"

Knowing when he was defeated – and not having the energy to argue anyway – Jesse settled back against the pillow. He shut his eyes, noting that he could still sense the lights even through his closed lids. At least they weren't blinking.

The corners of his mouth turned up a little when he felt his mom's hand stroke his hair back from his forehead. He opened his eyes, ready to tease her about her enjoying the opportunity to mother him while she could, but it wasn't his mom leaning over him. It was Jillian.

"Hi," she said with a rueful smile. "I didn't mean to wake you."

Confused, he shifted his gaze toward the corner. The tree glowed cheerfully, but there was no sign of his mother.

"I could have sworn my mom was just here."

"She was, but she had to leave about an hour ago."

"I guess I fell asleep."

"I guess so. But you started mumbling, so I was worried that you were having a bad dream."

A bad dream. That was a pretty fair description of his life since being shot.

Then he frowned at Jillian. "You met my mother."

She nodded. "And your father. And your grandparents, one of your aunts, a couple cousins and your brothers. Although I'd already met Jack. And it turns out that Jordan is going to be my self-defense instructor. I have to say that I prefer him in that role as opposed to prosecuting me for public intoxication."

"They dropped that charge, right?"

"Right."

Jesse lifted a hand, dismayed by how much effort it took, and dragged it down his bearded face. "I feel like Rip Van Winkle."

"I hope I haven't… overstepped," Jillian said. "By being here with your family."

Jesse cut her off with a Look of his own. "It saves me the trouble of having to arrange a dinner or something to make awkward introductions. And speaking of family and awkward introductions: how's your brother?"

Her expression clouded. "He's doing better. But Igorevich broke his legs. The doctors aren't sure if he'll ever dance again."

Jesse fumbled his hand toward the edge of the bed so that he could take hers. "I'm sorry."

She gave his a light squeeze, careful of the tubes that remained attached to it. "He's alive. Your friend LeRoy is still alive, and seems to be recovering. You're alive – the doctors have said that you're incredibly lucky in the way the bullet hit you. And Igorevich is dead."

Jesse knew that – someone had told him that, maybe Brian. "Are you okay?" Jesse had taken a life in the line of duty before, and though the man – like Igorevich – had very much deserved it, he knew that it took an emotional toll.

Jillian nodded. "Brian arranged for me to talk to one of the psychologists who work with you."

"Good." Figuring that was enough about that for the moment, Jesse returned her light squeeze. His memory as to what exactly had gone down was fuzzy at best.

"You dropped one of your hairpins," he said "in the storage room in your basement. It still had damp hair attached to it, so I knew you'd dropped it recently. I thought," Jesse closed his eyes, trying to remember. "I thought that you couldn't just have walked through the walls, like a ghost. And then I recalled how Igorevich – they called him The Ghost – had gotten into Losevsky's apartment without us knowing. And though this was a basement instead of an attic space, the thought stuck with me. There must have still been some plaster dust," he said "from where they'd worked on the new alarm system, and you tracked it because your feet were still a little damp. I found a faint bare footprint, seeming to head straight into the storage room wall."

"Brian told me that you were the one who figured it out. And that a quick records check showed that Robert Pratt didn't have a brother named Adam." The smile she gave him was rueful. "He also said that you were supposed to wait for backup to show up before you went inside."

Jesse lifted his good shoulder. The other one would be out of commission for a while, seeing as how a bullet had ripped through it, barely missing his throat. "I broke protocol. Entered through one of the back windows. But all I could picture was the Losevsky crime scene. You'd been gone for almost thirty minutes. That was more than enough time for him to have… hurt you."

"Are you going to be in trouble?"

"Maybe a little. But at this point, Mateyo – that's my boss – is just glad that I'm not dead."

"So am I."

Jesse shifted his head on the pillow so that he could study her face. The bruise from where the bastard had struck her was almost entirely faded, but there were dark shadows beneath her gorgeous green eyes. The past week hadn't been easy on her, either.

He made the effort to lift his arm so that he could brush his thumb over her cheek. Then he let it drop, and made a bigger effort to scoot over. "Come rest with me."

She looked alarmed. "In your hospital bed?"

"That's where I am, unfortunately, so yeah."

"I'll hurt you. Or they'll kick me out."

"You won't hurt me. And if they try to kick you out, I'm going with you."

"I don't think you'll be walking out of here under your own steam any time soon."

"Want to bet?"

She only shook her head. "I'll lay down with you. But only for a minute."

After she'd carefully climbed onto the bed beside him, Jesse pressed his lips to her forehead. "You know, they say that when you save someone's life, you become responsible for it."

"I've heard that."

"The way I see it, we kind of saved each other."

She was quiet for so long that Jesse tilted his head so that he could see if she'd fallen asleep. She hadn't.

"What are you saying? Exactly."

"I don't know. Exactly. Just that we should probably stick together."

She laid her hand on his chest, and began rubbing in gentle circles. "Probably a good idea."

They were quiet for several moments. "Like, permanently."

The rubbing stopped. "Are you asking me to marry you?"

Was he? That would be crazy. "Yeah, I think I am."

She cautiously lifted her head to peer at him. "Is this the pain medication talking?"

"No."

"Maybe the near-death experience."

The more she questioned him, the more he was certain. "Or maybe I'm just in love with you."

She smiled, her tired eyes lighting with happiness. "That's handy, considering I'm in love with you, too."

"So you'll marry me."

"Ask me again when you're not on any type of narcotic."

"I will."

She settled back down against him.

"When I ask you again, am I going to like the answer?"

He couldn't see her smile, but he sensed it.

"Yes."

Made in the USA
Charleston, SC
06 August 2015